The shadow turned, the blackness a slow-moving blur that stopped when the majority of it was facing Riley.

All Riley's senses honed in on his target. If there was fear inside him, it was so tightly corralled that it might as well have been nonexistent. His Special Ops drill sergeant had worked on replacing the deep-seated reaction to threats with a highly evolved set of survival skills. In a seasoned veteran like Riley, the fight-or-flight response was all but gone, and in its place, Riley ran through a series of analytical strategies, calculating the best odds for survival. *Plan A, Plan B, Plan C . . .*

The creature remained motionless. Then, slowly, it began to move into a vertical column, piling itself one mass atop another, almost like the sections of a millipede, reaching up into the treetops like a thunderhead. It threw back what might be a head and a hideous shriek split the sky.

It's challenging me, he realized. *It's going to attack. Plan D, Plan E . . .*

Buffy the Vampire Slayer™

Buffy the Vampire Slayer (movie tie-in)
The Harvest
Halloween Rain
Coyote Moon
Night of the Living Rerun
Blooded
Visitors
Unnatural Selection
The Power of Persuasion
Deep Water
Here Be Monsters
Ghoul Trouble
Doomsday Deck
The Angel Chronicles, Vol. 1
The Angel Chronicles, Vol. 2
The Angel Chronicles, Vol. 3
The Xander Years, Vol. 1
The Xander Years, Vol. 2
The Willow Files, Vol. 1
The Willow Files, Vol. 2
How I Survived My Summer Vacation, Vol. 1
The Faith Trials, Vol. 1
The Lost Slayer serial novel
    Part 1: Prophecies
    Part 2: Dark Times

Angel™

City Of
Not Forgotten
Redemption
Close to the Ground
Shakedown
Hollywood Noir
Avatar
Soul Trade
Bruja

Available from ARCHWAY Paperbacks and POCKET PULSE

Buffy the Vampire Slayer™

Available from POCKET BOOKS

Buffy
the Vampire Slayer™
ANGEL™

UNSEEN

LONG WAY HOME

NANCY HOLDER AND **JEFF MARIOTTE**

SIMON
PULSE

New York   London   Toronto   Sydney   Singapore

Historian's Note: This trilogy takes place between the fourth and fifth seasons of *Buffy*, and between the first and second seasons of *Angel*.

First Simon Pulse edition April 2002
™ and © 2001 Twentieth Century Fox Film Corporation.
All rights reserved.

SIMON PULSE
An imprint of Simon & Schuster
Children's Publishing Division
1230 Avenue of the Americas
New York, NY 10020

The text of this book was set in New Caledonia.

Printed in USA
2 4 6 8 0 9 7 5 3

ISBN 0-7434-1895-6

This one's for Joss!

Acknowledgments

The authors would like to thank the unseen people who make *Buffy* and *Angel* work—the makeup artists, costumers, transportations specialists, CGI technicians, carpenters, set designers, composers, editors, mixers, writers, directors, producers, and everyone else who works behind the scenes to make the shows the successes that they are. You folks aren't invisible, and you are appreciated.

Prologue

SUNNYDALE WAS THE TOWN THAT HAD THINGS IN IT THAT shouldn't have been there. Monsters shouldn't have been there. Vampires shouldn't have been there. Twelve cemeteries within its city limits shouldn't have been there.

But they were.

Sunnydale was Hellmouth Central, and in a better world, there would be no dot on the map for O Little Town of Bedlam, Mayhem, and Madness. It would be nothing. It would be nowhere. Unmissed, unmourned, and unseen.

But this was not a better world. This was the real world. And the one thing that should be in Sunnydale— the Slayer—was gone.

One moment she was standing beside Rupert Giles's sofa, arms at her sides, taking a breath as Tara finished her ritual. Then she had walked toward the shimmering golden circle that floated in the room like misplaced sunlight. Then she was gone.

Xander Harris was dumbfounded. This was what they'd been trying to accomplish—the candles, Tara's unceasing, toneless chanting, Buffy's visualization exercises, all of it. And he'd seen stranger things happen, around this group, things he hoped he'd never see again.

But somehow, watching Buffy walk into that circle, lifting her right hand to about waist height, as if she were reaching for a doorknob, and then swiveling her wrist as if she were turning that same knob . . . it was all just creepy. He tried to suppress a shiver. Anya noticed and put a comforting hand on his back.

"Cold?" she asked.

He didn't answer, just shook his head. A warm, gentle breeze had blown from the magickal doorway, and on the breeze he thought he could taste various flavors: cinnamon, rose, chocolate, maybe fresh-cut grass. It smelled like one of those teas Tara ordered at the Bronze, the kind that brought to mind a compost heap in a paper filter.

Xander realized he'd been hearing a distant bell chime, its tones spaced far apart, maybe every twenty seconds or so. It faded now, as the breeze died. He looked around—Giles, Riley, Joyce, Spike, Tara, Anya, all watched the circle that Buffy had stepped through, and they all wore faraway looks on their faces, as if they too listened to the bell.

The idea, Xander knew, was that Buffy would meet Angel on the other side of the door—wherever that was. Together, guided by the Three Witches of the um, Apocalypse?—Willow, Tara, and someone in Los Angeles named Doña Pilar—and a Russian girl none of the people in this room had ever met, they would rescue the teens who had been disappearing all over Los Angeles, and plug the hole through which monsters spilled into Sunnydale.

Hey, all in a day's work.

Anyway, that was the idea. Xander hoped it passed muster. He hoped this Russian girl with the funky machine knew what she was doing, and he hoped that Willow and Tara and Doña Pilar were as good at the witchly thing as they seemed to think. And there was also the part where Buffy and Angel would have to be good enough to fight whatever it was that lay on the other side of the door, in Monsterville. He had no doubt that the Slayer and her vampire ex were good, the best there were on this side of reality. But on the other side, who knew what rules applied? The locals behind Door Number One might be creatures who ate Slayers for breakfast and cleaned their teeth with demons afterward.

Giles broke the spell by speaking first. "Well, that's it then," he said. "I-I'm sure she'll be just fine, and will return to us in no time at all."

"She'd better," Riley said, glancing around the room as if looking for something he could punch. "I hate the idea of letting her go through that—"

"We know, Riley," Anya pointed out. "None of us feels good about it, but she's the Slayer, right? She kind of makes the rules. We're just the Slayerettes." She smiled brightly. "Hah. I'm a Slayerette."

Joyce interrupted his reverie. "Spike?" she said. Xander looked up. Spike had wandered very close to the golden circle, looking at it like a man trying to watch the picture on the screen of a TV that's been turned off, as it compresses to a single dot of light. Buffy's mom had put her hand on Spike's shoulder. "Don't get too close, dear," she warned.

Spike just shook her hand off, tossing a snarl over his shoulder at the others. "Bugger it," he said, "I'm going in."

He pushed himself into the fading circle, as if entering

water sideways, and disappeared before anyone could say a word.

"Wow," Anya said. "That was ballsy."

On the other side of Xander, Tara fell to her knees, gasping. She moaned and said, "He wasn't prepared, and I wasn't—"

"Tara?" Giles asked, crouching beside her. He put his hand on her back. "Are you all right?"

"I-I don't know," Tara said, grimacing. She smoothed back her hair. "The whole point of the ritual was to make sure that Buffy and Angel were protected going through, and on the other side. Spike jumping through like that broke my link with Willow and Doña Pilar, and it . . . it hurt."

"Go, Spike," Xander said with disgust.

"But he's all right?" Anya blurted. She looked first at Tara, and then at Giles and Xander.

There was real worry on her face, which irked Xander. Anya and Spike had a lot in common, and a couple of times, she'd seemed tempted to start something with the vampire. *Color me jealous, which is part of the rules of the pajama game. It means I love her.*

When no one spoke, Anya said, with a little hint of desperation, "Right?"

"I'm . . . I'm sure he'll be just . . . just fine," Giles stammered, as he and Riley helped Tara to her feet. Willow's sweetie appeared to be in considerable pain.

What will happen to Buffy and Angel without the link? Have we lost them? Xander wondered.

Anya settled into the couch and crossed one leg over the other. She frowned and said, "Okay. So what now?"

Tara wrapped her arms around herself in a protective hug. "I don't know," she repeated, shaking her head. "I don't know. This is all new territory, for all of us. We're just trying things out as we go along." She rocked back and forth. "I feel so sick inside. I feel so dizzy. . . ."

Riley walked into the kitchen. He poured a glass of water from the tap and brought it back to Tara. She shook her head but he kept his hand outstretched, giving her a curt nod. Unsteadily, she took the glass and gulped the water down as if she'd been lost in the desert for forty days and forty nights.

Xander stared at the circle, seeing not so much a shimmering, golden circle as one of the many masks that the Hellmouth wore, beckoning the Slayer to come in, make herself comfortable, and die.

Be safe, Buffy, Xander prayed, as much as Xander actually ever prayed. *Come back to us.*

He put his arm around Anya and she leaned her head against his chest, sighing heavily.

"If I had my powers, I could fix this," she said. She looked at Tara, who had closed her eyes and was leaning her head back against the sofa pillows. Her forehead was beaded with sweat. "Maybe I'm just lucky that way."

Riley took the glass and walked back into the kitchen. Buffy's soldier was *pissed*. Who at, was anybody's guess, but Xander put his money on Riley himself. He was blaming himself that Spike had broken ranks and done the predictably self-serving and unpredictable thing. He was probably also blaming himself for letting Buffy go through—*Hah, as if anybody can tell the Buffster what to do*—and he was no doubt blaming himself for not having thought of barreling in after Spike himself. Even though Riley knew better.

Cuz he's in love, Xander thought. *Plus, nice guy.*

Xander felt a bit mournful, remembering the time in his basement that Riley had told him that he knew Buffy didn't love him. Xander had been shocked. He himself had suffered from unrequited love for the Slayer, but that was because she'd turned him down for the Spring Fling and then, okay, slept with Angel.

Yeah, he'd been a geek, and a social pariah, and kinda dorky. And Buffy had been the new girl from L.A. And Riley was this handsome commando guy who could, like, order a nuclear attack on Kamchatka. Not love him?

In another universe, maybe, he thought.

Slayer, Slayer, wherever you are . . .

"Oh God, Buffy," he murmured, "be safe."

Chapter 1

BUFFY STEPPED THROUGH THE DOOR SHE HAD VISUALIZED, and over a plain wooden threshold, and that was the end of what could remotely be called normal. The other side didn't look anything like what she had expected—*although to be honest,* she thought, *what I guess I was expecting was to still be in Giles's living room saying "I told you this wouldn't work" to Tara. So pretty much anything is a surprise.*

But what she saw was more than just unexpected. It was unreal, a fairy tale landscape that she was sure had never existed on Earth. In the distance a castle perched atop a rolling green hill. Its walls and towers were a bluish gray, with pink pennants fluttering at the towers' peaks. Between her and the castle trees rose in columns, a kind of forest except that forests usually had all that underbrush and thorny parts, whereas this forest was all tall, strong trees with plenty of room between them for walking, picnicking, or whatever else came to mind, a carpet of lush green grass beneath them.

Hills rolled beyond the forest, topped by the castle, and in the far distance, snow-capped peaks that looked just a little too much like they were sugarcoated instead of frozen. Glowing above it all was a perfectly round, perfectly yellow sun in a crisp blue sky. It was all very bucolic and charming.

And then there was the dragon.

Where the rest of the scene was picture-book perfect, more charming than real and too real to be a dream, the dragon was absolutely horrifying. Sea green and vaguely iguana-like, if iguanas grew up to be the size of the Sun Cinema, with razorlike teeth that looked almost as long as Buffy was tall, a spiked tail, and leathery batwings. The beast turned its red, beady eyes on Buffy, shook its head from side to side a couple of times, and exhaled a blast of fetid breath.

Maybe they don't breathe fire, she thought, mentally holding her nose, *because they don't* need *to.*

It had seen her, she was certain of that. And if it wanted her for lunch, she couldn't imagine there was much that she could do to dissuade it. The idea of running occurred to her, but she discarded it a second later as impractical— the thing's legs were certainly long and powerful enough to cover ground faster than she could, even if she knew where she was going.

Just in case, she spun around to see what was behind her. *Forty yards of grass, and then nothing.*

The meadow ended abruptly at a drop-off that must have been incredibly steep, because from here she couldn't see a thing. In the distance, the fuzzy blue of an ocean stretched to the horizon. Her guess was that she was at the top of a cliff that fell away to the coast, but she couldn't tell for sure without advancing to the edge, and with the dragon behind her giving her the hungry eye, she wasn't overly excited to try that.

"Hi," she said to it, just in case it could talk because after all, here, who knew? "Buffy Summers. Slayer. You seen a guy in a black leather coat around here, spiky brown hair, dark eyes?"

The dragon lowered its head, front claws digging at the grassy earth.

"So probably not, is what I'm thinking," Buffy continued. "Because I was supposed to meet him here, and I'm not seeing any sign of him."

The dragon huffed again, and Buffy really wished it wouldn't. She'd hunted vamps in sewers that smelled better. For that matter, she couldn't remember having experienced a sewer that smelled worse.

And there was something about the way it was moving . . .

. . . *something,* she thought, *like a bull getting ready to charge . . .*

And then it did, straight for her, jaws wide, wicked-looking teeth glinting wetly in the sunlight.

Almost too easy, she thought. *Get it coming at me fast, then dodge and it can't stop, and it's bye-bye, dragon, over the cliff.*

She held her ground as long as she dared, looking into its red eyes, measuring its speed, watching for its tail and claws in case it led with one or the other. After it was practically on top of her, she took a running start and hurled herself toward the nearest copse of trees; and sure enough, the dragon started trying to brake, its front legs churning earth, rear legs locking. Clods of dirt flew everywhere.

Its momentum was too strong; it skidded and slid in a three-quarter turn, and tumbled over the edge of the cliff that must have been five hundred feet deep if it was an inch.

As it plummeted, it let out a dragon-size howl of distress, all the world's sirens turned on at once, ringing in Buffy's ears as it dropped away. Buffy almost felt bad for it—*probably acting purely on instinct. Walnut brain, saw me as a threat and it attacked, and I outsmarted it without even breaking a sweat.* She started toward the edge to see how far down it was, and to make sure that the dragon was really gone.

Which was when she heard the thunder of leathery wings filling with air.

Right, she thought. *They fly.*

That was when she decided running was the best idea, after all.

With no other goal in sight, Buffy struck out for the castle. Her Slayer strength coursed through her and she ran far faster than the strongest Olympic champion, eating the space beneath her with long easy strides. But behind her she heard the pitch of the wingbeats change and knew the thing had topped the cliff. She hazarded a glance over her shoulder and saw it craning its head on its rubbery neck and then, apparently spotting her, it flattened its body to cut wind resistance and came straight for her.

She ran a few more yards and then stopped, not wanting her back to it when it got to her. She turned and waited, hands on her thighs for a moment, catching her breath, trying to come up with another plan.

Absolutely nothing occurred to her. And the thing closed in, saliva glistening in its open mouth.

Now I know what a crab puff feels like at a party, she thought. *Except for the part where it's already dead.*

Buffy held still, waiting for it. Its hot breath blasted her as it grew closer, and still she froze, knowing the futility of dodging right or left. Its head grew enormous before her, the size of a bus. Then it really was on her, close enough for her to see its pink, ragged gums and sharp-edged indigo tongue, and finally she moved.

She hurled herself flat against the grass, and the dragon's lower jaw, swooping in at waist height, was suddenly above her. She kicked up with both legs, as hard as she could, into its long jaw. She heard teeth slam together, and thought she felt bones snap under her kick. The dragon lurched, mid-flight, and lifted off higher, as if to avoid another attack.

But it circled quickly, remarkably agile in flight, and dove toward her again, jaws open once more. Blood mixed with spittle flew from its open mouth. She waited until it was close, hopefully too close to maneuver, and then threw herself to the side. But its head followed, its huge jaw snapping shut, and one of its teeth snagged her outflung leg, ripping through her black leather pants and tearing her skin.

Buffy rolled to a sitting position, scooting out of the dragon's reach and glancing at her injury. It had left a long cut that already bled down her calf.

She didn't have time to worry about it, though, because the dragon had landed and was extending its snout toward her, mouth opening for another try. This time she flung herself right at it, bringing her hands down on top of its snout and catapulting herself up onto its neck. There, she spun and sat down quickly, legs clamped around the sides of its neck as if it were a horse and she a rider. The dragon shook its head violently, trying to dislodge her, but she grabbed two fistfuls of scaly flesh and hung on. It threw back its head, as if to crush her against its own back, but it wasn't flexible enough to accomplish that. It writhed and snarled and snapped. Buffy held on tight, digging in with her hands and legs, riding out every attempt it made to throw her off.

Finally, it took flight.

Its huge wings unfolded, spreading out to a full span that must have been thirty feet. The beast flapped them a couple of times, pushing its front end into the air with its powerful haunches, and then it was airborne.

This, I am not liking, Buffy thought. *At all.*

They gained altitude quickly, and within moments had climbed above the treetops. Buffy felt a rush of vertigo looking down at the landscape that passed so rapidly beneath her, and so far down. The dragon made it worse by soaring into a banked turn loaded with not-so-delicious and -nutritious G-forces. Her hold on the dragon started to slip—her hands were sweating, and her leg, slick with blood, couldn't grip well enough to keep her on if the thing kept this up.

Falling into a bunch of trees from a dragon's back was not one of the ways she had contemplated dying, and she had, she realized, considered lots of different ways.

But before she fell, the dragon righted itself and she settled back into the natural saddle where its neck met its shoulders. And the whole unsettling experience had given her an idea.

The thing was, she wasn't sure how to put it into action.

And the other thing was, if she did put it into action she might end up killing herself.

If it was a choice between killing herself and the dragon, or just dying, she resolved to take the monster out with her.

So she made the move.

She had to force herself to let go of its neck with her right hand. Her fist left a mark in its green flesh, which she found somewhat encouraging. She hoped she had hurt it, since it so obviously was intent on killing her. She didn't leave her hand empty for long, but instead leaned forward—rising out of her seat when she couldn't quite reach—and managed to clamp her hand down on its right ear. She pulled. The dragon loosed a roar that shook its entire body, and dropped twenty feet or so in the air. Buffy felt her stomach lurch.

She did the same thing with her left hand, grabbing the left ear.

The dragon bellowed, shaking its head as furiously as a dog coming out of the bath. Buffy was nearly torn from her hold, but she managed to maintain a grip.

The dragon dropped another few feet, its wings working at trying to swat the rider from its back instead of keeping them aloft.

And Buffy let go again, with her right hand.

This time, she had to trust the strength in her left hand and let go with her legs altogether, to reach out far enough. But she was able to do it. She balled her fist, and slammed it into the dragon's right eye.

The thing screeched with pain and tilted suddenly to the left, going into a spinning freefall.

Buffy caught hold with her right hand again, just below its right ear, and hugged as tightly as she could with her legs. Even so, she felt the centrifugal force and the rushing wind conspiring to tear her off. Every muscle she owned screamed with pain. She had never pushed her Slayer strength to this extent, but to let go was even more certain suicide than hanging on.

The world spun crazily toward her, faster with each passing second. She caught a glimpse of the meadow below, and knew she needed to do one more thing. Ignoring everything her mind shouted at her, she forced herself to let go again, and she took another swat at its eye. Again, it threw its head to the left, away from the attack, and its dizzying, spinning descent tilted that way.

Where there had been meadow below, now there were treetops, and Buffy and the dragon were heading straight into them. As if it realized suddenly what was happening, it arched its back and began to flutter its wings rapidly. For a brief moment, it seemed to slow its wild fall. But only for a moment, and then it was too late.

Buffy threw herself free at the moment of impact, curling herself as tightly as she could as thick-leafed trees slammed into her.

Over the crash of branches and the pain of a dozen sticks driving into her flesh, she heard the dragon's explosive impact. Buffy fell through the branches, snapping many, finally landing on the ground with the wind knocked out of her, bleeding from more cuts than she could imagine counting for the rest of her life. She kept her eyes open, though, not wanting the dragon to land on her.

But there was not much chance of that. Outweighing her by a thousand pounds or so, the branches parted like water before its mass—but the tree trunks didn't. The dragon had impaled itself on several straight, thick trunks. Stuck forty feet or so over her head, it hadn't quite died, but that was only a matter of moments away. Blood ran down the tree's bark like a fountain. The beast kicked fruitlessly, its wings twitching. Buffy felt another moment of pity, but when she tried to stand, the pain in her calf reminded her that it really had been a kill or be killed situation, and she had done what she needed to do to survive.

Bet that's the biggest stake I'll ever use in my career, she thought.

She looked away, toward the still-distant castle, but then she looked back quickly because she had one of those corner-of-the-eye things where something seems to be changing. And when she looked back at the beast in the trees, it was definitely changing. Its whole body shimmered, as if liquefying, and as she watched, it began to shrink.

So you can't dust 'em, but you can reduce them from giant economy size to miniature.

But even that was wrong, because it wasn't just shrinking—it was changing shape. Its neck became shorter, its wings vanished, its legs lengthened, and by the time it stopped transforming, it was a shape Buffy recognized all too well.

It had become a man. A man impaled on a single tree trunk, but a man nonetheless. He was as naked as the dragon had been—not that there would have been much of him left to hang clothes on if he did have clothes.

And the worst part was, he wasn't dead. Lots of pain, sure, but not dead.

Yet.

She raced to help him, pushing her way through the stubbly thicket, ignoring fresh scratches and cuts as branches smacked and sliced her.

He's got to be an enchanted prince or something. That'd fit into this whole fractured fairy tale theme that's going on here.

She'd always heard fairy tales had ancient roots that were darker than Madonna's, but had never really known quite how dark until she watched the man writhing in pain with a tree through his sternum.

"Hang on," she called, lifting a limb over her head and

throwing it out of her path. She was closing in on him, and she could smell his blood on the wood—*no vampire special power, just too much of it. Way too much.*

Then the trunk broke and the man tumbled to the earth, landing with a sickening, wet *thwop* about ten feet from her.

When it seemed like nothing could make things worse, the man spoke.

"Th-thank you," he said, in perfect though oddly accented English as she rushed up to him and landed on her knees beside him.

"Me?" Buffy replied without even thinking. "You're thanking me? I just shishkabobbed you."

"You freed me," the man said, writhing in agony. "From the-the curse."

The curse. Of course. Had to be a curse.

"This is better?" she asked.

He coughed, clearly weakening. "But-but you are not yet finished," he said. "She waits, in the tower. She needs you."

"She can wait," she said. *Whoever she is.*

The man coughed again, a wracking cough that seemed to consume all the strength he had left. When he spoke again, she could barely hear him.

"Th-the p-princess."

The princess, Buffy thought. *What else?*

"She was brought here against her will," he added.

Say what?

"Brought from where? How?"

"M-magick. She said she was from the land of Alay."

"L.A.?" she asked. "Is that what she said?"

Blood burbled out of his mouth.

He stopped coughing.

* * *

Angel saw Buffy in the distance as soon as he stepped through the door.

The landscape was obscured by a thick fog, wet and cold on his skin, but he spotted the blond hair and slender build through a brief parting in the mist. The woman was running, and from the breathless panting and the half-sobbing sounds she made, it was clear that she was in trouble.

He was already in motion, running down the hill toward her, when he realized that Buffy wouldn't make that noise. He was supposed to find her when he went through, so of course he assumed that the first blonde he saw was Buffy.

But whoever she was, she was in trouble, and Buffy didn't appear to be anywhere close by. At least, not that he could see through the preternaturally heavy fog.

Through another momentary break in the mist he saw what she was running from—two powerfully built men with long, loose hair and wild expressions, chasing her with ancient weapons in their hands.

When Angel reached the bottom of the slope, coming out into a kind of narrow valley, he had a better view of the whole bizarre affair. The men looked like historical barbarians of some kind—or fictional ones—wearing only loincloths of animal skin and some hammered metal jewelry. One swung a four-foot-long broadsword over his head in rapid circles, while the other clutched an ornate battleax in two oversize fists. The woman, now that Angel could see her, was similarly attired, in a metal breastplate that ended well above her belly and a long skirt made of leather that was slit up both sides. She was not adorned with any jewelry, and her waist-length hair flowed freely as she ran.

But her running was coming to an end, for the sword-wielding barbarian, who was as blond as the woman, caught up to her. He grabbed a fistful of her luxurious hair and yanked, tugging her off-balance. She fell into a heap at his feet, and the other guy, whose hair was as dark as tar, caught up.

They both stood over her and laughed. Their laughter sounded to Angel like that of men at a sporting event, like guys having a good guy-time together. But the woman's screams belied that appearance.

Angel didn't think twice, but let out a grunt of his own as he plowed into the two men. He caught the blond one in the ribs with his shoulder, lashing out with his feet to kick the other guy's battleax from his hands. Angel and the blond guy both stumbled over the woman and crashed to the ground. She screamed again, scrambling to her feet. The darker guy lunged for her but Angel reached out and snagged his wrist in both hands, trying to bend it like a pretzel. He heard bones break, and the man shrieked in pain, falling to his knees and cradling his arm in his other hand.

Angel began to turn back toward the blond guy but the man had recovered faster than Angel expected and sliced his sword toward Angel's back. The steel bit into Angel's flesh and drove through, the swordpoint finding the air in front of Angel's stomach a moment later. Angel grunted, falling forward, clutching at the sword as he did. He landed on his stomach in the dirt. The barbarian stood behind him, placed one foot on Angel's back, and withdrew his sword.

"I guess that will teach you to meddle in the affairs of others," the man said. Angel understood the words as if they were English, although somehow, he knew they weren't.

He waited there in the dirt, trying to gather his strength, biting back the incredible pain. As soon as the sword was removed, his healing process had begun, but it would take some time to get over a wound that major. In the meantime, Angel was weakened.

"Now," the man was saying behind him. "Where were we?"

"My arm," the dark one blubbered. "He broke my arm—"

"Silence," the blond guy said. "We have business with this little one."

"No, please," the woman's voice pleaded. "I beg you—"

"It's too late for begging, my lovely thing. It's your head they want in the Great Hall now."

The woman broke down into gulping sobs, and Angel knew he had to make his move.

Ignoring the pain, he shoved himself to his feet and leaped into the air, spinning as he did so. In midair, he kicked out at the back of the blond guy's head. His foot connected with a sickening impact and he saw the man crumple forward, toward the woman, his head exploding outward in a fine spray of red and gray. Her screams turned from piercing to soundless, her mouth working but no sound issuing from it. The darker guy raised his battleax in his remaining good hand, but Angel hit the ground, rolled, came up with his arm extended and straight-armed the man in the throat, inside the range of his ax. The man made a gagging noise and dropped.

Angel wobbled on his feet, pain nearly overwhelming him, but he managed to remain standing. The woman continued her soundless screaming, but he could see through squinted eyes that she was trying to control it, and it turned gradually into a series of hitching sobs as tears ran down her cheeks.

He inhaled and felt another sharp pang from where the

sword had gone through him. Holding in the breath, he turned his head toward the sun, and—

—*the sun.*

Angel was standing outdoors, in a valley. Here, the fog was light, and there was nothing but sky between him and a burning sun. It took him a quarter of a second to realize what was wrong with this picture, and when he did, it was the strangest thing yet in a whole series of strangenesses.

The sun's blue, he thought. *Not yellow, not white. The blue of a Bel Air swimming pool. Floating there in a clear green sky the color of emeralds, and baking the hard red earth under its rays.*

And I'm not even so much as smoldering.

It was a remarkable feeling, a kind of liberation. Whatever place this was, it was a place where he could walk freely in the daytime. Which, for Angel, hadn't happened very often in the past couple of hundred years. The sensation of warmth was unbelievable. Exquisite.

It only raised one disturbing question.

I'm safe in their sun, but what about their moon?

Chapter 2

THE THING HAD SURELY SEEN HER.

Salma de la Natividad brought a hand to her mouth to stifle her little gasp of fear, but it was too late and, truth to tell, it didn't matter anyway, if the giant creature had already noticed her. And she was convinced that it had. It had rushed by the tunnel in which she stood, pressed against the slick stone wall, and it had seemed to hesitate for the slightest moment, as if sensing her. Maybe it hadn't seen her—what use would eyes be to an underground monster, spending its life rushing through tunnels barely larger in diameter than it was? But it had other ways to know she was there, she guessed. Maybe it could pick up vibrations in the tunnels, where she had displaced the air. Maybe it had an abnormally sensitive sense of smell, or taste. Maybe it could hear the blood coursing through her veins, the double *thump* of her heart.

It rushed past the tunnel opening, with the speed and

impact of an express subway roaring past a platform. Salma had been to Manhattan on several occasions, and, while she usually traveled in limousines, or taxis, on her last trip there, with her parents, she had begged to ride on the subway. They had obliged her, and she remembered reaching the platform just as one rumbled past, remembered the great rush of wind and noise that seemed to recede even as the train was still right in front of her.

But the creature—she thought of it as a worm, even though it was unthinkably larger than any worm Salma had ever seen, or imagined—kept on going. It didn't try to turn around, didn't back up and come after her. *Am I safe here?* she wondered. *Or is staying here suicide?*

There was no way to know. She advanced, ever so slowly, keeping one hand always against the disgustingly moist wall for balance, to the opening of the tunnel down which the worm had just disappeared. As she neared it, a stench rose to greet her, a worse smell even than in the rest of the putrid tunnels. It was the odor of something unclean, something that never saw the sun or breathed the fresh air, but existed in its own universe of filth and death and degradation. Salma choked on it, and spat into the muck.

At the tunnel's mouth, though, there was no sign of the worm save the lingering smell. It was unlikely that the thing would come straight back through this same tunnel, she thought; it would have to be able to turn around to do that, and she doubted that it could. So she risked stepping out into that tunnel, blinking into the darkness to see if there were anything here that she hadn't seen in all the others.

The answer was no. It was exactly like the others, only stinkier, and something foul dripped from the ceiling to splash wetly before her, as if disturbed by the creature's passing. But one tunnel was as good as another to someone who had no clue as to where she was or where she needed to go. Salma headed in the direction away from where the worm had gone, not wanting to find herself coming up behind it.

As she made her way through the thick stew surrounding her feet, she passed three more tunnel openings. None of them seemed any more useful than any other, though, so she stayed where she was, figuring a steady course was better than roaming randomly through the maze.

But when she passed the fourth opening, it came at her.

It was only yards away, the length of a bowling alley. She couldn't tell if it had been moving before it saw her, or if it rested, waiting for her to come along. But as soon as she showed herself in front of its tunnel, the thing lunged, covering ground like a race car.

Salma screamed and ran. She sobbed until she realized that that used air and energy she needed for running, and then she clamped her mouth shut and held it in and ran harder. Fear gripped every inch of her, but she knew she couldn't allow it to freeze her or even slow her. Before her, she saw her parents, in the living room of their home in Los Angeles. She saw her brother Nicky. She saw her grandmother and grandfather. She knew what these images were telling her—*save yourself, so you can get home to us. We're waiting for you. Hurry home.*

I'm trying, she thought. She ran toward the images, as if she could run straight from here into her house—as if she could reverse the process by which she had come here, walking into a shimmering golden circle by accident and coming out in a field where she was captured by mounted soldiers.

But behind her, the worm charged. She felt its breath, sauna-wet and searing, against her back and legs, as she ran. It had teeth that clicked together, and its passage through the tunnels generated the familiar subway roar, but it had no voice, and she had seen no limbs. It was just a long tube with a horrible, fanged face at the front. And those fangs were mere feet behind her now.

The muck clawed at her legs with every step, slowing her down. The worm suffered no loss of speed from it—it was as if the thing was made for this environment, or had made the environment itself, carving or eating the tunnels into existence in the first place. There was no way she'd be able to outrun it for long. Already, it nipped at the flowing gown she'd been dressed in. One more good lunge and it would have her.

She forced herself on, despite certain doom, and came to another side tunnel. She hurled herself into it, barely making the turn, losing her balance and slamming into the side wall hard enough to make her see stars and fall into the goo. But the worm couldn't turn as fast as she could and it kept on, rushing down the tunnel she'd just left.

Salma sprawled in the muck, breathing hard. Tears threatened to return, but did not; instead of sorrow, she now felt the sudden heat of fury coloring her face. She had been made to run from something because she couldn't fight it. She knew she was no Buffy Summers, able to do battle against creatures like this. Running from problems had been her way of dealing with them—just as she had left home, to go to school in Sunnydale, where people didn't know who she was: a rich girl, a privileged child, who often wondered if the other kids had become her friends because of her or because of her wealth.

Compared to giant flesh-eating worms, she thought, *the aggravations of being a de la Natividad are tiny.* She could barely remember what it was she hadn't liked about living at home. Restrictions on her time and social life, of course, but not especially onerous ones. Always having to consider the needs and desires of her parents, grandparents, and brother. But that was what being in a family meant. That she wasn't alone in the world, that she had others to care about, others who, in turn, cared about her.

She was certainly alone now. And that worm could be coming back at any time. Charged up and angry, Salma stood, wiped the gunk off herself, and determined to find a way out of the tunnels no matter what.

Los Angeles

Helicopters buzzed over the city like so many enraged dragonflies or the soundtrack to a Vietnam war movie. Shirley Caine glanced up at them as she crossed the parking lot toward Foodstuffs Market; so many they dotted the blue sky like bugs on a screen door, and she couldn't begin to imagine what they all were. Police, she figured, and news stations. The images she'd seen on her TV at home were almost enough to make her not want to leave the house, but she didn't really have a choice—a family needed to eat, and she hadn't thought to stock up, as others apparently had, before things got so bad outside.

According to the news, more than a dozen people had been killed in the last twelve hours, caught in the crossfire between rival gangs. People were being advised to stay indoors and away from their windows, and to avoid any unnecessary trips. Los Angeles had become a war zone, and nobody was totally safe. In Monterey Park, citizens had formed a kind of armed Neighborhood Watch program, but three of them were wounded in a shootout with gang members, and they had disbanded, running back to the relative safety of their homes.

But these things hadn't been happening in Shirley's neighborhood, so she figured it would be safe for her to make a quick run to the market. After all, with two teenagers in the house—not to mention her husband, Henry, who, it seemed, could consume his own weight in food every day—the supplies dwindled fast, and if she couldn't feed them at home they'd just look elsewhere. That, she thought, would be more dangerous than just shopping herself.

As for Henry, he had sprained his ankle running from his office to his car, spooked by what he had thought was a gang member but who turned out to be his boss. Mr. D'Angelo was hurrying after him with some last-minute revisions on his report about a water treatment facility the firm was going to build in Encino. Now Henry was home, leg bandaged, ice pack in place, and she told him to stay home and watch the kids while she went to the store.

Actually, she was a little pissed off at him that he'd let her go without much protest, just a "be careful." When she'd left the house, he'd been lost in his report—*business as usual, water problems and riots in this godforsaken city*—and she tried to tell herself that his casual attitude meant that she was overreacting about the amount of danger her trip entailed, and not that he wasn't worried sick about her safety.

Still, the helicopters *did* seem to be almost directly overhead. And those screaming sirens might be drawing closer. She hurried toward the closed doors of the market, and whatever relative safety lay inside.

She had just reached the rubber mat in front of the automatic doors—thinking, incongruously, that perhaps she had always been wrong, it was probably an electric eye over the doors that opened them, and not some machinery concealed beneath the mat—when the two dark cars barreled into the parking lot. Brakes squealed as the first one charged in, slowing to avoid ramming into the few parked cars, then shot toward the lot's other exit. But the second car, anticipating that move, took a different route and zoomed toward that exit to cut the first car off. Both slammed to a sudden standstill, smoke billowing from their wheel wells. Then the firing started, gun barrels smashing windows in both cars, bursts of flame flaring from them, loud stuttering pops. Glass shattered, in their cars and the others in the lot.

Shirley, frozen on the rubber mat with the supermarket door hanging open, was suddenly aware of someone approaching her from inside. Her instinct was to run, but the only place to run was back into the parking lot and that had become a free-fire zone.

"Ma'am!" the guy inside the store said. She looked at him again, realized he was a store employee, with a green apron that had FOODSTUFFS stamped on it and a yellow plastic nametag pinned to it. "Please, ma'am, come in quickly!" He reached out to her from inside, as if he were afraid to extend any more than one hand outside the door. Shirley suddenly understood where she was and what was going on, almost as if waking up from hypnosis induced by the copters and sirens. She passed through the door into the darkened interior of the store.

There weren't many people inside—a dozen, at most. They huddled in the checkout lanes, presumably thinking the heavy counters could help keep them safe. Shirley saw them there at the same moment that the automatic doors swung closed behind her, and suddenly her eyes filled with tears.

Dammit, Henry, she thought, *you should have worried about me.*

"You are *so* not the chief of all Scoobs, Anya," Xander insisted, as they walked down Main, casting wary visual sweeps at the devastation around them. Sunnydale was beginning to resemble all those movies about the "projects," burned-out slums where society's outcasts dwelled like so many wounded animals. Though they'd seen monsters from afar, none had gotten close enough to pose an immediate challenge.

So we have time to indulge in one of our major forms of couple interaction, Xander thought, not unwarmly. *Pleasant bickering.*

"Who, then?" Anya asked, skirting an overturned trash can. "I have the experience. Are any of you a thousand years old? Have any of you been vengeance demons?"

"I'm not sure those are necessary prerequisites," Xander pointed out. He also pointed out a moving clump of something green and icky about a hundred feet down the street. They were coming back from checking the last-seen portal sightings, at Giles's suggestion. No portals had been visible, or any close-range monsters, either.

"And what are?" she asked, flaring. "Whatever you do? Telling jokes and . . . and making sure we have plenty of snacks?"

Ouch. "I didn't say I was necessarily the guy who should be in charge, with Buffy gone," Xander replied, feeling a bit huffy. "Just that I was the one who had been at it the longest. You know, in the beginning it was pretty much just me and Willow helping Buffy."

"Oh, and Giles wasn't there? Her Watcher?"

Xander looked at his feet, remembering the early days. He ignored the fist-size clump on the sidewalk, something vaguely organic and possibly, formerly alive. "Well, I guess he was. But he was, you know, pretty British in those days. Stiff upper lip, tweed suit and all that. He wasn't so big on getting out and mixing it up with the demons." Xander didn't bring up the times he himself had spent hiding from vampires, or sidelined by some minor injury, or simply paralyzed by fear. "She really leaned on me a lot."

"This isn't exactly how I've heard it," Anya said.

"Well, consider the sources," Xander shot back. "People who were . . . well, there . . . may not have the best recollection."

They turned a corner. In the yard of a big brown shingled house a monster carcass lay, flies buzzing around it. A neighborhood dog sniffed at it, marked it, and ran off, tail between its legs.

"Who else, then?" Xander asked, looking at the mound of decaying flesh. "You're too new to the whole, uhh, human world."

"What's wrong with Giles?" Anya replied. "We're out here because he told us to do this."

"I know," Xander said. It was why he had brought the subject up in the first place—because he and Anya had unquestioningly followed Giles's instructions, and now he *was* questioning. "Maybe he's the best, since he was a Watcher and all. But he's worried about Buffy and he's not making career decisions at the moment. Or even decisions that might keep us all alive for another, oh, ten minutes. And Tara is still suffering from linkus interruptus. So, that leaves you and me."

"Also, Joyce, but I agree with you there," Anya said.

"She's a wonderful woman but after all, this is not an art gallery."

"Well put," Xander said, impressed.

"It's not even an art exhibit. Although, I have to say that back when I was a vengeance demon, we did have sort of an annual 'show-and-tell' event. Once I brought a man I had cursed with incurable itching. It was his wife's idea. Seven-year itch, get it?" She looked very proud. "I received an honorable mention."

"And not for Miss Personality, I'm guessing," he said. At her look, he added quickly, "Although now, you would certainly win. Across the board. All the categories."

She looked pleased. "There was a leadership category," she said. "I would win that, too, you're saying."

"Ahhh . . ." *Curses . . . so to speak. Foiled again.*

"*And* I should remind you that I'm older than Giles. I possess much more wisdom."

"You seem younger, though," Xander said. "Not so mature." Even as he spoke the words, he realized what he'd done.

Anya spun on him. "Now you don't think I'm mature?"

"I mean mature in the bad way," Xander defended. "Not the good, mature way. The, uhh, old fogey, stick-in-the-mud way."

She regarded him for a long, uncomfortable moment. "I'm glad you don't think I'm an old fogey, Xander," she said finally. "Considering that I'm, you know, ancient. But not fogeyish."

"Hardly fogeyish at all," Xander agreed gratefully.

Anya started walking again, and Xander took a couple of quick steps to keep up with her. "I guess I don't need to be the Scooby Queen," she said. "I'm just trying to figure out my place in the group, you know. You have a place.

Willow has a place. Giles has a place. Even Tara is getting her place. What's my place? Xander's ex-demon girlfriend?"

"What's my place?" Xander asked.

She flashed him a warm smile. "Ex drifting wanderer, occasionally useful, brave and wonderful Xander."

"Wonderful?" He felt his face crimson.

"That's what I said."

"Well, you know," Xander said, "until Buffy comes back, I guess you can be the Scooby Queen. Anyway, you're always *my* Scooby Queen."

Anya stopped short, kissed him on the cheek, and took his hand. They continued back to Giles's place.

It worked! I'm in.

Spike felt a moment's queasiness and his vision blurred, but he blinked a couple of times, swallowed, and willed his eyes to focus. He glanced back over his shoulder, half-expecting to see Giles's living room and the Scoobies staring at him in shock, through a veil of gold.

But there was nothing like that behind him. He was just someplace else, and it was a sodding strange someplace at that.

And stranger still, he couldn't see Buffy anywhere. It hadn't been more than a minute after she'd gone through the door that he'd followed. It was impossible that she'd be out of sight so quickly; there was really no place for her to hide here, that he could see.

Spike hated nature. And yet he had landed in the middle of it, in a way. He found himself in a gently rolling meadow, with foot-tall grasses swaying in a summery breeze. Cries of night birds and the buzz of hidden insects filled the air, and the aroma was clean and earthy and natural. A full moon rode high in the sky, casting its shimmering light down on the meadow and glinting off the river that Spike could see and hear, maybe half a mile away across the fields.

But maybe it would be all right. Maybe it was just Earth nature he hated, and this was definitely not Earth. He blinked a couple of times, but it all remained: the moon, the sky, the grass, the river, no Buffy.

But, hullo, the moon was blood red, and the sky it dominated was a dark magenta color. The grasses seemed to have a pinkish cast, but Spike couldn't tell if they were their actual color or if the moon's luminescence merely painted them that way.

It's really fine that Buffy isn't here, he thought. *Slayer'd just get in my way, and probably go all girly-concerned when she found out what I'm up to.*

Watching Buffy prepare, back at Giles's, and then go through the magickal doorway, Spike had been struck by what the others were saying about the journey ahead. An infinite number of universes, where anything or anyone might be. Worlds where evolution had progressed down entirely different paths. Worlds where monsters ruled the days and the nights, where people would huddle in terror, knowing that they were only kept around as meat for the table. As Buffy left, Spike realized that nothing really held him to his old Earth, his old reality. Cheryce was gone. Drusilla would never return. Taunting Buffy and her soldier boy was all well and good, but not the kind of thing a man could make a lifetime's hobby of, especially when that man was immortal.

And then the thought had occurred to him all at once, full-blown: Somewhere in all those other worlds, there would be someone who could get the chip out of him. Or a world where the chip wouldn't work, or where humans weren't the dominant species and he could develop a taste for some other form of sustenance. The possibilities through the doorway were infinite, whereas at home they were far too strictly limited.

So he went, with no word or warning, and made it through the door moments before it blinked out of existence.

Now he had no idea where he was—no idea, really, how to even begin to define what "where" might mean under these circumstances.

But he wasn't getting anywhere just standing here in a meadow gazing at the moon, lovely color that it was. With no other destination in mind, no sign of civilization that he could see, he began to walk toward the river.

By the time he'd covered a quarter of a mile, he could smell it on the air. He stopped dead, inhaling deeply. There was no mistaking that unique tang, the coppery scent that he could taste at the back of his throat. Spike threw his head back with laughter, then resumed his course for the river, running now, leaping across the field with abandon.

When he reached the river, he descended its low bank and knelt beside it, bending his face toward it. The liquid was black in the moonlight, but he knew that come sunrise, if there even were a sun in this wonderland, it would run crimson.

Red as blood.

He pushed his face into the river and drank. Felt the thick liquid fill his mouth, cascade down his throat, and it was better than a lover's kiss.

The river ran with human blood. Nothing else came close to that flavor, that bouquet. Spike drank deeply, then rolled over on his back next to the river, laughing, scooping up handfuls and letting it dribble over his face, into his mouth. He had worried that he'd never taste this again, and here was a river of it, flowing freely, forty feet wide and who knew how deep or how long. *Cheryce would've loved to try skinny-dipping in this,* he thought pensively. *Stupid chip.*

Whatever this place was, it was a paradise for vampires. Spike had never imagined such a thing existed, and yet here it was, a simple matter of walking through a doorway and he was there. He rose, dusted the riverbank dirt from himself, and looked around in the moonlight.

I can build a house right there, he thought. *Run some pipes up from the river and have hot and cold running blood without ever having to leave my own place. Maybe put in a guest room in case Blondie comes through looking for something to slay.*

That thought brought another one to the surface—maybe there were others here, like him, vampires enjoying this heaven on—well, not Earth, but wherever. With no need to hunt, no fear of being found out and staked, there would be a real community, a sharing, a sense of family among them such as had never existed on Earth.

Hell with it, he thought, *might be fun in spite of that rubbish.*

He took another long drink from the river and started on his way again, determined to find out if anyone lived there. For a while, he kept to the riverside, but after twenty minutes or so, he came upon a bridge—primitive, but clearly made by humanlike hands. It was a low, stone structure, as if someone had painstakingly piled river stones on top of one another to achieve the necessary height, and then had mortared others together to create the span. It didn't look wide enough for any kind of wheeled vehicle bigger than a bicycle, and there was no road approaching it anyway. But as Spike scaled the bank to stand beside the bridge, he noticed that there was a path beaten through the grasses here, leading to the bridge and beyond it in one direction, and back, more or less the direction from which he had come, in the other.

He stepped onto the bridge and, satisfied of its solidity, crossed it. This was irrefutable evidence that someone lived here, he knew. Other vampires? Or prey? There was no telling, yet.

He followed the path, leaving the blood-river behind him.

The going was easy on the downtrodden trail, and Spike moved at a pretty good clip. As he walked, the scarlet moon slipped lower in the sky—*better keep a watch on that*—but still cast sufficient light to see clearly. He reckoned he had been on the move for about an hour when he saw something unnatural break across his view. At first, he couldn't make out what it was, but it marked a straight line, which, in these softly rolling hills, seemed very out of place.

Before he reached the line, Spike came to a point where a new path forked off the one he followed. He didn't know where it went, while this one promised to lead directly to this other sign of habitation, so he ignored the fork and kept on the main path. In another twenty minutes, he found out what the line was: a fence, a dozen feet tall, cutting across the fields. It continued as far as he could see in either direction. It was a simple wire fence, much as one would see on Earth, with four strands of barbed wire topping it. On the other side the fields continued, so he couldn't tell what the fence's purpose was— no way to know if he was fenced in, or out.

He picked up a piece of wood and tapped the fence,

gingerly. No shock, so it didn't seem to be electrified. Climbing it would not be a hardship, but the barbs at the top were not fun-making. It bothered him, the first stain on what had seemed like utter paradise. And he had a creeped-out feeling as he stood beside it, the old someone's-watching-me vibe that any vamp learned to trust and to hate.

Spike turned and strolled self-consciously back to where the path had forked, and took the side trail. He realized that he was growing tired, that all this walking was wearing him out. He didn't like to walk, didn't do much of it when he could avoid it. He was thinking about finding a flat spot off the trail to get some rest when he noticed that the path seemed to be dipping off the hills, toward a rocky area. *That might be better,* he thought. *I'll find a hidey-hole so if the sun comes up I won't be caught out in it.* He struck out for the rocks, realizing as he grew closer that they were larger than they'd looked from afar, twenty or thirty feet tall in spots. They seemed randomly scattered across the landscape, as if a giant toddler had been too bored to pick up his blocks.

Spike had just entered the rocky area when he was attacked.

There were six of them, dropping from the towering rocks and lunging from shadows. Spike took a half-step back, bracing himself for the onslaught. The first one reached for him, but Spike dodged his grasping hands, caught his wrist, and yanked, using the man's own momentum to throw him into the dirt. Spike found himself surprised that they seemed to be human, or at least humanlike. He hadn't quite known what to expect.

The next two plowed into him at once, knocking him off his feet. They all landed in a pile of flailing arms and legs. Spike tried to shove away the one who was right on top of him, crushing the wind out of him, but the other clawed at his arms and face. As he pushed and punched, he felt warm, ragged breath on his neck. He twisted and writhed but the guy came closer, and Spike heard the gnashing of teeth. When he felt a scrape on his neck, he exploded in anger. He thrashed and twisted and both guys went flying. Spike leaped to his feet, vamping out as he did so.

"Just what the bloody hell do you think you're doing?!" he demanded. "Keep your bleedin' fangs to yourselves!"

A hush fell over the group.

After a moment, one of them said, "He's one of us!" This one was tall and lanky, with straight, greasy hair hanging down around his face. A second vampire, stocky, bald, and goateed, touched one of his own fangs as if to make sure it was still there.

"If you're vampires, you bet your sweet bicuspids I am," Spike said.

" 'Course we're vampires," another one said. He had only one arm, and a stump of the other inside a taped-in sleeve. "Who else would be here?"

"What do you mean by that?" Spike asked. It dawned on him that they all seemed to be speaking English to him, though he clearly wasn't in any of the English-speaking nations he'd ever known. "You're all vampires here?"

"What else?" the greasy one asked.

"He's new here," another guy declared, striding forward confidently. He moved like royalty, and Spike instantly figured him for the Big Noise in these parts—this one had stayed back during the fighting, and didn't deign to step up until it was safe. But he was powerfully built, tall and broad, with short black hair and heavy-lidded brown eyes set into a handsome face. Spike hated him instantly. "Of course he doesn't know what's going on."

"Then why don't you enlighten me?" Spike asked, smoothing down his platinum hair.

The guy took up a position in front of Spike and the others dropped back a pace, letting their spokesman have the floor. "I don't know where you came from," he said. "For that matter, none of us knows for sure how we got here, or where we are. But we know what we're in. Did you see the fence?"

Spike shrugged. "I saw it."

"I thought you probably had. Then you should be able to figure it out. We're in a cage. Others—not vampires—come to watch us, to observe our behavior."

Realization dawned on Spike, and the idea turned his stomach.

"I'm in a sodding *zoo?*"

Chapter 3

Los Angeles

"I THINK YOU ALL KNOW, LADIES AND GENTLEMEN, THAT we're facing a serious problem here." The police commissioner for the city of Los Angeles stood at the front of the room in an expensive gray suit that matched the short, steel gray hair on his head. His cold blue eyes looked at the assembled officers. "In fact, a number of problems. This city hasn't been looking at this many problems all at once since the riots of the early nineties."

Kate Lockley watched him closely. He wasn't the kind of man who came to address the troops often, so when he did, it had to be something pretty significant. He was a politician, not a cop, though he had come up through the ranks. But that was a long time ago, in a different kind of city. His kind of policing didn't fly anymore, and his political skills were such that he had managed to alter the perception of himself so that he no longer looked, or even thought, like the hard-nosed cop he once was.

The room was a veritable who's who of police brass—captains, lieutenants, detectives from various squads, as well as an assortment of other law enforcement officials, including L. A. County sheriffs, the head of the FBI's local field office and some Special Agents, and a few U.S. marshals. All of them sat in silence, a few making notes on legal pads or small pocket-size notebooks as the commissioner continued.

"It isn't just the gang war, although that's the biggest immediate threat to public safety," he said, his voice grave. "And obviously, that's where the majority of our forces are necessarily deployed at the current time."

He has a cop's habit, Kate noted, *of using way more words than he needs to say something.* Even as a cop's daughter, she had never quite understood that impulse. She couldn't tell if they thought it made them sound more intelligent, or if it was some kind of reaction to coming into contact with too many lawyers, with their professional necessity for precise and ritualized language.

But he was continuing, and she realized she wasn't listening. He had turned toward a large map of the city spread out on a wall behind him, with red and yellow and blue flag stickpins stuck into it at various points.

". . . looting in these vicinities," he was saying as he pointed toward the red pins. "A power station in Carson was knocked off-line by an explosion, which is currently under investigation, and in the ensuing blackout a large number of businesses were broken into. We know of three deaths that have occurred as a result of this blackout, and when the suspects are identified and apprehended we have the district attorney's assurances that those suspects will be charged with homicide in association with those deaths.

"The blue pins represent teenagers who have disappeared. We know that there is, as yet, no knowledge or indication as to what may have happened to them, be they runaways, be they kidnap victims, or anything else."

Kate bit on her lower lip to keep from saying anything. She knew full well what had happened to them—not that she ever would have believed it, if she hadn't been at Cordelia Chase's apartment when Angel went through a strange doorway created by some Russian girl. The girl told him it would take him to a sort of parallel universe, where he could track down the missing teenagers and bring them home.

Of course, Kate couldn't tell her superiors that. If they believed her—*not a given*—they'd send a SWAT team to Cordelia's, take Alina into custody, and completely ignore the fact that they had no understanding whatsoever of the kind of forces they were messing with.

Kate's understanding was only sketchy, but more informed than her colleagues'. Ever since realizing that Angel was a vampire, she'd been studying up on things that rational people consigned to the categories of superstition and pure foolishness. Her discovery of Angel's nature coincided with the murder of her father at the hands of other vampires. She knew, intellectually, that Angel wasn't at fault, that he had, in fact, tried to save her father from them. But emotionally, that knowledge didn't help. Her relationship with Angel had been strained, at best, ever since. Learning about him, and his bloody past, only strained it more.

So now she was in the awkward position of withhold-

ing information from her department, and keeping knowledge about missing children from their worried parents.
She didn't know which she hated more.

". . . individuals of elevated position, including the
mayor, a California senator and several elected represen-
tatives," the commissioner droned on, "have expressed to
this department their concern over this situation and their
desire to have it resolved before another young person
turns up missing."

In other words, Kate thought, *the children of the rich
and powerful have disappeared along with the poor and
disenfranchised, so now it's become important enough to
care about.* She caught herself even as she thought it. *Am
I a cynic?* she wondered. *I always hoped I wouldn't be—
I don't think a cynic makes a good police officer, even
though so many cops are cynical.*

*And anyway, how does one "turn up missing?" Isn't
that a contradiction? If someone is missing, then he or
she hasn't turned up at all, right?*

She was relieved when the meeting was brought to a
finish without, she believed, much of anything accomplished. But the commissioner had been able to look like
he was involved and active, and her understanding was
that he was holding a press conference immediately after
the meeting at which he would declare it to have been a
great success. And if that helped to bring some degree of
order to the city, then she supposed it would have been
worth sitting through.

She worked her way through the room. The audience
was mostly men in dark suits, and she felt their glances,
coolly appraising, sizing her up, and not in every case
measuring her ability as a detective but her worth as a
woman. She was glad when she was out of there and back

in her car, headed toward her station house and the squad who knew her. She had a lot of work to do.

"Let me get this right," Buffy said. "I'm supposed to be scared of you? Because I just fought this dragon, see, and he was much bigger and, oh yeah, way scarier than you are. So how about if you just get out of my way and we'll tell people I was all trembly and everything, okay?"

The Black Knight was silent.

That was how she thought of him, as the Black Knight, capitalized. She had been continuing on a forested path toward the castle, and the princess from L.A. who was, supposedly, imprisoned in a tower there, and the Black Knight had stepped out of a stand of pines. He was completely encased in obsidian-black plate armor, from his helmet down to his metal boots, and he clanked when he walked like someone rummaging around in the pots and pans cupboard at home. His helmet was vaguely egg-shaped with a pointed visor that, if it was custom-made to fit around his nose, would have put him somewhere in the Cyrano de Bergerac territory, nasally speaking.

He stood across the path, blocking her way. In his hands he held a massive spiked mace, its handle almost four feet long, with at least a dozen three-inch spikes jutting from its bowling ball-size head.

It was the mace that made Buffy take him seriously. One good shot with that would do a lot of damage, and even her Slayer healing abilities would have a hard time bringing her back from, say, a blow to the head.

Trouble was, for all its weight and length, he handled it like it was nothing more than an aluminum baseball bat. It seemed virtually weightless in his gauntleted hands.

"So, not much for talking?" she asked him cheerfully. "That's okay. My boyfriend thinks I can pretty much carry a conversation all by myself anyway, you know, so . . ." she trailed off. "Umm, moving aside now?"

The Black Knight stood silent. Behind him, the sun was lowering over the castle, and his shadow was dark and weirdly proportioned.

"Because, you see, there's this missing . . . princess, in the castle, and I'm going to check on that," Buffy went on after a moment. "And I don't know what time it is or anything, but it seems like the sooner I get that done, the better."

The Black Knight said nothing.

"Okay," Buffy said with a shrug. "I'll just go around." She stepped off the path, intending to skirt past the Black Knight. He stepped off as well, blocking her way.

Angel all over again, she thought. He had the dark and silent part down. She wondered if whoever wore the armor was brooding inside there. She decided it was time to stop trying to engage him in conversation. She feinted toward the other side of the path, and the Black Knight lunged that way to block her. But her move was only a fake, and she doubled back to the Knight's right, hoping to leap past him before he could recover.

He recovered. He righted himself and swung the mace. Buffy flattened herself against the ground and it whistled above her, about where her waist would have been if she hadn't dropped. She didn't stay down for long, though, but shoved herself back up to one knee, then launched herself into the air. The mace was coming around again for another try, but she went above it and landed with both feet against the Knight's breastplate.

He staggered, but kept his balance.

Buffy landed, breathing hard, and only partly from the

exertion. *That should have knocked anyone to the ground,* she knew. *Especially a walking tin can whose balance can't be that great to begin with.* Now, examining the Knight with a fresh perspective, she noticed something else strange. His visor didn't seem to have any eye slits. It looked like seamless metal plate. *Which would mean that he's blind in there, but that's impossible. He knows my moves as soon as I make them.*

As Buffy considered, he advanced, raising the mace for another swing. She held her ground until he was in motion, then sidestepped it, spinning around and into a kick that landed just below his knee. She felt the impact all the way up her own leg, to her hip. But the Knight didn't seem to feel it at all. Before she could clear him, he let go of the mace with his left hand and batted at her. The back of his gauntlet slammed into her ribs, knocking her flying off the path.

He was coming at her even as she picked herself up, becoming more aggressive as the combat wore on. He retrieved the mace with his right hand and swung it in a tight circle over his head, like a helicopter's blades. As he bore down on Buffy, she prepared for a risky move. Once again, she waited until his attack was under way so she could gauge the arc of his heavy spiked club. On the mace's downward motion, she leaped into the air, caught the Knight's right arm, and used that to propel herself even higher, somersaulting over him. Midair, she twisted like a diver, so that on her descent she faced the Knight's back. She reached out and caught his helmet with both hands, using that to slow herself down. Then she planted both feet against his back and wrenched on the helmet with all her strength.

The helmet came free in her hands and she crashed to the ground with it. She rolled to an upright position, still clutching it. It was surprisingly heavy, and she glanced inside, hoping not to see a very messy mess.

It was empty.

She looked back at the Black Knight. Where there should have been a head, there wasn't. Armored shoulders led to empty space.

A chill passed through Buffy. Fighting vampires and demons was one thing, but she had thought this was a regular person in a suit.

"Good excuse for giving me the silent treatment," she said. "No head, hard to be a blabbermouth."

The worst part was, being headless didn't seem to slow it down a bit. Even as she stood, admiring the headless thing's mobility, it turned on her and raised the mace again. If anything, it seemed faster now, without a helmet to weigh it down.

The mace whistled past her, barely missing her own head. She dodged it, moving inside its arc and striking the armored breastplate with a combination—three swift jabs, right-left-right. The Knight took a step back but didn't falter. Switching the mace to his left hand, he grabbed at her, snagging her wrist in his powerful gauntlet. She shook, trying to free herself, but it did no good. His grip was unbreakable.

So she tried a different tack, and brought her own free hand to its wrist. Using that hand and the arm that it held as leverage, she bent the wrist backward as far as she could, finally feeling a satisfying snap. The armored hand broke off, and lost its grip on her wrist. Glancing inside it to ascertain that there was, in fact, no human hand there, she threw the gauntlet to the ground and skipped out of the Knight's way as he tried to close his left arm, still wielding the mace, around her.

Moving to the Knight's right side, to take advantage of its lack of a right hand, she aimed a quick trio of powerful kicks at its midsection, where the breastplate overhung the leggings. The Knight rocked unsteadily back and forth, the mace in his left hand waggling as he tried to maintain his balance. Buffy launched into a flying spin-kick and slammed into the Knight in the same spot, putting everything she had into it.

The Knight flew apart. His upper section clattered to the ground behind him, and his legs wobbled for a second and then tipped over where they were. When his upper part crashed, the left arm snapped off and bounced a couple of feet away, the mace finally slipping from its relaxed gauntlet.

Buffy surveyed the damage. "If I knew country music, I'd sing a few bars of 'I Fall to Pieces,' " she panted. "But, you know, country music?"

She hoped that this would be the last obstacle before she reached the castle. The sun was almost down behind the hills that ranged beyond the castle, and going into that place in the dark wasn't exactly something she looked forward to eagerly.

She had taken two steps when the right gauntlet closed on her ankle with a crushing grip.

Los Angeles

"No!" Nicky de la Natividad shouted. Then, seeing the hurt on his grandmother's face, he lowered his voice. "I won't just sit and wait for her," he went on. "I can't."

"But you must, *mi angelito*," Doña Pilar pleaded. They stood in her little kitchen, where she stirred a huge iron kettle that bubbled over a burner. Nicky wore a loose white tee shirt that exposed his muscular arms, still bearing scorch marks from his adventure at Del DeSola's oil field. His head was totally devoid of hair, with even his eyebrows burned off, and the faintest breeze felt oddly cool on his head. He supposed it would take some time to get used to. "Buffy has gone after her already. Willow and I are doing what we can to help, but—"

"But what you can do isn't much, is it?" Nicky interrupted. "Since you've lost contact with her . . ."

"Still, if anyone has a prayer of finding Salma and bringing her home, we must believe that it is Buffy."

"You have more faith than I, *'buela,*" Nicky said. "But then, you always have."

His grandmother stroked his cheek tenderly, gently. Nicky felt a pang deep in his gut. He was terrified. He wanted someone to tell him that everything was going to be all right.

"I have tried to instill faith in you since you were an infant, Nicky." Her voice was shaky. "We have not always been as successful as we would have liked. The fact that you were able to accomplish the ritual of the Night of the Long Knives means that I had some impact on you, no?"

"Impact, yes," Nicky replied, not quite understanding his hostility. Wanting very much to confess that he wished he had more faith. "I guess I learned a trick or two at your knee. But you have that unshakable belief that things will work out, which I can never even approach. You look at how to make things right, while I worry about what will go wrong."

He scowled and turned away from his grandmother. For some reason that he couldn't put into words, watching her stir her potion infuriated him. He felt guilty, and he didn't want to see her doing something he had also done—work magick, and change reality with it.

He flung at her, "It's not working. And all we know is that Buffy is someplace other than she was, but we don't even know if it's the same someplace else where Salma is."

"But we are trying—"

"All this is wrong," he said flatly. "We shouldn't have done it."

"It was done." She sighed. "We cannot stop now."

He balled his fists, imagining himself with thirty *camachos* at his side, thirty Latin Cobras to kick the butts of whoever did this to Salma. They'd be sorry they were born.

"She's my sister," he said, turning around to face her, "so she's my responsibility."

"Do you not understand, Nicky?" Doña Pilar asked sadly. She sniffed at her kettle, made a face, and reached for a jar of some greenish herb on a rack nearby. She unscrewed the lid and tossed in a pinch of whatever it was. Nicky knew she rarely labeled her jars, trusting her memory and senses to keep track of what was in each. "If there were a way to send someone directly to Salma," she continued, "we would have. Finding her will be a challenge, even with Willow and me helping, and Buffy is the best person we know—the best person on Earth—for that task."

"Because she's a Slayer?"

"*Sí,* absolutely. Because she is *the* Slayer. The one and only. Even as a young girl, growing up, one heard whispered rumors of Slayers from the *brujos.* There is no one as powerful or as able to face whatever might be encountered in the alternities where Salma has been sent."

He wanted her to convince him. "Sure, she's tough, I guess. From what you say, so are Willow and the others. But I'm tough too, you know."

His grandmother put a loving hand on his shoulder. Nicky was grateful, but tried to keep the color out of his cheeks. "You are strong, *papi*. And dangerous—no doubt too much so for your own good." She lowered her hand as he moved away. "But the kind of strength you possess is not the kind one needs over there."

"So I'm supposed to what, just sit around this house?" Nicky threw his arms into the air, as if to emphasize what house he referred to. "While Salma is in danger, and maybe Buffy is tracking her down someplace in an infinite number of realities, but maybe she's not? Even in Oaxaca you heard about the needle in a haystack, right? What if you don't even know which haystack to look in? Or which field of hay?"

"Which is why Willow and I need to help guide her," she said patiently. "And don't forget, Angel is looking, too."

"Great," Nicky said sarcastically. He was practically begging for her reassurance as he shot down her attempts to comfort him. "Two people, searching an infinite number of possibilities. Don't you think it would be better if there were three? Then we could divide infinity into thirds and be finished, oh, sometime before the sun goes nova, maybe."

"Nicky," Doña Pilar said. She made settling motions with her hands. "We could send a million people through and it wouldn't be enough. Without help from this side, there's no hope of finding Salma or the others. The ones we're looking for left from this reality, so there are traces we can follow. It is not a matter of having enough people, it is simply a matter of guiding the ones who are there."

"I can't, *mi abuelita*," Nicky argued. "I can't just sit here while my sister is missing. Especially if it's my fault—"

"Oh, Nicky, it isn't!" Doña Pilar took his wide hands in

her tiny ones. "This is not your fault." She dipped her head. *"Bueno,* I do believe that the passage into Sunnydale was partially your fault. When you began the rituals for the Night of the Long Knives, you affected the atmosphere in Sunnydale. But you never could have anticipated that Alina would be testing the Reality Tracer at the same time you were working powerful magick."

"So because I was using magick, and she was using her machine," Nicky said, "we created monsters that tear people apart?"

"The shadow," she said softly. *"Bueno."*

"What are you not telling me?" he demanded, his voice shrill. " *'Buela,* what did I do?"

She hesitated. "All right. You have asked me for the truth. I think you either created the shadow monster that appeared in Sunnydale, and that either you or Alina opened the passage that let it into Sunnydale."

"Ay, Dios," he murmured. "That and all the other monsters."

"You couldn't know that Sunnydale was on a Hellmouth. That bad timing would also work against you."

"Did *you* know about Sunnydale?" he asked her.

"No." She gazed at him steadily. "Truly, I did not. I wouldn't have let your parents send Salma to school there if I had known. And I don't think you had anything to do with Salma disappearing."

He grimaced. "You don't think so?"

"I am sure of it." Her smile, meant to be reassuring, only reminded Nicky how much this old lady loved him. If she were dying in front of him, she would tell him that she was fine, if only to spare his feelings.

Nicky shook his hairless head. "I wish I could be as certain as you."

Doña Pilar shrugged. "It always comes back around to that," she said. "I don't know how to persuade you, how to make you as sure as I am that things will work out. Buffy will find Salma. Salma is fine—she's missing, but not necessarily in any danger. She will come home soon. Then you will know that I was right all along. We just need to show patience, and Willow and Tara and I need to be able to reach across to Buffy again."

She brought the spoon out of the kettle, and sniffed the contents again. Seeming more satisfied, this time she took the tiniest of sips off the spoon and nodded her head.

"Please, grandmother," Nicky begged her. "Please let me go through. I can help Buffy, I know. I couldn't stand to be here while something bad happens to Salma, and I can't shake the feeling that she's in trouble." He paused, looking at the tiny woman before him, the woman who shared his eyes and his smile and his sister's strong cheekbones. "I couldn't live with that."

Doña Pilar frowned at him. "Very well," she said. "I suppose you won't leave it alone, will you?"

"No chance," he replied. "You know me, *'buela.*" His smile was sour. "I'm the spoiled little rich kid who always gets want he wants."

She sighed. "Then go to see Cordelia Chase. Alina and the machine are there. Perhaps they can prepare you and send you over. If they succeed, Willow and Tara and I will try to keep an eye on you from here."

Then she crossed herself, and that frightened him.

Have I cut myself off from the protection of the Holy Mother, because I invoked the power of ancient Aztec gods?

"Is that what you're brewing?" he asked harshly.

"Some kind of potion to help you restore contact with Buffy?"

Doña Pilar smiled. "This?" she said, lifting out another spoonful and taking a healthy swallow. "No, this is soup. *Albondigas* soup. Would you care for some before you go?"

Nicky shook his head. "I'll pass."

"You need strength," she said. "Not just *cojones.*"

He was shocked to hear his grandmother speak so. His startled reaction amused her, and she smiled briefly before returning her attention to the soup.

Grandmother and grandson stood in silence for a few moments. Nicky sensed they were having some sort of standoff, but he didn't know what to do or say to move them forward again.

At last, he blurted, "Please, *'buela,* just give me Cordelia Chase's address."

"Someone needs to deny you sometime," she said wistfully. *"Ay, hijo,* if I could go back in time, I would be a different grandmother for you."

"I don't want a different one," he said, trying his old grin on her. "I like this one."

She didn't smile back. "Because she gives you what you want."

He touched her wrinkled brown hand, and in that moment, she seemed solid to him again, not some ghost or wish, but a real person who could feel sadness and disappointment in him. *I'm a shallow bastard,* he thought dismally. *She can see right through me. I'm the ghost of the grandson she really wanted. A nice man. A good man.*

I'm his shadow, that's all.

"Because she loves me," he said.

"Her address is on the refrigerator," she murmured, as

if it didn't matter to her one way or the other, and went back to stirring her soup.

When he left with the slip of paper in his hand, she said softly, *"Que te vayes con Dios."*

Go with God.

"Gracias, grandmother of Nicolas de la Natividad," he said feelingly.

Chapter 4

Sunnydale

Giles was not loving Wesley.

The Brit was on the other end of the line, giving Giles what-for about "letting" Spike go through the alternity door, despite Giles's attempts to explain that there had been no "letting" in the situation, none whatsover. Meanwhile, Xander, Anya, Tara, Riley, and Joyce Summers were sitting on his couch and in his chairs, facing him with glum, hopeful expressions on their faces, which put him in mind of the year Principal Snyder had forced him to be in charge of the Sunnydale High School Talent Show.

With the naïveté of a foreigner, Giles had mistakenly assumed that a school event with the word "talent" in it ought to require the presence of same, and had decided to hold auditions. After each audition—charmingly referred to in the vernacular as "a tryout," the vast majority of which had been screamingly awful—the performer had sat in just this precise way as these four now, practically begging for a spot on the program. Then someone in the teachers' lounge had made some comments about "somebody's British elitism," and Giles had quickly realized the error of his ways. As a result, every single student who auditioned got a spot, and all was well with the fabled American democratic process, not to mention their highly cultivated passion for exercises in appallingly bad taste.

"Well, you should have kept Spike locked up somewhere," Wesley was now saying. "Serves you right, letting him gad about." His tone changed as he said, his mouth away from the receiver, "What's that? Yes, quite." Into the phone, he added, "Cordelia would like to remind you that Spike had Angel tortured while he was in L.A., and that he threatened to kill her. And yet *you* allowed him to live."

Giles pursed his lips shut. He was tempted to say, "Tit for tat," since Angel had once tortured *him,* but that would have been in exceedingly bad taste. And of course he didn't want anyone to kill Cordelia.

He shook his head at the hopeful quartet. "So let's recapitulate. It was Spike's going through that broke the link among Tara, Willow and the grandmother."

"Yes."

"And the link has not been reestablished, and we don't yet know why," he said, mostly for their benefit. Joyce grimaced and Anya shrugged, reaching for the bowl of barbecued potato chips Xander had picked up at his parents' house. Tara sank lower into the overstuffed chair, looking defeated. Riley got up and began to pace.

"How's the research going?" Giles asked Wesley.

"It's been difficult to do much of it," Wesley said tightly. "It's a bad deal up here. Gang violence, and—"

"Well, it's status quo here, too," Giles cut in. "We're overrun with demons." As if on cue, something slammed against the exterior wall, making Giles's place shake. Everyone jumped, then resumed course. There'd been so many attacks the group had become rather nonchalant about them.

"And monsters," Anya added. At Xander's quizzical frown, she said, "Everyone always tries to blame demons for everything. Not all episodes of mass destruction are their fault." She gave him a little smile and said to Giles, "So, we're also overrun with monsters."

"And monsters," Giles told Wesley.

Anya looked proud of herself. "I'm a loyal thing, aren't I? Sticking up for demons?"

"Ex thing," Xander reminded her. "You're a full-bodied—I mean, full-blooded human now."

"I'm not talking status quo," Wesley insisted on the phone. "It's become rather worse than that. The gangs are warring against each other. Mass shootings, fires. The bodies are piling up, and plenty of them were innocent bystanders. It's insane, Giles."

"Then one can assume that nothing we've attempted so far is helping. And, in point of fact, may be making the situation worse." Giles pushed up his glasses and rolled his shoulders to work out the kinks. "Do you really think the Russian girl knows what she's doing with that thing? Perhaps she's only telling us what she wants us to believe. Perhaps she's creating all the mayhem herself."

"Like the Initiative," Anya filled in. "Wow, they really messed things up, huh?"

Riley looked pained and Xander made a *"sssh"* at his girlfriend.

"Tell you what," Wesley snapped. "I'll just pull out my

trusty mayhemometer and see if you're right." Then he sighed. "Sorry, old boy. I'm just tired and frustrated."

Giles winced. He didn't like being reminded that he and Wesley, by virtue of both birthplace and occupation, had a lot in common. He had found Wesley Wyndam-Pryce to be a bit of a prig, too rigid by half, and rather lacking in humor. Which was, to be honest, Buffy's original assessment of Giles when she and he had first met.

He sighed and said to Tara, "Would you care to speak to Willow?"

Shyly, Tara got up and took the phone from his hand. He took a few steps away, to give her some small amount of privacy. Xander and Anya had begun squabbling about something, and Joyce Summers was clasping her hands, her forehead creased. She had been aware of Buffy's role as the Chosen One for two years, but her fear for her daughter was palpable. Joyce was quite aware that Buffy had already enjoyed a longer lifespan than many of her predecessors. It was the Slayer's fate—at least, thus far in the annals of time—to die young.

Riley, meanwhile, had picked up his gun and was checking it, ostensibly for ammunition.

"Hi," Tara said softly. "I'm fine." She shrugged and touched her hair. "A little tired, actually. Have you figured out how to reestablish the link?"

She listened and ticked her glance at Giles, who raised his brows. Then she said, "I'll try that." Her cheeks grew rosy. She was a lovely girl, really, looked a bit British. She murmured, "You, too."

She handed the phone back to Giles. He took it, and said, "Willow?"

"Giles, hi," Willow said. "Listen, Alina's going to try to psychically link with me. Cool, huh?" Her voice was tinged with excitement. "Since Tara and Doña Pilar and I were able to do it magickally, we think we might have a shot at it with, you know, her gift."

"What do you hope to accomplish?" Giles asked. "Locating Buffy?"

Riley looked at Giles sharply. Giles held up a cautioning hand, which did little to curb the young man's intensity.

"Or Angel, or both," she answered. She lowered her voice. "Or maybe even Spike. They all ended up in different places."

"How do you know?"

"Before everything went kerplooey, Alina could see their surroundings. Mentally, I mean. The backgrounds didn't match up. Alina's getting kind of close to the edge, Giles, and I don't know why I'm whispering about it because she *can* read my mind, after all."

"Indeed," he said, concerned. *I do wish Riley would stop staring at me.*

"It's so weird. She's hardly ever been out of her house. Everything's new and different. It's creating quite a strain on her. And she's worried about her boyfriend," Willow added.

"Oh. Where is he?" Giles asked.

Willow cleared her throat, "Oh, hi, Alina," she piped. "Gotta go. Tell Tara to rest up. If Alina and I manage the link, maybe we can bring her in later."

"I shall."

"Please tell Buffy's mom we'll find her soon," Willow added sweetly. "She must be worried sick."

"Quite."

"Okay, gotta go. Bye."

"Good-bye, Willow. And good luck," Giles said, to the dial tone. He cleared his throat and smiled pleasantly at

Joyce and Riley. "They're working on the search for Buffy," he said.

"How?" Riley demanded.

"And Spike?" Anya asked. Xander frowned. She gave him a look and said, "And Angel. I'm worried about all of them, okay?" She smiled at Riley. "I'm just worried sick about Buffy."

Riley stuffed his gun into a holster and said, "I'm going on patrol."

He stomped out of the room and left the others staring at Giles.

And to think I minded *directing that talent show,* he thought glumly.

Los Angeles

It doesn't take a mind reader to understand what she's saying, Willow thought, as she watched Alina pacing and muttering to herself in Cordelia's living room. *Or a Russian dictionary.*

She's really getting scared.

Cordelia walked into the room, precariously balancing a tray with three coffee cups, an open carton of milk, and some packets of Equal. Also, a single spoon and some half-wadded-up paper napkins. Cordelia did her best when it came to the social graces.

"Here," she said, setting the tray down on her coffee table. She smoothed her hair away from her forehead. "Wow, when you make it from scratch . . ." She sighed and wrinkled her nose. "But I wanted you guys to have the best."

"Cordelia, really," Wesley said, as he laid the phone on Cordelia's end table beside the sofa. "You had the beans ground at Starbucks. All you did was put some of them in the basket and pour in the water."

"I had to insert a coffee filter," she said, as if she'd caught him in the most devious of base fibs.

"Yes. Quite." He shook his head and surveyed the cups. "Is one of those for me?"

She raised a brow. "After that? I don't think so." Then she shrugged. "If you want. I'm going to have some tea. Herbal." She smiled at Willow. "Caffeine ages the skin."

Willow got ready to take umbrage, but the Cordelia of Los Angeles was not the Queen of Mean, as had been the Cordelia of Sunnydale. True, she was still the Queen of Major Sarcasm, but the sharp edge had been slightly dulled. She seemed to have matured, gotten some compassion under her belt.

Refreshing, Willow thought. *Also, kind of spooky.*

Alina picked up one of the cups of coffee and drank it quickly. She was a pretty girl, her outfit of a pair of jeans and a rather nondescript turtleneck sweater. From what Willow had heard of her life, she had never gotten to experiment with makeup or even go shopping at a mall. She had been a virtual prisoner.

"Yes," Alina said, gazing at Willow over her cup. "A prisoner."

Willow started. She said anxiously, "I didn't mean to offend you or anything with . . . what I was thinking about you in the privacy of my own mind."

"Is okay." Alina looked tired. She put down her cup and raked her fingers through her hair. Tears slid down her cheeks and she crossed her arms over her chest, letting out a shuddering sigh. "Soon you and I must try to bond. The longer we wait . . ." She didn't finish her sentence.

"Okay, then." Willow swallowed hard. "What do you want me to do? Do we touch each other's temples and chant, 'I am Spock'? Which, since no TV for you, um, you don't get. It's a joke."

"Vulcan mind meld," Alina said. She drained her coffee and put the cup down with a decisive gesture. "You can go into trance?"

"Yes." Willow nodded. "I'm Trance Girl. No problem."

"Then, privacy," she said to the others.

"Why don't you go into my bedroom?" Cordelia suggested. "We'll stay out here." She gazed around. "You, too, Phantom Dennis."

As if to indicate his agreement, Alina's empty cup rose from the table and floated toward the kitchen.

Alina nodded at Willow. The two stood and Willow followed Alina down the hall, into Cordelia's bedroom.

It was a spacious room for an apartment. Alina indicated the bed and said, "Lie down, please. I will join with you."

"Um, I'm in a committed relationship," she said, then flushed and did as the other girl requested. Alina lay down beside her, both of them on their backs, and took Willow's hand in hers.

"Breathe deeply and slowly. Close eyes," Alina said gently. Willow liked her. She was really sweet, and Willow felt sorry about the crummy life she'd had to lead.

"Willow, you are also sweet," Alina murmured. "For an American, especially."

"Americans are actually fairly nice. Well, except for hate crimes and stuff."

"I hope to see much of America," Alina said.

"I hope that for you, too."

"No, breathing."

Willow listened to her breath, matching her rhythm to

Alina's. Slowly in, slowly out . . . she heard a muted buzzing sound and felt as if she were floating a few inches above the mattress. The vague scent of oranges wafted around her.

Behind her eyelids, golden light glowed.

She heard her own heartbeat, and then what she guessed was Alina's as well.

She kept pace with Alina's slow, rhythmic breathing. Then suddenly she saw an enchanted landscape of gentle hills and a splendid stone castle in the background. She could almost feel the sunshine on her face, almost smell the lush vegetation.

We're doing it, she thought.

Then Alina caught her breath, and Willow lost the image.

The Russian girl groaned in frustration. Before Willow had completely regained her composure, Alina sat upright and buried her face in her hands.

"I saw something," Willow offered.

"I am too nervous. I cannot do." Alina dropped her hands to her lap. "I am so, so sorry."

"No, it's okay," Willow said anxiously. She was flooded with disappointment. *What are we going to do?*

Alina looked at her uncertainly. She looked terrified as she said, "Perhaps my parents will repair the Tracer."

"And force you to do whatever they want with it," Willow said, biting her lower lip.

"Mischa could help, perhaps." The other girl closed her eyes, then grimaced. "He must be blocking his thoughts. I can't find him."

"Don't worry," Willow said worriedly. "We'll figure something out. We'll get this working and boy, watch things happen."

Alina let out a little cry and grabbed Willow's shoulders. She said, "They're coming!"

"Who?" Willow asked, wide-eyed and freaked out.

"Someone is trying to get through my barrier," she said. "Someone very powerful." She raked her hands through her hair. "It must be my parents."

It occurred to Willow that they were sitting ducks in Cordelia's apartment. With Angel out of the picture, they didn't even have anybody on their side who could hit very hard. She wondered if Cordelia had a gun—*eeuuuw, not liking that idea*—but if people did trace Alina here, what were they going to do about it?

Alina shook her head. "This whole scheme. It is crazy, isn't it." She wasn't asking Willow a question.

Alina got up off the bed and paced. "When I was a little girl, I could feel my parents' excitement. Their love." She looked pensive. "They loved me. But more than that, they loved the possibilities I represented. The hope. It was all still a happy dream.

"But this path they've chosen . . ." Her shoulders slumped. "Somehow, it has warped them. They don't see that what we're doing is wrong. They don't care. The consequences of our actions are unseen to them. What counts is making the dream come true."

"Um, well, that's called drive here in America, and a lot of times, we think it's pretty neat," Willow ventured.

"Obsession is the correct word," Alina cut in. She touched Willow's shoulder, then dropped her hand to her side and walked some more. Seeing Cordelia's mirror, she stopped and peered at her reflection. "My parents have stopped seeing me as flesh and blood. As their daughter. I'm only part of the machine." She gestured toward the magic toaster-thing resting against the pillows.

"No," Willow protested. "I'm sure that's not true, Alina. You're just tired and scared. Plus you probably have low blood sugar."

Alina shook her head. "I believe that if my father finds me, he will force me to make even more people disappear."

"He wouldn't . . . force . . . hurt . . . his own daughter," Willow chewed her lower lip. *Just us.* "Would he?"

Alina looked dejected. "I don't know what my parents are capable of anymore. When I think about what we were doing . . ." She ran her hands up and down her arms, as if trying to warm herself.

"The only true friend I have is Mischa, and I can't find him. I can't lock onto him." She covered her mouth as if she were going to be sick and whirled on her heel. "Willow, what if he's dead?"

This is one of the problems with life as I know it, Willow thought. *Cuz, like, if this was a TV show, I would tell her not to worry and we'd have a big hug, and then we'd cut to commercial. Then my father, played by Stephen Collins, would have a long chat with her parents and those guys on* Roswell *would bring everyone back. And Pacey and Joey would live happily ever after.*

Problem is, this is real life, starring us.

And in my real life, people die. A lot. Well, not the same people. Most of them die only once.

But I've mourned more deaths than I ever imagined I would, and I'm not even out of college.

"You see?" Alina whispered. "You cannot lie to me, just to comfort me. It's very possible that Mischa has been killed."

"Do you want me to do a protection spell for him?" she asked.

"Is it traceable?" she asked reluctantly. "Would someone with highly developed mental powers be able to track him following its magickal trail?"

Willow was intrigued. "I honestly have no idea," she said. But it occurred to her that it might be. Hadn't Doña Pilar believed that the nightmare that surrounded the de la Natividad home with blackness had followed one of her spells back to its source?

"Then don't do it," Alina said. Her misery was palpable. "My parents taught me that no one outside our family was to be trusted. But I have found several people more trustworthy than they."

She sat down on the bed. Then she swung her legs onto the mattress and lay down. "I'm so tired, Willow. Do you mind if I rest?"

"Of course not." Willow made as if to leave.

"But don't go. Please," Alina pleaded. "I'm afraid to be by myself. I feel like I will melt into the bed and no one will ever find me again."

Wow. What an imagination, Willow thought. "Okay. Of course I'll stay," Willow said. "You go to sleep. I'll . . . I'll make sure you don't melt."

Alina smiled faintly and closed her eyes. Within seconds, she was asleep.

Willow looked up toward the ceiling and sent out an audible thought:

Tara, can you hear me?

Yes, Willow.

I love you.

And I love you.

All this stuff is really weird, don't you think, Tara?

Yeah. Someone should write a book about it.

They giggled together.

Then Willow felt her own lids growing heavy; she lay

down beside Alina and folded her hands over her abdomen.

Suddenly so tired . . .

"There are places between waking and dreaming where awareness lingers, but volition does not," Dream Giles said to Dream Willow. "Where you know that something's approaching your bed, say, or even touching you, yet you are powerless to move. You can't quite wake up, either. It's terrifying."

"That's happened to me," Dream Willow told him.

It's happening to me now.
Something's in the room now.
Something that shouldn't be here.
Something that means to harm us both.
Kill us both.
Something that is bending over me . . . stop it, go away . . . help . . . Buffy . . . where are you? . . . stop, stop—

Something very cold and evil slid into Willow's brain; something that wanted nothing but the worst for every living thing; but it was not a piece of alternity that had slipped out or slipped through. It was the residue of what was left after some of the world's goodness had been sucked into the portal Alina had created to send the youth of Los Angeles into oblivion. It was the absence of good, which is worse than evil. Apathy, which is far worse.

It was something that was in the world all the time, although invisible.

Willow didn't know about the eternal battle between good and evil, not really; she didn't know there were Powers That Be that kept track of the rules, and demons who maintained the balance, as Whistler had done. That there were Protectors and Judges and Keys; she didn't know any of that. She knew about the Hellmouth, of course, and she knew about the Slayer, but she didn't realize that the matters of life and death were very much like games, with playing fields and regulations.

But when good got sucked out, the field tilted badly. The rules went out the window.

The lack of goodness hurt as it bored into her, traveling down her spinal column, lodging itself inside her like a pestilent tumor.

But then she slept, and dreamed—not of Tara, but of Oz, her lost love, her sacrificed love, her unworkable love—

The absence of goodness is despair.

Her chest rose only slightly.

It is death.

Her chest rose . . . not at all.

I am thinking of Moscow in winter, Mischa thought. *The Kremlin domed with snow, and the thick fur coats and hats, and people rushing home to the samovar and the vodka.*

He was making good progress on the road. He figured he must be across the Arizona border by now, almost halfway to the Grand . . .

Muscovites everywhere, walking through the snow; city snow is often dirty and gray. The old ladies are wearing their woolen babushkas. No one can make borscht like my Aunt Vera.

Oh, God, is Alina okay? What if she—

His blood froze as he glanced into the rearview mirror.

A Highway Patrol officer had just pulled onto the blacktop about fifty feet behind him. There was no one but Mischa on the road, and he was topping eighty.

He swore in Russian and took his foot off the gas. If he

braked, it would be admission of guilt, and the cop would be more likely to pull him over. Mischa knew all the tricks. They had served him well both here and back home. Authoritarian minds were the same everywhere.

Gradually, Mischa's stolen Saturn slowed to a more acceptable seventy and he swallowed hard. Sweat glistened on his forehead, gelling in the air conditioning as he trembled. Hitchhiking hadn't worked—too slow, not enough forward motion. He'd been afraid that Alina would somehow get there before him, and, thinking he wouldn't be coming, would give up on him. So he'd given up, finally, and stolen a car from a parking lot in San Bernardino. The car's owner had run inside a convenience store, leaving the motor running, so Mischa had simply slipped inside and helped himself to it. He'd been on Interstate 10 in no time, heading east, but the knowledge that the car would be the object of a search was always on his mind, as was the equally chilling knowledge that Alina's parents would be scanning for his mind.

For all he knew, the patrol officer was calling in his license plate and discovering that the car had been stolen. Any moment now, the siren and lights would blast on, and Mischa would be faced with a choice: try to outrun him, or surrender?

He drove on, breathless, beyond tense.

Moscow in the snow. It's just beautiful.

Chapter 5

THE YOUNG WOMAN LED ANGEL THROUGH AN INCREAS-
ingly dark and forbidding forest. After he had beaten the
men who had accosted her, she had looked at him with big
blue eyes, and said, "Please, sir, you must accompany me to
my grandmother's cottage, or they'll just come after me."

Angel looked at the bodies on the ground. "Not them,"
he said.

"No, but there are many others," she said. "I beg of
you."

"I have to be . . . somewhere," Angel replied. Except
the thing was, he really didn't know where that "somewhere" was. Buffy wasn't here, but that only left an infinite number of places where she might be. And as he
didn't know how he could travel from one reality to another without some contact from Alina or Willow, Tara,
and Doña Pilar—whose presence he hadn't felt since ar-
riving here—he figured one place was probably as good

as another. He agreed. She introduced herself as Tan-kia, and he told her his name.

"What did they want with you?" he asked her as they followed narrow trails between tall trees. The green canopy overhead was so dense that Angel could no longer see the sun or sky.

"To enslave me," she said matter-of-factly, as if it were something he should have known at a glance. "I am of the Forest People."

He ducked a tree branch that she walked easily beneath. "And they enslave the Forest People?"

This time she held a branch for him as he passed. "Of course, when they can."

"Your grandmother is also a Forest Person?" he asked.

"Yes, she is—one of the most respected of us all," Tan-kia said, letting the branch go. "She is a witch of some repute. They would never have attacked me at her cottage, but when I foolishly wandered away from the Forest—I only wanted to see what lay over the ridge—they took me." Her face hardened as if at bad memories. "I had been enslaved for several weeks before I made my escape, and then they chased me, thinking they could have me back again. Thanks to you, Angel, they learned their mistake."

"Did you see it?" he asked. "Whatever is over the ridge?"

"I saw only another ridge," Tan-kia replied, smiling ruefully. She shrugged. "I am sure that there is more to see over that one, though."

"And where do they live, the men who meant to enslave you?"

"A town, in a nearby valley. There are big houses there, made of stone, not just wood. And those who live in the big houses all want slaves, like me."

Angel had heard of parallel universes, but he wasn't

sure just how parallel they were. This young woman, still in her teens, leading him to her grandmother the witch, reminded Angel of what Buffy had told him about Salma de la Natividad and her grandmother, Doña Pilar, back in L.A. *Maybe they're this universe's version of those two,* he thought. *They might be able to locate Buffy.* It was the best shot he'd had since he'd arrived, so he determined to take it.

The woods reminded Angel of those in Romania in the old days, so thick with growth that to step off the path meant risking becoming hopelessly entangled in the brush and lost in the trees. He was sure some forests like that still existed in parts of eastern Europe, but most had been logged, built over, roads graded through them. The forests that had inspired so many frightening fairy stories on Earth were being defanged, their teeth and their terror removed by the ever-increasing population. He had a sense that the same process had not yet happened here—that if he were to fly up above the canopy of the trees, he would see that these forests went on for hundreds, if not thousands, of miles. This was a place like those from the fairy tales back home.

As Tan-kia passed through the woods with which she seemed so intimate, leading Angel down paths that he couldn't even make out until they were on them, she kept up a constant chatter, telling Angel about her home, her grandmother, the trees and birds and animals they passed. He tried to be polite, but he listened for sounds of pursuit, watched for possible ambush sites, and was generally preoccupied with making sure that Tan-kia would get home safely. Besides, if there was anything her witchy grandmother could do to help reunite him with Buffy, she would be inclined to do so because he had brought her granddaughter home safely.

Perhaps three hours had passed; having been to Hell for centuries, Angel was aware that time moved at different speeds in different dimensions. They came to a clearing in the woods, where patches of unchanged sky showed through the trees, and in the center of the clearing was a small cottage, built from local materials so that it almost blended perfectly with the trees surrounding it. Gray smoke plumed toward the sky from a chimney. *If I didn't know a witch lived here,* he thought, *I'd swear a witch lived here.*

"This your grandmother's place?" Angel asked.

"Yes," Tan-kia responded. "This is where I grew up, where she raised me after my parents were taken away."

"By the same people who took you?" Angel guessed.

"Yes," Tan-kia said. "They have taken Forest People for their slaves for as long as anyone can remember." She took Angel's hand and gave it a quick, shy squeeze. "Thank you again," she said, "for what you have done for me."

She turned away and walked to the door. Before opening it, she cooed loudly once, some kind of signal, Angel assumed. Then she tugged the door open, calling, "It's me, grandmother!" before entering. "I'm home!" She passed into the shadows for a moment, then returned to beckon Angel in.

Having been invited across the threshold, he followed her. Her grandmother met them just inside, in a room that might have been built for those same fairy tales Angel had thought of earlier. The floors, walls, and ceiling were all hewn from the same wood, as was all the furniture—chairs, tables, and other items notched and pegged together. The place was a woodworker's dream, no metal or plastic to be seen, and only a small amount of stone where a fire crackled in a fireplace. The cozy den looked like the dwarves' house from *Snow White*, but the woman who lived here, Tan-kia's grandmother, was no dwarf.

She was taller than Angel by a good head and a half. Her deeply lined face was drawn back in a smile that was at once friendly and a little intimidating. Angel amended his earlier estimation of the house, and wondered if in fact it was carved from gingerbread, because this woman certainly looked like one who could eat Hansel and Gretel and still be hungry for dessert. Her hair was white and stringy and hung straight down her back, nearly to her knees. She wore a simple burgundy dress with a plain white apron over it, tied at the waist by a white sash.

After locking Tan-kia in an embrace that Angel feared might crush the girl's spine, the grandmother sat and listened quietly while Tan-kia told her story, describing Angel's dispatching of the two barbarians with great relish. She glossed over the period of her imprisonment, and Angel was struck again by how second nature the whole idea seemed to be to the people here.

When she was finished, her grandmother looked steadily at Angel. After a few moments, she smiled again. "You have done my granddaughter a great service, and asked for nothing in return," she told him seriously. "Had you asked for a boon, I could not have granted it. But since you did not, then I can. What would you have?"

Angel didn't have to think about it twice. "There's this girl, Buffy . . ." he began.

"You would have her fall in love with you?"

Angel finally let himself think what he'd been trying not to think about ever since he got involved with alternities.

There must be hundreds of realities here where Buffy and I can be together again. Places where I'm just a man,

and she's a woman. No vampire, no Slayer. Just . . . us.
Or if she needs that, if she needs to be more, where she is
still a Slayer, and I . . . I'm free . . .

He lost himself in reverie as emotions washed over
him. He still wanted her. They had agreed to stay away
from each other, and she didn't remember the twenty-
four hours they had spent together when he had regained
his mortality. But he had never agreed to stop loving her.

Nor could he forget what it felt like to hold Buffy, and
feel his heart thundering in his chest from her nearness,
and her love and her desire for him.

"I need to find her," he said simply.

Tan-kia's grandmother nodded again. Tan-kia had
turned away as soon as Angel mentioned another woman,
and he thought maybe he'd been misreading her interest
as simply gratitude, when there was more there.

"I will need to look inside you to find her," the grandmother said quietly.

"I'm a vam . . . a lot of people can't see inside me," he
cautioned.

"I can. I already do, to a degree." She gave him a look
that he couldn't read—had she seen that he was a vampire?

She straight-armed herself out of the chair she sat in
and came to Angel, taking his head between her hands.
She brought her face very close, her cloudy blue eyes
looking deeply into his. He fought the temptation to re-
sist—he didn't really know her, or Tan-kia, and this
whole thing could be some kind of a trap, for all he knew.

But he found himself trusting her anyway, so he didn't
struggle. After a moment, she released him.

"Her name is Buffy," she said.

"That's right."

She traced a circle in the air with a fingertip, and an

image appeared there, as if it were an old, fading TV screen. "This is she?"

Inside the circle, Angel could see Buffy. She was under attack—by pieces of armor, it seemed, clutching at her, kicking at her. She tried to fight back, but there were so many of them, it looked as if they'd overwhelm her at any moment.

"Yes, that's her!" Angel said urgently. "She needs me. Can you send me now?"

"Of course," the witch said. "It will only take a few moments. A few preparations."

"Grandmother!" Tan-kia said sharply. She had gone to a window, looking out at the woods beyond the clearing. When she turned around, the look on her face was one of mortal terror.

"Soldiers," she said. "Dozens of them. They must have followed us."

Angel took her place at the window. At the edge of the clearing, a force had massed—barbaric-looking men like the ones he had saved Tan-kia from before, but armed with bows and arrows and sharpened spears, in addition to swords.

There were at least thirty of them. And their weapons, their arrows and spears, were all wood-shafted.

Any one of them could kill him with a lucky shot.

"That the posse?" he asked. "Search party for you?"

"And my grandmother," she said anxiously. "They rarely venture so far into the woods, so we must have truly angered them."

"Or scared them," Angel added.

Tan-kia nodded.

"What about the girl? Buffy?" the grandmother reminded him.

Not that I need reminding.

"If you go," Tan-kia said, "they'll kill us both. Without hesitation."

The disembodied wrist held Buffy in place.

Then one of the Black Knight's armored legs twined itself between Buffy's legs and kicked, knocking her off-balance. When she fell to the ground, the other arm snaked around her throat, gauntleted fingers cutting off her air. She tugged at it with her own hands, but she felt her strength rapidly slipping away, and as the other body parts pounded her, the sky began to darken before her eyes.

Not the sky, she realized. Her vision was clouding. The battle had been going on for hours. At least, that was how it felt. And after dealing with the dragon, she was already tired. It would be so easy just to drift off. But she knew if she lost consciousness she wouldn't be waking up again. This wasn't slipping away into a dream, this was the end if she let the thing beat her.

Forcing herself to stay alert, she pulled harder at the gauntlet, feeling its metal dent under her grip. She ignored the increased pinch and continued to tug it away from her, finally breaking its grip. When it released, she threw it as hard as she could.

She rolled to a sitting position, kicking at some of the pieces of armor that still assaulted her. She gained a moment's respite, which she used to inhale deeply a couple of times. But then the various sections of animated armor ganged up on her again, metal bruising her flesh, grabbing at her appendages.

There's got to be a way to stop this, she thought. But just as suddenly, she thought, *Why? If one is going to enchant armor, why not enchant it all the way? Keep it at-*

*tacking until it's pulverized to its very atoms, and even
then it can still do some damage. Try breathing in an entire suit of armor and see what it does for your lungs.*

But she wasn't willing to give up. She snatched up one
of the metallic legs and used it to bash at the other pieces.
They fell back from her ferocious barrage, but as soon as
she moved on to the next piece, the last one resumed its
attack.

One of the arms clutched the big war mace and swung
it awkwardly at her legs. Buffy dodged it easily, then
swooped down with one hand and grabbed it by the grip.
She shook the arm, but it wouldn't release the mace, so
she drove it into the ground as hard as she could, handle
down. The arm shook loose, and she quickly reversed it
and brought the weapon's spiked head down on the arm,
crushing it into the earth.

That arm lay still for a moment, then twitched a couple
of times, apparently trying to continue the battle.

But Buffy had a different idea. She dodged and jumped
over the armored bits, heading for the helmet, which had
managed to stay away from the worst of the fight. As she
approached the helm, it tried to scuttle away. Buffy was
faster, though. She swung the mace, whirling it over her
head twice to get up some speed, and smashed it into the
helmet.

Metal flew everywhere.

She raised the mace and crashed it into the helmet
again, or what was left of it.

The armor lay quiet.

The helmet was the brain, she thought, breathing hard.
Kill it, kill the whole suit.

Should have thought of that sooner.

Buffy wiped sweat from her forehead and looked at the

castle, straight down a wide pathway worn by animals pulling carts or wagons. In the highest tower's window, she thought she could just make out a vague form.

The contender from L.A. for Miss Alternate Reality? No rest for the weary.

"You're kidding me, right, mates?" Spike said.

The other vampires had explained the way things worked to him. He shook his head disbelievingly. "You don't hunt. You get your blood from that river—all right, handy, but can anyone say boring? Every now and then you see someone watching you, taking notes, taking bloody pictures! And you don't ever get ticked off and just *charge* them?"

"Fence is electrified, Spike," the dark-haired, handsome bloke said. He had introduced himself as Malon. Spike wished he'd quit doing the Robert Mitchum thing with his eyes and either open them or close them. "When they want it to be. Somehow, if anyone tries to make a break, they know and they power it up. Couple of us tried going over it once. Fried 'em."

"What about under it? What about taking a running jump or something? Haven't any of you ever seen *The Great Escape?* Or bloody *Chicken Run?*"

Issak, the one-armed one, wagged his stump at Spike. They were all sitting among the jumbled rocks. Seemed that the sun—which had risen about half an hour earlier, was not his friend here, either, so he had found refuge with the others among the shadowed outcroppings, to avoid the Mother of All Sunburns.

"Easy for you to talk big," he said. "You just got here. You haven't actually tried getting out. You haven't lost a limb to their weapons."

"That what happened to you?" Spike asked.

"You bet," Issak said. "They have these energy poles. You get too close, they burn you with them."

"You tried it and lost an arm?"

Issak nodded.

"Then you didn't try hard enough," Spike said coldly. "Shouldn't have backed down until they killed you. At least the ones who went into the fence were committed to it."

"Man, you're full of talk," the greasy-haired one interjected. He had given his name as Ren'chlad. Spike wondered where these blokes were from—and why there didn't seem to be any women here—but the answers he got when he asked were even more confusing than not knowing. "Haven't seen you try it."

"I haven't been here long enough to try much of anything, have I?" Spike rejoined. "And I haven't seen any of your people with their sodding 'energy poles' or whatever, or you'd have seen some action. You know if you all banded together, they wouldn't be able to stop all of you."

"You're full of it, Spike," Malon said. "Like you said, you haven't even seen them. You don't know what we know, so maybe you should just keep your accusations to yourself."

Spike shrugged. "You just watch me when they show themselves. Maybe you're content to be on exhibit, but I'm not. I've got things to do. I can't afford to cool my heels in here for the rest of eternity."

He looked around at the other vampires, each with his own spot in the shade of the big rocks. *Bunch of useless louts,* he thought. *Never catch me behaving like that.*

But in the next moment, he amended that view. If he didn't get the damn chip out of him, that was exactly what he'd be like, sitting in his crypt in Sunnydale drinking butcher's blood and playing canasta for the rest of time.

If I ever get home.
The thought made him sick.

Salma de la Natividad ran full out. In spite of her terror
and her weariness, she had latched onto a rhythm and she
held it, doing a Marion Jones plus a Kathy Freeman
through the disgusting damp closeness of the tunnels.

Of course, she had inspiration.

Behind her, the worm-thing barreled forward, its teeth
clacking together as it—*what, slithered?* she wondered—
after her. She was managing to outpace it, but barely. One
slip, one stumble, one misstep and she was worm food.
The knowledge propelled her forward, kept her legs
reaching out, her footing firm.

But she wasn't a runner, and she couldn't keep the pace
up much longer. She threw herself around corners, but the
thing seemed to have learned that trick. It held back just
far enough that it always managed to make the corners
behind her.

As she kept going, lungs sucking in great gasping
breaths that felt like they were tearing her apart, the germ
of an idea came to her.

I can still breathe, she thought. She worked with that
for a moment, keeping her legs charging, her arms pump-
ing back and forth. *If I can breathe, there must be air. I'd
have used up all the air in here—well, me and the
worm—if it wasn't being replaced from someplace.*

So there's ventilation.

And where there's ventilation, there's a way out.

Which meant that as she ran, not only did she have to
watch her footing, she had to keep an eye open for vents
or ducts or passageways—whatever might be admitting
air into the tunnel system.

But she saw nothing, just expanses of rock walls, slick with worm-whatever.

And meanwhile, the worm kept up with her, waiting for that slip, that misstep.

When she came to a corner, she half-stepped to spin herself around it, hoping to throw the creature off and earn herself a breather. It didn't work, though. Not only did the creature clear the corner, but her half-step landed wrong, and her right foot skidded out from under her as she rounded the corner.

She went down in the muck with a splash, catching herself on her hands. She pushed herself back up immediately, but it was too late. The worm-thing rounded the corner behind her and sped up, mouth opening to swallow her whole. The inside of it was all soft pink flesh and yellow teeth.

But as she struggled to regain her footing, she noticed something, down low on the wall, that she never would have noticed from a standing position. It was a slice in the stone, a dark hollow, barely as wide as she was. And the air before it smelled cleaner. With less than a second to spare, she threw herself into it, jamming herself into the stone crack, feeling its rough edges cut her open in a dozen places.

The worm whisked past her, even longer than she thought it was; it reminded her of the Chinese dragons people maneuvered on Chinese New Year. This one was at least two dozen people long.

It continued down the tunnel—it would have to go to another turn and work its way back around, since these were one-way tunnels as far as it was concerned. She could get out of the crevasse, go back, try to find another way out.

But she was here. And there was definitely breathable air coming through the crack. If she pushed . . .

I'll never fit, she thought.

But what's the worst that could happen if I try? It'll kill me?

Like the worm won't.

She shoved herself farther into the rock slit. It was tight—too tight, she was sure. But her own blood lubricated her passage and made her skin slip across the rock. More jagged spurs cut her, everywhere, but still she forced herself on, pushing herself inch by inch with her fingertips. Nails splintered on the rock; one pointy spot dug a trench in her back as she shoved her way through.

The farther she went, the more it hurt, and the more claustrophobic she grew. Her nose pushed against the rock, scratching across the tip. She tried to look to her right, to see what she was edging toward, but she could see nothing.

But as she kept going, the air smelled fresher.

She continued.

When it seemed that she could go no farther, that her screaming muscles would rebel against her and refuse to take her another inch, she felt herself moving into a wider space. A few moments later, it was wide enough to allow her to turn her head, so she could see, for the first time since she'd entered the crevasse, where she was headed.

And there was light.

From there, it was easy. She had room enough to push off with her hands and feet, propelling herself toward the opening through which beautiful white light spilled. The light picked out details—a rosy vein in the gray and black speckled rock, a bit of an upthrust that looked to her like a rose thorn—and they were beautiful. Light was beautiful. Air was lovely beyond all measure. It tasted like gold, like chocolate, like a piano concerto.

Three minutes later, she was standing in a field.

She had emerged from a cliff face. At the top, built of gray stone that blended almost seamlessly, was a wall of the castle she had seen before, when she was brought here to be sacrificed. But she could see no one on the wall, no windows facing her way. There was only a long meadow of tall grasses, and in the distance, a forest and the mountains.

She didn't know where she was, or what lay inside the forest, or how far to those mountains.

But she knew what was in the castle. She started to walk, glorying in the sunshine on her face.

After an hour or so, she guessed, she still hadn't crossed the entire meadow. Although she was near exhaustion, she'd made some progress. The forest was ahead, less than a third of the distance she'd already covered. From here, she could see that the trees were incredibly tall, their tops higher than the tallest redwoods or giant sequoias she'd seen in California.

They were intimidating—but beautiful, and she couldn't wait to be back in their shade.

But before she could reach them, she heard a decidedly unnatural sound, behind her—a fanfare of trumpets.

She spun around. Coming from the castle—thundering her way—was a company of soldiers, trumpeter at their head. They were mounted, on the same strange beasts she'd been carried on before. And they rode at full gallop.

Once more, Salma started to run.

Chapter 6

Los Angeles

LOS ANGELES WAS AN INFERNO.

Ernesto Hernandez rode shotgun while Flaco Montoya drove the SUV. Nicky was in the back, compulsively chewing cinnamon gum, tapping his fingertips against his thigh. The two bodyguards were chatting in the singsong Spanish of the lower classes, and Nicky was eavesdropping. Their boss, Ruben Velasco, was down in the hospital in Sunnydale. Someone had done a job on him, and everyone on the de la Natividads' private security force was jittery. Of course, Nicky's family wouldn't just let him go to this Cordelia Chase's home unaccompanied.

"L.A. is a freakin' war zone, *hombre; pues,* worse than the last set of riots. *Orale,* it's crazy to go out in this," Ernie drawled.

Flaco nudged Ernie, who lowered his voice and

changed the subject. Neither of the buffed-up machos wanted the son of the family to think they were cowards.

But they're right, Nicky thought, as he gazed out the window. Flames blurred in shimmering curtains as they passed block after block of burning buildings. Police cars screamed everywhere, like a bunch of hysterical chicks who'd seen a spider on the floor of the school gym or something. Nicky heard the familiar hollow sound of gunfire, and reflexively looked for the shooter. Two men were chasing each other down the street.

He shook his head. Maybe Salma was safer, wherever she was, than being in the midst of this chaos. *Is bringing her home really doing her a favor? Maybe I should just leave her there.*

But he didn't believe it. He didn't believe it for one single minute. He had to know. He had to see her, to talk to her. *And for all I know, she could be dea—*

"Nicky? Okay if I turn on Radio Latina?" Flaco called to him.

"Sure, *mano.*" Nicky gave Flaco a grim smile and decided to try to be sociable. "You ever see Los Tiranos in concert? They're awesome."

"My older brother saw Selena once," Flaco said. "She was a hottie."

Till some lunatic shot her, Nicky added silently, and fell back into brooding.

Anyone hurts Salma, I am invoking the worst demon I can find, and I am tearing them apart. He clenched his fists and gritted his teeth, feeling the rush that anger brought. He had no more powers. His Night of the Long Knives was over.

My grandmother will help me.

But he was not sure of that. He was sure of nothing.

Except that I will do whatever I can to make up for what I have done. I would even die.

The round globule of burning goo caromed off Xander's mighty shield—which he had snatched off the nearest trash can—and arced into the sky like a flyball from Hell.

"Just let it bounce!" Giles cried, as Joyce held out her trash can lid in an effort to capture it. Startled by his shout, she yanked the lid away, and the thing bounced on the ground and came to a rolling stop.

Tara and Anya gingerly approached it. It was smoking, and the grass surrounding it was catching fire. Tara did something with her fingers and the fires went out.

My daughter knows the most interesting people, Joyce thought wryly. *The other women in my book group get to brag about their children's accomplishments, but I'll bet not one of their kids' pals has ever put out a fire with magick.*

"So, was that, like, an Initiative guardian droid or something?" Xander asked, smoothing back his hair. "Did you see how I deflected it?" he added, preening for his girlfriend.

"You were like Mickey Mantle," she said. "And did you notice that I knew who to compare you to?"

"I certainly did." He blew her a kiss. "All that pop-culture work you've been doing is paying off."

Giles forced open the door to the building and gestured for the others to come inside. It was an old-fashioned fraternity house, rather like one might find in the movies, with oak wainscoting and brass trophies in a glass case in the living room. Joyce found it almost impossible to believe that Riley had been a soldier involved in covert operations below this very building, and that the government had since filled the entire subterranean laboratory with concrete.

This was their second attempt to access the lab. First they'd gone to where Spike had showed Buffy "a back entrance"—a secret door concealed in a rock face. Nothing remained of the door, however. Or of the rock.

It's kind of like the X-Files, Joyce thought, *only it's real, and there are no commercials.*

At the back of the upstairs hall, next to what had once been Riley's room, Xander opened a small compartment and pressed a button. The four of them waited.

Nothing happened.

"It's still deactivated," Xander said to Giles, who nodded.

"One may assume they've permanently scrapped the entire project," Giles said. To Joyce, he added, "We've checked periodically. Thought perhaps they might secretly resume operations, or some such."

"Riley would t-tell us," Tara insisted.

"Right," Xander bit off. "Like he told us he was in the Initiative in the first place."

"Or B-Buffy," Tara added.

Xander still looked unimpressed. "Yup. Like she told us about Angel when he came back from Hell."

Someday, Buffy will bring home a regular boy, Joyce thought wistfully. *And I'll just keel over and die from shock.*

"So, snooping around the Initiative still not an option," Xander continued, moving his shoulders. "Do we ask Riley if he knows anything about flying goo globs, therefore necessitating the fessing up that we have, yet again, not trusted him?"

"Why should that shame us?" Anya shrugged. "He didn't fess up to us. We only found out he was in the Initiative by accident."

"But that's because he didn't t-trust us," Tara pointed out. "Because he didn't know us. B-but we trust him, now. Because . . . he's a good guy, like us."

Xander frowned at her. "Only, with a rank, serial number, and really big guns."

Tara said, "I l-like Riley. He's not hiding any-th-thing from us."

Xander cocked his head. "Except that maybe this whole thing is something *else* the Initiative cooked up, and that girl in Los Angeles who's supposed to be from Russia is just an undercover U.S.D.A.-inspected Dr. Walsh drone looking for a free trip to Mars?"

"Well, we oughtn't jump to conclusions," Giles said, but Joyce saw uncertainty flicker across his features. "Why on earth would they want to go to Mars?"

"Why would anyone want to make supersoldiers out of used people and demon parts?" Xander countered. "But they did."

Joyce felt a little queasy. "Maybe Buffy should sign up for one of those video dating services," she said to herself. "Of course, I haven't done much better with men." When she realized she'd spoken aloud, she flushed and glanced at Giles. "In the actual boyfriend department, I mean. I was thinking of Ted, my homicidal robot."

Anya smiled at Joyce. "Don't be too hard on yourself. Look at how many monsters Xander dated before he found me."

"You have a point," Joyce said wistfully.

"Besides, those cookies were really awesome," Xander said, also sounding wistful. "Okay, mind-numbing ingredient, but that guy knew how to properly exploit the chocolate chips."

"Well, shall we move on?" Giles pushed up his glasses. "We're not going to find any clues here."

"Maybe Wesley will figure out the problem first," Anya offered. "That would save us a lot of trouble."

"Not to mention pride," Xander drawled. "That would just make your Watcher-guy day, wouldn't it, G-man?"

Giles closed his eyes. "I have told you, many times, not to call me that."

"Sorry." Xander smiled brightly, not at all contrite.

Joyce said to the Watcher, "Maybe we should go back to your place, and look in some more books."

"Indeed." Giles looked relieved. "Books."

Xander moaned. "More reading. Yuck. I want to go where the action is."

"I wonder if R-Riley's found anything," Tara said, "on p-patrol."

"Maybe something found him," Anya piped up. "And ate him."

"Is this girl's glass half-full or what?" Xander said warmly.

"Children, please." Giles sighed and led the way out of the fraternity house. Joyce took up the rear, feeling rather like a den mother.

"Any more goo globs, I got dibs," Xander announced.

"You can have them," Anya told him.

"It's not just a glob, it's an adventure, in this Slayer's army," Xander said gleefully.

Joyce looked nervously left and right, and followed after the rest of the troops.

Riley patrolled, acutely alert, staying on task despite the fact that memories of life in the Initiative strayed through his mind's eye. Buffy had often ridiculed Forrest for referring to the team as "the family," but they *had* been a family. The military knew how to build camaraderie, and forge ties between men who might otherwise not bond. Maybe the feelings of brotherhood had been engineered by Maggie Walsh and the rest of the corrupt scientific community in charge of the operation, but for Riley and the others, those feelings had been real.

Buffy had a family—her mother and the Scooby Gang—but she did not rely on them the same way Riley had relied on the other guys in Ops. She still held herself aloof, and he wasn't certain she realized it. Never quite let anyone in—kept secrets, held back—and never quite let herself feel that closeness he longed to share with her.

Was she different with Angel? he wondered. *She gave herself to him. He was her first lover . . . and her first love. Did the hurt teach her to withdraw? Or did Angel feel it too, that place she goes where no one else can reach her?*

Or is it just a place she's found where she can maintain some distance from me?

He sighed, heard a noise, whirled around. He almost laughed aloud; here in Madness Central, a plain old chipmunk had startled him. It darted up a tree, turned back around, stared at him, chittered, and disappeared into the foliage. It gave him pause to consider that even on a Hellmouth, nature kept on doing what was natural.

He continued on, scouting, watching, staying calm and keeping his reflexes at the ready. He wondered what the gang was doing.

Reading, probably. Giles probably has them at those books, and by the time I get back there, he'll have a theory about what's going on . . . and a good one, too.

He thought of Maggie Walsh, and sighed. *Damn fine scientist . . . but damn crazy, too.*

He felt the shadow before he saw it: a frigid puddle of darkness that slipped across Weatherly Park, consuming into blackness the trees and bushes. He unsnapped his pistol, knowing as he did so that it would be useless against the shadow monster. But he had no idea what else to do.

Buffy's not here, he told the shadow. *But I am.*

The shadow slid along, a living being. He wondered if it was sentient. Was it aware of him? He stood his ground, watching, alert, spinning a dozen strategies for combating the monster.

I should have brought Tara along, he thought belatedly. *We make a pretty good team, actually.*

They don't give her enough credit for the things she does. She contributes a lot, especially in the magick department. But they probably just see her as a hanger-on. Willow's girlfriend.

Kinda like me and Buffy.

The shadow turned, the blackness a slow-moving blur that stopped when the majority of it was facing Riley. It stood transfixed, perhaps ten feet across and fifteen feet high.

All Riley's senses honed in on his target. If there was fear inside him, it was so tightly corralled that it might as well have been nonexistent. His Special Ops drill sergeant had worked on replacing the deep-seated, reptilian reaction to threats with a conscious and highly evolved set of survival skills. In a seasoned veteran like Riley, the fight-or-flight response was all but gone, and in its place, Riley ran through a series of analytical strategies, calculating his best odds for survival. *Plan A, Plan B, Plan C . . .*

The creature remained motionless. Then, slowly, it began to move into a vertical column, piling itself one mass atop another, almost like the sections of a millipede, reaching up into the treetops like a thunderhead. It threw back what might be a head and a hideous shriek split the sky.

It's challenging me, he realized. *It's going to attack. Plan D, Plan E . . .*

The police car remained on Mischa's tail. He knew the stolen Saturn would never be able to outrun the California Highway Patrol. Mile after mile slipped by, each one bringing the Arizona border that much closer. If he could make the border, he realized, the CHP officer would have to give up, turn back. He might alert the Arizona authorities of the stolen car entering their state, but that might still give Mischa an edge he could use.

I need something that goes faster, he thought. *Something that doesn't need a good road.*

As if reading his thoughts, the police car's light bar came on. Red and blue lights flashed in his rearview, illuminating the Saturn's interior.

Stop? he thought.

Alina's waiting.

Alina needs me at the Grand Canyon.

He floored the accelerator and the Saturn lunged forward.

Back to seventy-five.

Eighty.

Ninety.

Behind him, the police car kept pace. Its siren wailed.

Mischa combed the road ahead for the border, but it didn't appear.

A voice boomed from the police car, almost godlike in its power. "Pull over!" it commanded. "Gold Saturn, pull to the side of the road *now!"*

Mischa ignored it, kept going. The speedometer crept higher. Ninety-five. The car shuddered as if it would break apart. One hundred.

Ahead, a patch of light shone beside the road. An exit sign flashed past, promising a gas station.

The police car stayed right on his tail. Mischa knew that the cops wouldn't give up until he had reached Arizona, but Arizona kept not appearing. *Any moment they might start shooting.*

I won't be any good to Alina dead, he thought.

But maybe there was another way.

At the last moment, he pulled off the freeway, catching the little patch of gravel beside the exit. He fishtailed, a plume of dust and rock kicking into the air behind him, but then his front wheels found the pavement and he shot up the exit ramp.

The police car stayed right behind.

At the top of the ramp was a Gas-N-Go station, a beacon of light against the evening desert sky. There was an old truck parked close to the minimart, and a newer SUV sat at one of the pumps. Mischa turned into the lot and stomped on the brake at the same time. The Saturn started to spin, but its ABS caught and the car corrected and slid to a stop in the gravel lot.

Mischa bolted from the car, leaving the door wide open, and made for the minimart. Behind him, lights and siren going, the police car lurched into the lot.

Los Angeles

Cordelia stood in the kitchen with a cup of her very own, homemade coffee in her hands, when the front door burst open.

She said to Phantom Dennis, "Don't be so dramatic. You can't flounce out the door like some huffy housewife just because life's not fair and it's your turn to do the dishes when there are actually dishes to be done."

"Yes? Hello?" Wesley asked, giving her a look as he went to the door.

"It's just Dennis," Cordelia informed him. "He's having a temper tantrum because he thinks it's my turn to do the dishes. But I did the lunch plate." She looked victorious. "It's not my fault if there was only one thing to wash when it was my turn. And besides—"

"May I help you?" Wesley asked, with a touch of exasperation.

"Angel," said a woman's voice, in thickly accented English. "Is he here? He gave us this address."

Cordelia left the kitchen and hurried toward the door. Behind her, the kitchen faucet turned on. Dishes began to rattle. She smiled to herself and kept walking.

Three people stood huddled in the entry to her apartment. They were clearly a family, Mom, Dad, and a little boy, all three with warm, cocoa-colored skin and black hair. They looked tired and frightened.

"I'm Rojelio Flores," the man announced.

Cordelia's eyes widened. *The guy from the jail,* she filled in. *The one Angel saved from the Big House.*

"Come in," she said. "Angel's not here right now. He's . . . elsewhere." At their sagging expressions of disappointment, she added hopefully, "But we have coffee."

"Ay." The woman touched the man's shoulder. A tear slid down her cheek and she sort of caved in on herself, as if she'd only managed to keep going until she hit Cordelia's threshold. "If you don't mind . . ."

"No, come on in," Cordelia urged. "I'm used to having people dropping in without calling first. Really."

"Actually, we tried to call, but we got your voicemail," Rojelio told her as he put his hands on his son's shoulders and gently herded him inside. The boy's eyes were bleary and there were lines under them.

"Huh." Cordelia frowned. "Dennis," she called, "did you use the phone?"

There was no answer—*like I was expecting one*—and she crossed into the living room, the Flores family trailing behind her. She picked her cordless off the end table and pressed it to her ear, avoiding impaling herself with the post of her large silver hoop. There was a *sshing* noise like dead air on a radio station, which did not go away when she pressed the disconnect button. She set the phone in the cradle.

"It must be off the hook in the bedroom," she said.

"We couldn't stay in the motel," Mrs. Flores explained as she took a seat on the couch. Her son scooted beside her, pressed very close. "It wasn't safe anymore."

Across the room, Cordelia's very favorite floor lamp toppled over with a resounding crash.

"Dennis!" she called.

Mrs. Flores looked at her husband, who sighed. Then the little boy said, "I'm sorry, lady. I'll pay for it when I have some money."

The woman's eyes welled. She put her arms around her son and held him against her body as his huge brown eyes stared fearfully into Cordelia's face.

Cordelia peered into the kitchen. A sponge attacked some stubborn, baked-on grease in a glass casserole dish, then *sploshed* in the soapy water in the sink. Dennis was otherwise occupied.

"My son and I have powers," Rojelio said.

"Oh." She smiled at the little boy. "It's all right," she said. "Please, don't think a thing about my lamp." *Or anything else in my apartment,* she added silently.

The lamp began to lift, then slammed back down to the floor. It was followed by a trio of books that flew across the room.

The boy cried out and buried his face against his mother's shoulder.

Wesley said, "It's all right. Please, just take a breath." He looked at Cordelia. "Psychokinetic episodes generally increase in strength and unpredictability when the sender is agitated."

"Carlos, Carlitos, mi amor," the woman soothed. Still standing behind the couch, his father patted the boy's head and the boy mumbled something.

Then the father came beside his family and sat wearily down. The Flores family sat there like See No Evil, Hear No Evil, and Astrally Project No Evil. Surveying her domain, perhaps taking an inventory of the breakables, Rojelio pinched the bridge of his nose and wiped his eyes. He said, "Maybe we shouldn't stay here."

"We have nowhere else to go," Mrs. Flores murmured. She held out a hand to Cordelia. "Someone has been shooting at us. It may be the friends of those men who framed my husband. And the motel is overrun with gang members."

"I saw a man get shot," the boy informed Wesley. "Blood spurted out!"

"Oh, my God," Cordelia said, moved to tears. She looked at Wesley. "We have got to get Angel back."

"Back?" Mrs. Flores echoed.

"Whoops," Cordelia muttered to herself as she went down the hall. "Um, checking on the phone, okay?"

She was about to knock on her bedroom door when it opened. Willow stood in the doorway, looking kind of white and not so good.

"Hey." She wiped the sleepiness from her eyes, smudging what little mascara she had bothered to apply oh, maybe yesterday. "I'm so tired. I feel dead."

"You look okay, though," Cordelia informed her. She glommed onto Willow's arm and drew her down the hall. "Did you guys use the phone?"

"Huh?" Willow yawned.

"Never mind. I'm glad you're awake. I can use your help."

When they came into the living room, Cordelia put her arm around Willow's shoulder. "Willow," she said cheerily, extending her hand. "Meet the Flores family. They are psychotic."

"Psychokinetic," Wesley corrected.

She smiled brightly at Willow. "Could you maybe help the Floreses tone down their powers or something? Immediately, if not sooner, especially before somebody breaks something really valuable, like the shot glass the bartender at D'Oblique told me Leo DiCaprio had a tequila boiler in?"

"Which is patently ridiculous," Wesley began, but Cordelia silenced him with an imperious wave of her hand.

"I'm not sure I can actually stop a mental power like that," Willow said thoughtfully. Her speech was a little slurred. "But I could set up some wards."

"Great." Cordelia pulled her into the center of the living room. "Ward it up."

"Where's Alina?" Wesley asked.

Willow shrugged. "She decided to take a nap. We're both . . . I'm so tired," she said again.

"Where is Angel?" Carlos piped.

"Angel is . . . helping a friend of ours," Cordelia said brightly. *In another dimension, but I don't want to frighten Carlos, cuz we know what those wacky folks with psychic powers can do.*

Another book fell out of the bookshelf.

"Wow, Cordelia, you never used to read," Willow said. "Now you *own* books."

"Yeah, well." Cordelia glanced anxiously at Carlos. "There's a lot about me that you don't know, Willow. I'm very different from when I lived in Sunnydale. So snap it up, Rosenberg. I mean, *please.*"

Willow trudged into the living room and smiled uncertainly at the people on the couch. Cordelia said, "Angel helped this family with some problems. Now they're here. For more help, which we are more than happy to provide."

"How do you do?" Willow asked politely. "I'm Willow Rosenberg." They regarded her with uncertainty. She said, "I'm going to do a little magick, all right? Just a safeguard, for protection."

"Ay," Mrs. Flores said, crossing herself. "We're Catholic."

"That's okay," Willow assured her. "So is Doña Pilar, and she's a *bruja.*"

Cordelia smiled. "Besides, Willow's Jewish."

Everyone looked at her as if trying to discern the importance of that fact, and when Cordelia realized she didn't know, either, she merely said, "I'll go check on Alina and put the phone back on the hook."

She left the group, then turned around and said, "I'll make some more coffee when I come back. And . . ." She thought for a moment, wondering if there was anything in the fridge. *Good thing Xander didn't come along,* she thought. *He'd have scarfed down everything in sight by now.*

Not that there's any food in sight right now, but anyway...

She walked back down the airy hall of her large, airy apartment, thinking to herself that she would be eternally grateful to Dennis's mom for walling him up alive. It was too bad that she had persuaded so many former tenants to kill themselves before Angel, Doyle, and she managed to exorcise her so Dennis could blast her to Hell or wherever.

But that's why the rent was cheap, which is why I get to live in this beautiful place.

She rapped lightly on the bedroom door. "Alina?"

There was no answer, which confirmed Cordelia's suspicion that the Russian girl had fallen asleep. She turned the knob and went inside.

Alina was flat on her back with her mouth hanging open. Her left arm was outstretched, her hand hanging limply over the side, and the phone was on the floor. Cordelia bent gracefully down—her parents had paid a fortune for charm school lessons back in that hub of charm, Sunnydale—and picked up the phone.

A strange buzzing emanated from the headset. Frowning slightly, Cordelia put it to her ear.

Wind and death and something very cold . . . something very wrong . . . something that was the lack of goodness . . .

"Eek!" she cried, and dropped the phone.

Alina kind of gasped and bolted upright. *"Мама!"* she screamed.

Cordelia screamed back, and the two screamed one

more time for extra measure, and then Wesley was in the room, grabbing Cordelia's arms and saying, "What is it?"

"I don't know!" She shuddered. Her knees buckled. "I really have no idea."

Alina said, "There is something in this apartment that should not be here." She stood up on the bed as if a snake was winding around her ankles.

"Okay, you know about Dennis," Cordelia said, a bit put out.

Just then, the bed slid about two feet to the right. Alina fell off, and Wesley let go of Cordelia in time to catch Alina before she hit the floor.

She said, "Something is unbalanced. The world has gone the wrong way."

"You got that right," Cordelia ventured.

"Like . . ." Wesley contemplated the vast field of metaphors and similes at his disposal. "Like a rift in the Force?"

The girl looked confused. "Rift?"

"He means, is something broken in the um, world-space?" Cordelia offered, belatedly realizing hers was a metaphor with no basis in English.

Wesley frowned at her. " 'World-space?' "

"Precisely," Alina exclaimed. "And now it's in the phone."

"Oh, great. My phone's possessed," Cordelia said, sighing. "It was probably Carlos."

"Cordelia, he doesn't possess things," Wesley said patiently. "Go get Willow, and ask her to depossess your phone." As she crossed the room, he turned back to Alina. "Did something follow you here? Is it something that was somehow seeking you out?"

She shook her head. "I don't know. I think . . . I think

something happened when we tried to use the Reality Tracer. But something is very wrong."

Cordelia found Willow in the kitchen, slowly drinking a glass of water. Dennis was still working on the dishes.

Willow said, "I'm feeling better."

"Good, cuz you have work to do," Cordelia announced, grabbing her by the hand and dragging her back toward her bedroom. "Something is majorly wrong with my phone, and do you know what it means to an actress to be lacking a phone? No jobs! No work!"

"I thought your job was helping Angel," Willow pointed out.

Cordelia gave her a look. "Excuse me, but I happen to aspire to something better."

"Better than saving the world from the forces of darkness?"

"Well, yeah." She shrugged, a tiny bit abashed, but just a tiny bit. *Angel knows what I mean.* "Just last week, I very nearly got a callback for an antiperspirant commercial." She gave her head a toss. "I just didn't have the stinky chick look down."

Willow nodded. She moved her shoulders. "You know, I feel lots better," she reflected. "Not just a little better."

They walked into the room. The bed was on the other side; Willow turned to Alina and said, "Rearranging the furniture because?"

Alina blurted something in Russian. Wesley, Cordelia, and Willow stared at her in total bewilderment. Then she said, "Is no longer in phone. Is in bed."

As if on cue, the bed started to shake. Willow reached out a hand and intoned a spell of protection.

"Hecate, heed my plea. Keep me and mine free from all

harm, without and within. Make safe all who dwell within these walls, and banish all evil from our midst."

While they looked on, something black and smudgy rose from the bed, like sooty smoke, and curled up toward the ceiling. It hovered there, then moved right, then left, as if searching for something. Cordelia slid a glance toward Willow, to see how she was reacting, and was not comforted by the expression of confusion on Willow's face.

"I think we need to try the Reality Tracer again," she said. "I think this is something that's not supposed to be here."

"But nothing could come *into* this reality," Alina protested. "We were sending outward. Here, in Los Angeles, no one can come through. I made sure."

"But that thing's not working right, right?" Cordelia observed. "So you can't be sure of anything."

"Cuz, like Sunnydale has a lot of into going on," Willow said. "Monsters and stuff. Oh, but you didn't do that, right?"

Alina nodded. Cordelia found herself thinking that the Russian girl was kind of . . . colorless. If someone asked her what she was like, Cordelia wouldn't know what to say.

Alina hesitated and looked at her. "I'm afraid," she confessed. "Think of if you lived your whole life with people who could read your mind. It is a very hard way to grow up."

"I didn't mean . . ." Cordelia began, then trailed off. *I see what you mean,* she said silently to Alina, who nodded slowly in reply. *It sucks.*

Alina said to both the girls, "Someone was trying to find me. I don't know if the black thing was because of that. But whoever it was, it wasn't Mischa."

"We'll protect you," Wesley promised.

"Yeah. We'll get the Flores guys to throw lamps at any-one who breaks down my front door," Cordelia said dryly. Then she made a face as she watched the smoky trail slither across her ceiling. As it undulated along, cracks appeared. A piece of plaster wedged loose and landed with an unceremonious *thunk* on the floor.

"On second thought, Dennis might be able to help with some kitchen knives," Cordelia suggested. "Get cracking with the toaster, okay, girls?"

"It's like an entropy current," Wesley mused. "I wonder if I have some information on that. Cordelia, those books I brought over . . ."

"The ones Carlos has been throwing all over the floor?" She flushed and rolled her eyes. "Okay, Willow, so I haven't bought any books in L.A., all right? But only because Wesley and Angel buy all the ones I would have bought, except they buy them first."

"I'm thinking *Theoretical Alternatives for Entropical Permutations,*" Wesley said to Willow. "I've got the new edition."

"Ooh." Willow's eyes widened. "The one with the in-troduction by Stephen Hawking?"

"No, my copy's got the alternative intro. It just falls apart," Wesley retorted, and the two shared a moment of amusement that Cordelia just did not get. To Cordelia, he said, "Would you mind? It's that big heavy red one Carlos hefted out of the case."

Relegated to errand girl, Cordelia thought. *Next thing you know, they'll be asking me to—*

"And do you think you might make some more cof-fee?" Wesley added. She was just about to growl at him when he said, "It's so delicious. It must be the way you load the beans into the filter just so."

She scrutinized him for mockery, found it absent, and preened. "All right," she said brightly. "I'll be back in a little while."

She trotted down the hall, saw the Floreses, who had gotten to their feet and were huddling together, and said, "Everything's fine."

"What was the screaming about?"

"My bed is kind of smoking. Or it was." She tried again. "Evil was in the phone. Or something. Do you know what entropical alternatives are? Anyway." She smiled at them. "Who wants some more coffee?"

Sunnydale

"Very well, old boy," Giles said to Wesley. "Entropy currents. I'll look into it." Smiling faintly, he hung up and looked at the group. His smile faded. "He thought of it first because it happened to him first. Something crawled into Cordelia's phone and also made her bed smoke."

"I said nothing," Xander said innocently, as Anya glanced his way. "I have nothing to say about Cordelia's smoking bed."

Tara hid a little smile as she remembered hearing about the time Willow accidentally set her own bed on fire. *I miss her so.*

"What's an entropy current?" Joyce asked.

"Well, entropy is the principle that eventually things return to chaos. So, an entropy current is like a . . . a channel of disorder."

"Oh," Joyce said blankly.

"Like when someone's orbit decays," Xander explained.

"Actually, that's an inaccuracy. An orbit doesn't actu-ally decay. Rather, it . . ." Giles began, then caught himself, as he realized his explanation was starting to decay. "At any rate, there's a theory that there are chaos currents in the magickal atmosphere, much as there are thermal currents in the natural world." He wandered over to his bookcase and scanned the titles with obvious eagerness.

Joyce looked tired. Tara could definitely relate. Worrying about Willow was taking quite a toll on her; Joyce was the Slayer's mom and she must have certainly accumulated a lot of stress and worry over the years. Every day just added more.

Giles pulled out a few books and began handing them out, saying, "Well, you all wanted to do research, and here we are."

"Much joy," Xander mumbled. "Or not."

Then something crashed against the apartment wall and they all looked at each other.

"More monsters," Anya announced. "They seem to come in bunches."

"Hmm. Perhaps reinforcing the theory of entropy currents," Giles said.

They set to reading. Now and then something would roar outside or shuffle past the building. Everyone fairly much ignored each individual occurrence. But Tara could feel herself becoming agitated. She looked down at the book in her lap and the letters swam.

Finally, she said to the others, "I need to get some fresh air."

Giles raised his brows and said, "Do you really think that's a good idea?"

"Yeah," Xander added, "the fresh air is filled with fresh monsters."

Anya chuckled and gave him a peck on the cheek.

Tara felt thwarted, and claustrophobic. She remembered that this feeling had come over her once before, when she had realized the Scooby Gang didn't consider her one of their own.

Am I having a panic attack? she wondered.

"I-I need to go," she blurted, fighting her stammer.

"Then I'll go with you," Xander suggested. "You shouldn't go out there alone."

"Xander, you're such a he-man," Anya cooed. "Even if I get my powers back someday, I will never, ever eviscerate you."

"An, how romantic. Yet oddly comforting," he said. He looked around. "Riley leave any Uzis lying around? Bazookas? Wish we still had the rocket launcher."

"That was a fine weapon," Giles said wistfully.

Joyce Summers stared at him. "When was there a rocket launcher?"

"I'll get a mace. I like maces," Xander suggested, as he crossed to Giles's weapons trunk. He rummaged around, then hefted a wood-handled weapon topped with a metal sphere covered with spikes. "How about you?" he asked Tara. "Would you like a shishkabobber or something?"

"I-I'll stick to magick," she said shyly.

"Giles, *when* was there a rocket launcher? Did you give my daughter a rocket launcher?" Joyce persisted.

Xander said to Tara, "Let's blow this popstand while they duke it out." He flashed his friendly grin at her and together they walked to the door.

"Don't let anyone bite your head off," Anya called.

"We'll just step right outside door number 217 so she can breathe in the smoke and ash particles," Xander promised. "Then we'll come right back in. Good, Tara?"

"S-sure." She ducked her head. She liked Xander and Anya. She wondered what would happen if the others discovered that all the women in her family were demons. That was why she'd left home and come to Sunnydale . . . to escape, if not that legacy, then at least to keep her terrible secret to herself. But she figured that if Anya found out, she would forgive her for not coming forward . . . and she might actually like her even better.

Not that she's unfriendly now, Tara thought.

"Perhaps you should also have a proper shield," Giles suggested, crossing to his weapons chest and foraging around for something. He stood up with an impressive circular leather shield in his hand.

Xander took it, testing the heft, and said, "And to think they used to laugh at my Dungeons and Dragons group down at the comic-book store. My Dungeonmaster would be so proud. Of course, my Dungeonmaster is dead," he reflected. He turned to Tara and said, "He got eaten during graduation."

"That's—that's too bad," Tara said sincerely. Her chest felt as if it were about to burst at the same time that her throat was closing up. *This is a panic attack,* she thought.

"Actually, it was the way he would have wanted to go, if he'd had a choice. Of course, he would have preferred to be eaten during finals. Or a pep rally. Not a lot of Razorback spirit in the ol' D.M."

Unaware of her distress, Xander strolled to the door. Tara reached forward, turned the knob, and yanked the door open. She practically bolted across the threshold, and she knew she was becoming more and more irrational.

Then she knew why.

"Riley!" she said, as waves of sensations, all unpleasant, washed over her. "I think he's in trouble."

Xander cocked his head. "Because . . . ?"

She didn't know how to explain. "I have a feeling."

"Works for me." He popped his head into the apartment. "Giles. Tara thinks Riley's in trouble."

"Really? How so?" Giles asked.

"She's a witch," Xander reminded him. "So let's go, okay?"

Giles appeared less than five seconds later, a crossbow in his hand. Anya was right behind him with a small hand ax. And Mrs. Summers, with what looked to be a machete.

"Do you know where Riley is?" Giles asked Tara.

Tara shook her head, sorry she didn't have more to go on. "I only have a s-sense that he's in danger."

"We'd better split up," Giles decided. "Tara, go with Xander. Anya and I will go . . . somewhere you two don't. Joyce, stay by the phone. Please."

"I . . ." Joyce Summers nodded and lowered her machete, as if realizing that really was the best thing she could do. "It's too bad Spike's not here," she said. "He could listen for messages."

"See? Some guys will go into an interdimensional reality to avoid the littlest bit of work," Xander bit off as they hustled down the stairs. "Slacker."

All the buildings facing them were ablaze. There were no fire trucks, no ambulances, no police cars. They had all been dispatched to other emergencies. All Sunnydale was one big emergency.

A fiercely ugly troll zipped past. Xander took a half-hearted swing at it and missed. The troll shot him a sneer and kept going. Xander shrugged and said, "Okay, Tara, find Timmy!"

Tara gave him a look. "I'm not Lassie," she said. But she pointed to their right and said, "Let's try over there."

"We'll go look at the ruins of the school," Giles suggested. "Riley likes to patrol there."

"Yup. Some of his happiest moments with Buffy were spent there," Xander said sarcastically. He sighed. "So were mine. Well, there was watching the place blow up."

Tara and Xander moved out, walking briskly. Xander put the battleax over his shoulder and started humming "Follow the Yellow Brick Road." Tara used to be shocked by the way these people joked during times of crisis, but she had come to realize that they did it to keep themselves from wigging out. Being wry and cynical was a way to ground themselves, poke fun at death. It was the same with fighter pilots and emergency room doctors.

"If you're the scarecrow, who am I?" she asked, as the sky thundered and rolled, making the ground shake.

"Well, let's see. You definitely have a heart," he said, smiling at her. "And a brain."

"I'm the Cowardly Lion," she ventured shyly.

"No way." Xander chuckled. "You're one of the bravest people I've ever met in my life."

Tara was surprised . . . and very pleased. "Thank . . . thank you."

"It's a fact. I'd be terrified to do half the stuff you do. And coming out . . . that was really brave of you and Will." He grinned at her. Then his smile fell a little. "She's happy, right?"

He still loves her, Tara realized. *A part of him will always love a part of her. And that's fine with me.*

There's so much more to relationships than what meets the eye. The pairing up and the being couples and the being in relationships . . . that's just the surface stuff.

"She's happy," Tara said. "I promise."

"That's great." He meant it.

Tara smiled at him. Then she suddenly turned her head. "Oh, my God, Xander! Look!"

The chain link fence that surrounded Weatherly Park had been severely compromised, as they say in the military. Translation: ripped to shreds. The section directly in front of them was nothing but small collections of links, most torn in half, lying in scattered piles on the ground. The bushes behind it had been shredded to mulch. A tree had fallen over.

In front of the collapsed section lay Riley's pistol.

Of Riley, there was no trace.

Chapter 7

Bɪʟʟʏ Bᴏʙ Mᴏꜰꜰɪᴛᴛ ᴡᴀs ᴀ ᴄᴏᴘ, ᴛʜᴇ sᴏɴ ᴏꜰ ᴀ ᴄᴏᴘ, ᴀɴᴅ the grandson of a cop. Law enforcement, his dad used to say, ran in the men of the Moffitt family as surely as big hair and varicose veins ran in the women. Billy Bob had always found that somewhat more amusing than either his mother or his wife did. He'd been offered the job after making friends with a couple of Sunnydale officers at a law enforcement convention. He'd thought his wife would be reluctant to leave Carthage, Tennessee, where they lived in a perfectly nice split-level next door to his parents, for a home near the Pacific, but when he had suggested that, she had simply looked at him, shaken her head, and tried to suppress a smile.

Out of his eleven years as a police officer, three had been back home in Carthage, and the remaining eight had been here in Sunnydale. He knew—one didn't have to be on the force long to know—that things in Sunnydale were, well, different than elsewhere. What was rare in other towns was commonplace here; the impossible, in Sunnydale, was merely unexpected. There were whispers, rumors, things people talked about in the locker room after a long shift, or after a few beers at a cop barbecue, after the food was gone and the sun was setting and the women had gone inside to wash dishes and gab about whatever it was they found interesting.

About things that came out after dark, things a less sensible person might call monsters. About the victims found occasionally in Sunnydale's back alleys and deserted lots, their blood drained from their bodies. About a young girl who faced down the really bad stuff and kept it in line—though, having been the first to arrive at a few of those crime scenes, Billy Bob wondered about the truth of that rumor, because there was no denying some bad stuff hit Sunnydale now and again.

But never had it been like this.

In the last twenty minutes, he'd seen a skittering thing, not more than three feet tall, with at least fifty legs, run underneath a car—in motion—and upend the vehicle, tossing it onto a sidewalk. He'd seen a tall, gaunt man in a flowing black coat that looked as if it had been manufactured in the 1800s walk by. The man—if he was a man—wore a tall silk hat and carried a cane. The man had smiled at Billy Bob, revealing precisely sharpened teeth, and the sensation was not unlike having someone drop an ice cube down the back of Billy Bob's uniform shirt.

A grocer, closing his store, turned his back to the sidewalk long enough to draw down the security gate that he locked over his store windows each night. He nodded to

Billy Bob, who returned the nod. But then, in full view of the police officer, the gaunt man in black had twisted the head of his cane, revealing a sword blade concealed inside. He'd driven the sword through the grocer's back, puncturing his heart and maybe a lung, then had turned back to Billy Bob and, sheathing his dripping blade, tossed another of those malevolent grins his way.

Billy Bob had pulled his weapon and shouted at the gaunt man to halt, but the man had simply gripped his shoulders in his own hands and somehow *folded* in on himself, until he was nothing more than a point of blackness, then not even that, just gone.

Billy Bob had watched in open-mouthed astonishment, not even remembering to summon an ambulance for the grocer until the gasping, bubbling man had died. Any other week, Billy Bob would have felt intense remorse for that failure, but this week it was just one more body. And after that, he saw a shape glide by in the night sky, black against black, but as the shape passed through the glow of a street lamp, Billy Bob saw that it was nothing more than an oversize human-looking face, the size of a watermelon, with wings, dripping some kind of saliva as it flew past. When Billy Bob looked at the street where the saliva had fallen, he saw that each drop sizzled like acid on the pavement.

So, while there had been a lot of bad weeks in Sunnydale law enforcement history, there had never been one like this that he could remember. He walked the streets alone because there had been so many emergency calls, every pair of officers had had to split up to have any hope of responding to even half of them. And the enormity of what he faced overwhelmed him. Finally, he holstered his weapon, snapped the flap over its butt, and sat down on a step, simply watching the madness go by. There was nothing one cop could do, not even a cop whose father was a cop and whose grandfather was a cop.

All Billy Bob could think about was moving back to Carthage.

Thirty barbarian warriors, dressed in animal skins and crudely worked metal ornaments, ringed the cottage where Angel had taken refuge with Tan-kia and her grandmother, the witch. Angel observed them through the narrow windows, watching them spread out across the rim of the clearing. The cottage was a sturdily constructed little place, but it was only wood, and if they had discovered the trick of firing flaming arrows here, they'd be able to burn it down in no time. Even if they hadn't, if they approached it with war axes they could hack their way in. Angel had killed plenty in his time, but he'd never single-handedly faced a force like this. For one thing, the age of barbarism had been over long before he'd been born.

"Angel won't let us down," Tan-kia told her grandmother.

Angel turned. The young woman stood behind her grandmother's chair, stroking the witch's long silver hair comfortingly. The old woman's shoulders were slumped, defeat apparent in her posture. "You should have seen him fight those other men," Tan-kia went on. "He was unstoppable."

Oh, I'm stoppable, he thought. *See all those arrows and spears? Made of wooden shafts? Only takes one to stop me once and for all.*

Buffy is in trouble, he reminded himself. *That's where my priority has to be.*

He glanced out the window again. The soldiers were getting themselves into position. In another few minutes, he guessed, the attack would begin, and then the air would be thick with flying shafts of wood.

If he was going to do anything, it had to be now.

And, as much as he wanted to just leave, he knew he couldn't do that, couldn't sentence these two women to death.

"Grandmother," he said, his voice soft, "can you create illusions? Tricks to fool the eye?"

The old woman waved one hand. "Of course," she said. "That's nothing."

"These would have to be good," Angel continued. "Convincing."

She shrugged. "Nothing," she repeated.

"And there'd have to be many of them. Thirty or so."

She made eye contact with Angel, and he saw a gleam of understanding there. "How many warriors did you say are outside?"

"About thirty," he said.

"And precisely what is it I'm to create the illusion of?"

"Me," Angel said.

"I can do that." She began to speak words in a language Angel didn't recognize, describing intricate patterns in the air with her fingertips.

"Wait," Angel said. "Not yet." He let the change happen, bringing his vampiric side to the fore. When he was done, Tan-kia let out a small gasp. "Now," Angel said.

The grandmother continued with her spell. After a few moments, the small room was full of Angels, but they had no physical substance. Angel passed his hand right through one of them. Others walked through solid objects, or stood with furniture inside them.

"Each of them is a shadow of you," the grandmother

explained. "Or a reflection, if you will. These shades have no will of their own, but to follow your bidding."

"But they cannot hurt the warriors," Tan-kia said. "So what good will they be?"

"Maybe they won't need to hurt them," Angel said. He experimented. He raised his right hand into the air. The other Angels raised their right hands. He stepped to his left. They stepped to their lefts. *Too bad the Rockettes didn't have this woman,* he thought.

He wasn't totally comfortable with this plan, but didn't have time to come up with another one. Buffy was waiting. He went to the door, his doubles mimicking his motions. "Close the door behind me. Us."

Without another word, he threw the door open and charged out of it, screaming wordlessly. Behind him, thirty additional Angels roared out of the door. Like the original, they all ran full bore at the barbarian warriors. He mentally commanded them to spread out, directing them at the barbarians ranged all around the clearing, and it seemed to work.

As he ran, Angel sensed arrows being nocked in bows, spears raised for throwing. He waited another half-second, still running, until he heard the *thwip* of bowstrings. Then he launched himself into the air, gaining some height, spinning twice and then coming in for a landing. The first volley of arrows thudded into the ground beneath him.

Around him, the other Angels had duplicated his move, and even where arrows were fired higher than their leaps had taken them, they sailed through the Angel doubles without pause.

Barbarians screamed in mortal terror. Some of them fled their positions, throwing bows or spears to the dirt. Others, though, held their line, firing again and again. Arrows passed through the Angel shades, some of them flying toward the cottage.

Finally, Angel met one of the barbarians. The man threw his bow aside and drew a long, heavy sword. Angel paused, and the warrior feinted toward him. Angel dodged to his left. The barbarian sliced right, and the tip of the sword nearly grazed Angel's stomach. When it was safely past him, though, he moved in fast, slamming his left fist into the soldier's right wrist to disable his sword hand, and driving his right into the man's chin. The barbarian crumpled. Angel scooped up his sword just in time to raise it in defense as the nearest warrior attacked him. The blades clanged together, vibrations traveling through Angel's shoulders. This barbarian drew his blade back for another swing, and Angel took advantage of the moment to thrust forward with his sword. The tip of the blade shoved through the man's leather breastplate. Blood bubbled up from his lips, and he fell to the ground.

Angel's shades mimicked his actions, but without the same results. It almost didn't matter, though—the sheer horror of all these vamp-faced Angel-beings moving around and through the barbarians was enough to send them running for their lives.

The fight only took a few minutes. Angel had to best only six of them in battle, and the rest retreated at top speed. Angel, winded, watched them run, then stabbed the sword into the earth and turned back to the cabin. It looked like a pincushion, with arrows and a few spears stuck into its wooden exterior from every angle. The alternate Angels followed him to the cabin, until he reached the door, at which point they all vanished.

"Thanks, guys," he told their disappearing forms.

He went inside. Tan-kia knelt on the floor, sobbing. In

her chair, the grandmother sat where Angel had last seen her, but now an arrow had pierced her chest, sticking her to the chair's back. A thin trail of blood leaked down her stomach.

"Angel . . ." Tan-kia said, her voice catching.

"I'm not dead," the grandmother uttered weakly. "Yet. I have a . . . few moments left."

"I'm sorry," Angel said.

"You did what you . . . could," the grandmother assured him.

"It came through the window," Tan-kia said sharply. "I should have been there. I should have stopped it."

"You couldn't have," Angel argued. "Then it would just be you dying instead. There were just too many of them."

"There is no . . . fault here, child," the grandmother managed. Her breath sounded ragged and wet. "What is, is."

"But . . . I'll live here alone?" Tan-kia asked, holding her grandmother's hands. "Without you?"

"There will always be traces of me here," the old woman whispered. "And . . . you have much to learn. It is your turn to protect these woods."

"I'm to be the witch?"

"I meant to tell you sooner . . . in a different way. But, yes."

Tan-kia looked at Angel, something like panic in her eyes. "Isn't there something—?"

"Sorry," Angel said. "I'm no doctor."

"Don't worry . . . about me," the grandmother declared. "Don't you have somewhere else to be?"

"Yes," Angel said. "But—"

"I don't have strength enough to do . . . what I promised," she replied. "But Tan-kia does."

"But I don't know how, grandmother!"

"Do you know how . . . how to listen?"

"Of course I do," Tan-kia said.

"That's all you need, then. Just listen fast, while I can still . . . still talk."

She began to describe the process, and Tan-kia set about learning to be a witch, as Angel paced the floor of the little cottage. *Hurry,* he thought. *Just get it done. Before it's too late.*

Los Angeles

When someone began pounding on the door, Cordelia took a quick head count. The Flores family was in her dining area, gathered around her table. Alina sat in the living room, still fiddling with the Reality Tracer. Willow, in the bedroom, was in a trance. Dennis hadn't been seen for a while—*but hey,* she thought, *what's new?*

Wesley was seated at the dining room table, reading the big red book, and apparently didn't even hear the door. The knocking continued.

Cordelia headed for the door. *Not bad guys, cuz they don't usually knock. And people I know would just barge in,* she reasoned, *so it's not a friend or someone I owe money to. And it's not someone who owes me money, because, sadly, those don't exist.*

She opened the door.

A strange young man stood there, completely hairless, in a tee shirt and baggy black pants and big sneakers.

"I need to find her," he said, forcing his way in past Cordelia.

"Excuse me? Find who?" She felt aggravation at the way this guy just walked in, but something in his demeanor—well, that and the frankly kind of scary way he looked—made her not want to argue with him.

"My sister. I need to go after her." The look in his eyes was blank, like a lost—or searching—child.

"And that sister would be . . . ? Have we met?" Cordelia asked. "Because, you know, looking at you, I think that'd be something I'd remember."

"Salma," he said angrily, as if his incoherence were Cordelia's fault. "My sister."

"You're the brother?" Cordelia asked incredulously. She turned to Alina, who watched from the sofa. "Hey, I found Nicky!" she called.

"He was already found," Alina pointed out.

"Good Lord," Wesley said, snapping the book shut and looking up. He pushed back his chair. "You're Nicky de la Natividad?"

Cordelia raised her chin. "I still get credit. I found him again."

"It's Salma who's missing," Nicky said. "She went somewhere else. My grandmother said you could send me through."

"Oh, right," Cordelia agreed sarcastically. "You *do* know she spent a lot of time and energy looking for you, right? So if you go off looking for her, and then you get lost and she gets found, then we're right back where we started from, which doesn't really do anybody much good."

"I need to find her," he insisted.

Cordelia looked from Nicky to Wesley to Alina and back again. Alina had the machine in pieces on the table. "Alina, could you even send him?"

"Not just now," Alina said frankly. "Maybe later, if I can get this working right. But I'm no engineer."

"And if we had a train to drive, that'd be a problem," Cordelia said. "But can you fix it?"

Alina sighed. "I don't know."

"Plus, my concern about the currents may hold some additional problems," Wesley added. "This may be something not even the Vishnikoffs know about."

Cordelia smiled at Nicky. "There's your answer. Sorry, maybe later." She started toward the door, to open it and let him out. Instead, he came farther inside and plopped down on the couch, arms folded across his chest, his mouth a flat line.

"I'll wait," he declared.

"We have coffee," Wesley said. "Cordelia?"

"Not a problem," she said, gritting her teeth.

The castle looked to Buffy like something out of a storybook, if storybooks were written by demented homicidal maniacs. It was built of heavy gray stone, but the walls were grown over with mosses and lichens, which gave it an unhealthy, greenish tinge. Soaring to heights of thirty or forty feet, the walls were broken here and there by narrow slits of window, perfect for shooting arrows or pouring boiling oil. As if to confirm that impression, she noticed that the walls beneath some of the slits were stained a darker color than the rest of the stone, and no moss grew on the stains. The tops of the walls were crenellated, broken every fifty feet or so by towers that spiked toward the sky. Some of these peak-roofed towers had balconies or larger windows, and it was in one of these that Buffy had seen the "princess" she was supposedly here to rescue.

According to a dying dragon-guy-thing, anyway.

The rutted roadway she had taken here led straight to a

gateway, but a portcullis and heavy double doors, each a dozen feet across, blocked the way. The portcullis was stopped a foot or so off the ground, so that Buffy could have scooted beneath it if she'd needed to. But its iron bars ended in razor sharp points, like enormous teeth, and she had no desire to risk it. A few feet along the wall from the big gate, though, there was a smaller door, dark wood with rusted metal straps across it at the top and bottom and an ancient metal knob.

Pedestrian access.

She approached the door. A knocker adorned it, in the shape of a demon's horned head, with glowing red eyes. At first Buffy thought the eyes were jeweled, but when she looked more closely, she couldn't see facets of any kind—they looked vaguely liquid, burning with illumination from within.

She couldn't force the thought away. *They look alive.*

Knocking didn't seem like a good idea anyway. If whoever—or whatever—lived here didn't already know she had come, announcing herself made no sense. Better to let herself in if she could, try to find that back tower from the inside, save the girl and get out.

She wished there were some contact from Willow, or Alina. This was her first rescue and she wasn't sure what to do once she accomplished it.

And Angel, the thought came to her. *What's happened to him?*

Trying not to look at the demonic knocker, Buffy pushed open the door. It swung in easily, though with a moan that could have come directly from the Universal Studios sound effects library. *So much for the element of surprise,* she thought. *Better than any burglar alarm.*

She stood still for a few moments, listening to see if the

creaking door stirred up any activity from inside. Satisfied that it hadn't, she left the door ajar and went in.

The door opened into a courtyard, the same place that the big gate gave access to. There was room for a few wagons and horses, or a couple of dozen cars, she guessed. It didn't look like it had seen much traffic lately, though. The cobbled courtyard had weeds growing up through the stones, silver in the moonlight. In one corner, a wooden platform of some kind had rotted and fallen in on itself. Buffy couldn't make out its function, but couldn't help thinking it looked like a gallows or a guillotine.

Such a cheery place, she thought. *Needing that Martha Stewart touch.*

Across the courtyard a set of stairs led up to another door. This one, tall and narrow, must be the door to the castle's insides, she thought. The only other way out of the courtyard was up rough-hewn stone steps that led to battlements along the castle's outer walls—defensive positions, she guessed. Left without a lot of options, Buffy crossed the courtyard, walking with determined purpose, not trying to hide herself. She climbed the steps to the big door and tried it. This one also opened easily, though more quietly. She went inside.

A warm, welcoming glow met her as she crossed the threshold; a glow emanating from several dozen burning candles. She pushed the door closed and investigated the Great Hall in which she found herself. The welcoming part of the candle's glow vanished when she realized that in the shadows beneath the candles, their holders were wall-mounted skulls—many of which looked human. Others were clearly animal, but not animals with which Buffy was familiar. The candles themselves were fat and greasy, filling the Hall with unpleasant odors.

Someone, certainly, had lit the candles. But she could see no other sign of habitation. In the upper reaches of the Hall, cobwebs hung thick as clouds. The floor was covered with a layer of dust.

There were three ways out of the Hall—a grand staircase that led up into darkness, and two doors, one to the left and one to the right. None of the choices looked any more promising than any other. The stairs might make sense, since Buffy knew she had to get up to the tower at some point. But what if they led to a second level here, and the tower could only be accessed from the ground level? It might be better, she decided, to try to find the tower's base first, and then figure out how to get up.

From the main entrance, the tower in which she had seen the girl was on the rear right corner, so she picked the door to her right. It stuck a little, but she shoved and it opened for her. More candles illuminated a dining hall, with a vast table, empty except for three candelabras spaced about eight feet apart, ringed by dozens of heavy chairs. The furniture was all wood, blocky and cumbersome looking. Tapestries hung on the walls, depicting scenes of creatures that were not familiar— white fish-faced things with six legs, bearlike beasts rearing up on two legs, but with faces that resembled big-eyed aliens more than bears, and various other arrangements of body parts. Buffy could easily have spent more time exploring this one room, but she wanted to get to the girl and get out of here as quickly as she could. She continued through the dining hall to another door on the far end.

This door led into a kitchen area—acre after acre of counter space, seven big stone ovens; and off to one side, chunks of meat, bigger than any dead cow Buffy had ever seen, hanging from hooks in an alcove. The stench of the old meat overpowered the nasty smell of the candles here, so Buffy hurried through the kitchen and out another door.

She found herself inside a tiny room with only one candle burning in it, mounted on another skull-sconce on the wall. Other than the candle, it contained only dust and cobwebs—and no other doors. *Wrong turn—there must have been another door out of the kitchen,* she thought. She went back through the door she'd come in.

But there was no kitchen on the other side. She was in a long hallway, lined with suits of spiderwebbed armor and triangular-shaped wall hangings. Her first thought was of the Black Knight she had defeated. These suits of armor didn't come at her, though, so she cautiously walked between them, down the hall. There was a door between every suit of armor, and she had no clue where any of them led. She found herself growing concerned.

Because this hall shouldn't be here at all, she knew. *I went from a kitchen into the little room, then went back through the door seconds later. So this should be a kitchen, which it so definitely is not.*

Feeling majorly creeped out, she went from door to door, hesitating about opening any of them for fear that they'd just lead to . . . well, she didn't know. She finally figured that she just needed to pick one and try it. She put her hand on the knob of the first one—and froze.

From the other side came a scratching, skittering sound.

She remembered her dream, the one she'd had where she'd opened door after door to find no one there. It had been one of their earliest clues to the existence of the alternities. The dreams of Slayers were like that; sometimes prophetic.

So if I open the door . . .

The skittering got louder, as if something really, really hoped she would.

Chapter 8

Los Angeles

CASA CORDELIA: A MADHOUSE, A MADHOUSE. CORDELIA thought it was amazing how much activity there seemed to be in her apartment, yet in reality, the Flores family had decided to take a nap, and everyone else was sitting around her kitchen table, freaking out, staring at Wesley as if he had just invented the contraption pressed to his ear. Except for the new boy, Nicky, who was off pacing up and down her hall like a bull at the run in Pamplona.

"I see. And did Giles say anything about my theory before he ran off to help Riley?" Wesley asked as calmly as he could. "Oh, that he would have thought of it first had he known about the phenomenon. Typical." He looked huffy. "No, no. Can you tell me if you've found anything in the research books?"

I'm thinking nada, Cordelia thought, and Alina looked

at her blankly. "'*Nada*' is Spanish for 'nothing,'" she said aloud.

"No Tara?" Willow asked softly.

Wesley held up a hand. "Now *that's* interesting," he said, nodding. "That's very interesting indeed. Thank you. Yes, please have Giles call the moment he gets in. Thank you again."

He hung up, looking pleased. "We may be getting somewhere. It appears that Buffy's mother has continued reading while the others went in search of Riley Finn. She's come across some information that suggests that entropy currents may actually be caused, or enhanced, when an individual's reality is shifted or changed."

"Or enhanced?" Willow asked, then appeared uncomfortable. She was seated next to Alina at the kitchen table. The Reality Tracer lay in pieces all around them. "Saying no to enhanced reality. Sounding like druggie talk."

"You see, the machine that Alina's parents created—the Reality Tracer—actually creates a sort of entropy current, in conjunction with Alina's own ability to project a change in reality. If a person has had a true reality shift, they may be able to move within alternities even if they're not completely properly 'beamed,' as it were, by the machine."

"Sounds Star-Trekian," Cordelia said.

"Wesley *Crusher,*" Willow added, grinning faintly.

"He crushes?" Alina asked uncertainly.

"Pop-culture reference." Willow picked up the main chassis of the Reality Tracer with both hands and examined it. "If this really was *Star Trek,* we'd have this puppy fixed in forty-eight minutes. Less, if you account for the fact that they usually introduce the problem in the second act."

"Hello, real life, and you've been trying to fix it for a lot longer than forty-eight minutes, and you know, this thing really does look like a cheesy movie prop." Cordelia glanced over Willow's shoulder. "It's a real mess, isn't it. How come your parents never, you know, made an extra one or got nicer parts or something?"

"Some of the components were handmade," Alina said, "by people who are dead now. We would have to disassemble it to re-create it. In the new world order, we would be able to produce as many as we liked."

"In a dazzling array of exciting decorator colors," Cordelia said waspishly.

"So, send me through, then," Nicky said as he came into the kitchen. The refrigerator door opened and Phantom Dennis offered Nicky a Corona. Nicky waved it away with an impatient sneer.

"Look, I think the theory is interesting, but I haven't been able to discuss it with my colleague directly," Wesley said.

Nicky launched into a string of exciting Mexican swearwords, some of which Cordelia even knew how to spell. He said angrily, "Look, I heard what you said. I altered my reality, okay? I made myself invincible with the Night of the Long Knives. I can go through!"

"We aren't sure of anything. We don't know what will happen if we try it with the broken Tracer. My best conjecture is that some good was sucked out of this world, or evil was released by an alternity, and we have no knowledge how that affects anything. We're still working out our premise."

"This is what I am wondering," Alina said. "What about people who are not precisely *of* this reality? I am thinking of your Slayer and her vampire lover."

"And Spike, who really loused things up," Willow said.

Alina looked thoughtful. "Perhaps he loused the things up because he is too close to this reality. The other vampire, the one Buffy loves, he is unique, you told me. He has a soul. No other vampire has a soul."

"Only, Buffy doesn't love him," Willow said quickly. "She loves Riley. A lot." She nodded. "A whole lot."

"It could be that instead of entropy currents, we are dealing with something like . . . uncertainty fields," Wesley mused. "Since they're not entirely of this reality, the field of uncertainty around them protects them."

"Well," Willow said slowly, "I'm a witch. I probably have an uncertainty field. Maybe I can go through." She made a face. "Not loving that idea, but I could. Not . . . love it, I mean. I could go."

Wesley crossed his arms over his chest. "We need you here, to help with the machine."

"Por qué?" Nicky barked. "She's not helping with it. None of you are helping with it. You don't know what the hell you're doing!" He slammed his hand down on the kitchen table. Willow startled, nearly dropping the Tracer. "You shouldn't have played with fire, Alina!"

"Oh, but it's all right for you to set oil fields on fire, huh?" Cordelia snapped at him. "Do magick from recipes you had to steal from your own grandmother?"

"Spells," Willow murmured, "not recipes."

"Whatever." She glared at Wesley. "I say we give it a try. We're not getting anywhere, and all our really unreal-reality superhero types are in Oz or wherever, and if he gets ground up into taco meat, I say, 'Sorry, you were warned.' "

"That is racist," Nicky said through gritted teeth.

"Taco meat? Get over it," Cordelia said. "I could have just as easily said 'Hungarian goulash.' "

"Ghoul-ash," Wesley said, smiling faintly. "That's actually rather clever, Cordelia."

"Thank you." She pointed to the Tracer. "They've jiggled things around forever. For all they know, they could put those pieces back in and it could be even better than new. So let's let Guinea Pig Boy have a try."

"All he wants to do is find his sister," Alina sniffed. "He doesn't care about anyone else."

Wow, some personality emerges, Cordelia thought, then remembered that Alina could read her mind. *Well, you haven't really had much of one,* she added. *No offense.*

"Family loyalty, imagine that," Nicky flung at her. "All *you* people have is Party loyalty."

Alina looked pointedly at the gang tattoo on Nicky's hand and snickered.

"Let me go," Nicky said to Wesley. "I'm ready to go."

"I can't permit it. You're just human, after all," he said to Nicky. "The others were . . . others. More than human."

"In Spike's case, subhuman," Cordelia added.

"Well, who else do you have who is like that?" Alina asked. "You have many surprising individuals here. Is there not more than one vampire with soul? More than one Slayer?"

The answer came to Wesley and Cordelia at precisely the same time.

"Oh, my God," Cordelia murmured. "Yes, there is." She looked at Wesley, who raised his chin. His eyes grew cold and hard.

"Yes, you're quite right, Cordelia. Indeed there is."

Cordelia exhaled. She thought of the Slayer who had tortured Wesley for hours. The one Wolfram and Hart had hired to kill Angel. The one who was trying to find her way back into the light.

The one she did not trust at all.

"Oh, boy," she muttered.

Alina frowned at her. "What has faith to do with it? Religion is for the masses."

"Praying wouldn't be a bad idea right now," Cordelia said aloud.

In the middle of the prison was a barren square of crabgrass referred to by the "Correctional Facility Administrator" as "the Commons." In the old movies, "the warden" called it "the yard."

Faith the Vampire Slayer called the CFA "the bitch" and the area "the field." There were some dandelions in it, and a couple of patches of wild daisies; it was the closest thing she had to the dreams she had had of the Mayor and her, picnicking, when she was in the coma. Those dreams started out so nice . . .

. . . and like most dreams, ended very badly.

I put myself here on purpose, she reminded herself, at least a hundred times a day. *I'm after redemption, same as Angel.*

But for Faith, she had thought that would mean being able to sink into invisibility. Just become an anonymous number, confined (not really) to some small space with plenty of time to pull up the weeds, one by one. Sometimes she wanted to grab them by the handful and yank, but you didn't get them all that way. No, you had to do it one at a time.

"Yo, Faith, you need anything?" asked Shirl as Faith walked past her. It was a question she would answer at least a dozen times before "the exercise period" was over. Lots of her fellow babes behind bars wanted to be friends with Faith. She was strong and brave and she didn't take any crap.

It was difficult to maintain one's anonymity when

everybody wanted to face down the newest gunslinger to stride into town. But word got around as fast as rich white girls got parole that Faith was the bitch to beat if you wanted to rule the block. So each new bad girl, eager to outbad everybody else, took Faith on. She didn't give as good as she could; she'd kill most of her opponents. So she held back an awful lot; sometimes she let them beat the crap out of her just because it was too much work to dodge them.

"Yo, Faith." Carrie Grimes stepped up to Faith. Her face was an overripe plum and her lips were split. One eye was swollen shut.

"Who?" Faith asked. Never "why?" Never "how?" It didn't matter. Carrie was one of Faith's own.

"Julia Swank." Carrie's split lip started to bleed. "And all's you can see is my face, Faith, but she beat me black-and-blue all over."

Faith cast a steely gaze across the field to the northeast quadrant. That was where Julia held court. She was a three-striker, and she had no hope of parole. She didn't mind solitary—the warden had given her a private cell of her own, and she seemed to have a lot of leeway in when she had to stay in it. But she had a hell of a lot to lose if she lost respect among her girls—like maybe even her life.

Faith reflected tiredly on how stupid it all was, and remembered how stupid she had been before Angel made her soul crack open and all the infection started pouring out. Though she kept staring at Julia, to give her the message that she, Faith, knew what she'd been up to and that she wasn't about to let her go free over it, her mind traveled down other roads: to the rage, and the pain, and the grief she had caused for others; and in so doing, had brought these things down upon her own head.

She thought about what Angel had said to her: *Feeling is good, even when it hurts.*

It hurt almost all the time.

Julia must have felt Faith's gaze on her—had probably been waiting for it—and turned her head to look at her enemy. Julia had once been very beautiful—still was, from the right angles—but her stepfather had taken care of that. Faith didn't know the particulars—in prison, there were way too many particulars to keep track of, and sometimes they changed over time. Faith was fairly certain it had been Julia's stepbrother who had deformed her when Julia had joined the block.

Anyway, it didn't matter. The bitterness and the rage were the particulars that didn't change. Julia was just the face they were wearing today.

"She beat me, Faith, she beat me," Carrie sputtered, blood droplets forming on her lower lip. It was the universal command: *Give her payback.*

The weird thing was, Faith used to wonder what this hellhole had to do with redemption. How voluntarily submitting to incarceration with enraged, hostile women was gonna make her better. But seeing the fury that powerlessness caused, she got it: she had gone so bad and so crazy because she felt powerless; powerless to be good, powerless to save her Watcher, powerless to be loved, like Buffy. Add an ugly childhood and you wound up in places like this with blood on your hands and shadows in your cheeks.

I'm gonna look like I'm a hundred and two by the time I get out of here, she thought dully.

She started across the field. Julia's lips parted in a faint smile. She was jonesing on the action to come.

As Faith approached, a line of hard-faced women, *the*

minions, Faith called them, took up their stations between the interloper and their leader. Faith just sneered at them and kept walking in a straight line, forcing the two in the center to drop back. Julia looked mildly disgusted, but took two giant steps forward and cocked her head.

"This my territory," she proclaimed.

"And that certainly is something to be proud of," Faith shot back. "My friend is hurt."

"Honey, you so ugly you don't got friends," Julia said. Her Juliettes cackled.

This is so lame, Faith thought. *I'm so glad Angel's not here.*

"Payback," she said.

"Right here?" Julia replied. "In front of God and everybody?"

"No. In my own good time. Maybe you'll see me coming."

Faith turned on her heel and cracked her knuckles.

Sunnydale

Anya said what everyone else was thinking: "Something ate Riley."

Xander shook his head, "No way."

"I don't believe it," Giles insisted. "Riley's a very capable soldier."

Tara moved from the group and walked to the destroyed fence. She bent down and said, "Look. Whatever was here left a trail."

Anya joined her. Giles looked at the two, heads earnestly bowed, and felt a moment of fear. *They're all so very different from one another,* he thought, *except that they can be killed. And I couldn't bear it. I can't even imagine my Slayer actually dying.*

He came forward, joining the group crouch, at which point a shuddering roar split the air and made everyone cry out in surprise. There was another roar, and then a gunshot.

"Which way?" Anya cried. "Which way should we go?"

"The trail doubles back," Giles said, pointing. "It appears that whatever advanced, doubled back and retreated. It's somewhere in the park."

"Riley?" Xander bellowed as he ran to Giles and the girls.

There was another gunshot.

The four raced past the piles of vegetation, leaping across long, gaping gullies that appeared to have been lasered into the ground, the concave surfaces of the depressions shiny and glassy.

Caused by intense heat, Giles surmised. *Perhaps a Lindworm. Haven't seen one of those since we worked with the Gatekeeper . . .*

"Get away," Giles shouted at them, as they both taunted the creature with their weaponry. "For God's sake, go!"

Then another gunshot echoed through the park, and the worm collapsed. It twitched, shrieking, then mewled like a kitten, then made absolutely no sound at all.

There was a bunch of rustling as some of the overturned tree branches got thrown out of the way and Riley emerged, covered with mud and bloody stripes. He looked terrible but he had all the main parts.

He said, "Run."

"But you shot it," Xander pointed out, as he rolled back off Giles. "And now we're all safe, right? And man, you must carry lots of guns."

"At least two." Riley shook his head. "The worm's not

the problem. The problem is this other thing. That I was hiding from, before I had to save you guys."

As if on cue, an enormous, black mass reared up, towering over Giles, Riley, and Xander. Everyone scattered backward, with Riley putting himself between the others and the shadow monster.

Then Tara yelled to Riley, "I-I can make it solid. Like before."

"Go," Riley said, never taking his eyes off the large, black form.

As Giles looked on, she performed an incantation. The thing appeared to be pulled down by gravity, and as its movements became more labored, Riley began to shoot it. Giles let loose a crossbow bolt, and Xander hefted his mace.

Then it whipped out some section of itself and grabbed Riley around the left leg. It began sucking him toward itself, and Giles had a fleeting, awful memory of what Cheryce had looked like after an encounter with one of these things.

"Ohhhh, crap!" Xander yelled, as he dashed forward and began pummeling the creature with the mace. Giles shot it again. Riley fought to get loose, kicking with his right leg, pounding with both fists as Xander continued to compress that portion of the solidified shadow into shadow lite. Together they kept working on the piece until it began to tatter and separate from the rest of the creature.

Then a fresh section glommed onto Xander and slithered around his waist. Xander shouted and dropped his crossbow. Riley, kicking free, picked it up and slammed it into the bands constricting Xander's hips and torso. Giles got off another shot, and Xander was freed as the piece of the monster released him.

Then, just as it appeared that they had the monster on the defense, it grew higher. Shadow upon shadow shot into the sky and began to crest over like an enormous tidal wave. Within seconds, it would easily engulf them all.

Giles closed his eyes. From somewhere deep inside himself, he felt a surge of power. He could see it in his mind; it was a scintillating blue, all simmering and filled with magick.

"By the power of Hecate and the Goddess, I demand that you return whence you came!" he shouted.

The creature roared and began to tumble over into an arch, its mass dwarfing Xander, Riley, Tara, and Anya, as they tried to scramble out of its reach.

"I order your return!" Giles thundered.

It furiously twisted its wounded body.

Then a golden semicircle popped into the air, began to glow, and the thing was literally sucked into it. Like a powerful vacuum, it was dragged in, bit by bit, until it was completely swallowed up.

The portal disappeared.

"Wow," Xander said, blinking at Giles.

"That was definitely a shadow monster," Anya announced. "They eat magickal residue." She looked at the others.

"Residue?" Xander echoed, confused.

"Some magicks throw off a lot of energy. Some are negative, some are positive." Anya smiled at Xander. "That's why they work. For example, a love spell throws off wonderful sensations of lust and desire, and—"

"We were checking out psi-residue particles at the Initiative," Riley said, wiping the blood off his face. "It was a pet project of Dr. Ping's."

"That monster, that shadow creature, was drawn here

because someone's performed powerful magick," Anya explained. "Someone here in Sunnydale, I'm guessing."

"Us?" Tara asked. "M-me?"

"I don't think so," Anya said. "Otherwise, they would have shown up here before. This is something different. Someone did something that hasn't been around here before, I'm guessing."

"I'm going to Los Angeles," Riley said.

"Why?" Tara asked, unmistakable dismay in her voice.

"I think I know what brought those monsters through," Riley said. "I think it's that girl's brother. I'm going to make sure he doesn't do it again."

"That's not why," Xander said, looking steadily at him. "Can't stand it, can you? All those macho protective urges coming over you. Hey, man, chill. She's the Slayer. She'll be okay."

Riley looked just as steadily back at Xander.

"Riley," Giles said, not unkindly, "Xander's right. We need you here. We've got more to deal with than we can handle."

The soldier wavered, and Giles knew he had him. Riley would stay. He wouldn't let civilians go unprotected.

But he didn't have to like it, and Riley clearly didn't; he was silent during the rest of the way back to Giles's apartment. His shoulders were hunched, his jaw set and hard.

He really loves her, Giles thought. *It must be difficult for him, knowing that Angel's joining up with her on the other side of reality . . . hopefully, anyway.*

"Hi," Joyce Summers said from the doorway, as the five trudged wearily past the fountain in the courtyard of Giles's building. "Wesley called. They want Riley to go to Los Angeles."

"What?" Giles asked, startled. "Why?"

Joyce looked equally ill at ease. "They want him to help break Faith out of jail."

They're gaining on me, Salma thought.

The soldiers on their terrifying horselike beasts thundered after her. She couldn't tell if they were hunting her down for sport or because she represented some kind of threat. Either way, she was their quarry, and as she panted and stumbled over rocks and tree roots, she didn't have much chance of eluding them.

What will they do to me? Why am I here?

Mad, giddy laughter nearly burbled out of her, but she still had her wits about her. She had to keep focused, keep ahead of them.

It's always so easy in the movies or on TV. The hero always finds an alley or a little cave or something.

There was nothing here but trees and grass. Incredibly, birds were singing and she saw something that looked like a rabbit dart across her path. It was all so normal, and yet so bizarre, that again, she had to suppress the urge to laugh.

The stands of trees were dense and thick with foliage; she whipped through the undergrowth, barely stopping to push branches out of her way as she caromed back and forth, bashing into trunks and outlying limbs like a brand-new skier on a bunny slope. Adrenaline and terror made her clumsy and unable to slow down; she was mindless as she forged ahead, losing track of every conscious thought. Her survival instinct had completely taken over.

Run, run, run.

It barely occurred to her that she was flying through total darkness now. She didn't care. She could hear the hooves of the fantastical beasts. Hear the trumpets . . .

The trumpets . . .

Salma stumbled. She was on an incline; she dropped to the ground and rolled, moving swiftly, tasting the mud and dead leaves in her mouth and her nose. She made herself roll faster, faster . . .

The trumpets . . .

The incline dropped and became a cliff; she covered her mouth with both hands as she sailed over the edge, unable to see a single thing around her. . . .

It seemed she fell for hours, keeping herself from screaming; she had enough time to think about her parents, and her *abuelita,* Doña Pilar, and Nicky. . . .

I love you all. . . .

When she landed, she blacked out. Perhaps for a moment, perhaps for a week.

She woke up in darkness.

And in stillness.

Silence.

For a moment, she thought she was alone.

But then she saw the soldiers, bearing down on her. . . .

Chapter 9

Her hand on the doorknob, Buffy paused and listened to the sounds from the other side. Something was over there, trying to get to the side she was on, in the big hallway. She didn't know what it was, but she knew she didn't want to let it out. She released the knob and backed away.

And the door rattled, then bulged toward her.

She felt the rush of adrenaline that accompanied slayage course through her veins. Her senses were instantly sharpened, mind alert, body poised for action. Fight or flight, it was called, when the body prepares itself, in a time of crisis, for one or the other.

Flight seemed like the best course of action here, not having any idea what was over there, or even if it was a foe. But to complicate things, she didn't know where to run—there were at least twenty doors off this hallway, and she didn't know where any of them led—and, as she had learned, where they led one minute didn't necessarily indicate where they'd lead the next. The castle was a giant maze that cheated by changing the rules as it went.

Finally, the door burst open, and Buffy's mind was made up.

They looked like rats—long, twitching snouts, dirty brownish fur, pink hairless tails, four legs tipped with little claws that made that skittery noise she'd heard on the flagstone floors—but they were the size of spaniels, and there were dozens of them.

They zeroed in on her like she was made of cheese.

Definitely flight, Buffy thought. She dove for the nearest door, yanked it open, and bolted through, slamming it behind her. The swinging door hit one of the rat-things on the snout and knocked it backward into its brother and sister rat-things with a high-pitched squeal of pain, and she took a fleeting satisfaction that she had caused it some pain, because it and its fellows had certainly freaked her out enormously.

The room she found herself in was some kind of library, with big leather-bound volumes scattered on bookstands, and chairs and tables at which to read them. Like the other rooms she had passed through, it was empty, and she didn't take time to look at the books to see if she could read them, because those rat things had broken down another door, and at this point there was only one door separating her from them. But the library had another exit, so she headed there, tugging open the door even though it stuck like a door swelled by damp weather. As she passed through this second door, the first door flew open and the dog-size rats charged in, squeaking and scampering straight for her.

"Stupid, stupid rat creatures!" Buffy shouted at them as she pushed this door shut. She couldn't even tell what this room was for, maybe taking private meals. A small table stood in the center with four chairs around it, and a heavy sideboard abutted one wall. Buffy ran to the sideboard, which two normal humans couldn't have budged. But she was the Slayer, and she leaned against it, pressed her feet against the stone floor for traction, and, feeling the muscles in her arms and shoulders strain from the weight, she slid it across the floor in front of the door.

The door rattled in its frame as the rat-things hurled themselves against it, but with the weight of the sideboard there, it held. The skittering stopped.

Buffy took a deep breath, and let it out.

But what she hadn't noticed was that there was a pass-through from another room, probably a way to serve meals in here, and it was covered by a sliding wooden panel.

She noticed it only when it splintered, and one of the whiskered ratty snouts shoved through it, forcing its wiggling body all the way through. If she hadn't moved the sideboard it would have landed on top of it, but instead it dropped to the floor with a heavy thump, and then another one came through, and another.

Buffy realized that not only weren't the rat creatures that stupid, they were probably smarter than the rats she knew back home. Except possibly for Amy, who was, after all, more of an enchanted witch than a rat.

She lunged for the door that led out of here, thankful that most of these rooms seemed to have at least two ways in and out. *Probably,* she thought, *because the place is a maze, and a maze isn't much good if it doesn't allow for lots of progress in entirely the wrong direction.*

This time, the rat creatures were closer to her, and she didn't even manage to get the door closed before a few of them had wedged their bodies in the doorway. She heard squeals of pain and felt bones crunch under the pressure of the door as she pushed it closed, but she knew she couldn't close it all the way without shooing them all out of the doorway, and there didn't seem to be much chance of that happening. She gave up, ran across this room, which was completely devoid of furnishings, and through the next door. Rat things nipped at her heels as she ran, and she felt her heel kick one in the teeth.

Another room, another door. Buffy felt herself growing winded. With each room she passed through, the rats seemed to get closer and closer. *There'll come a time,* she thought, *that I'll have to fight them. Maybe it should be sooner rather than later, while I still have some energy to devote to it.*

She slammed the door, just ahead of them, of a room that seemed to be some kind of armory—swords, axes, and pikes lined the walls, organized by size in racks. *Good place for a battle,* she realized. *At least there are plenty of weapons—and the rats, I believe, are a little short on opposing thumbs.*

She was reaching for a double-handed war ax when she caught a movement out of the corner of her eye. Snatching up the ax, she whirled, raising it—and stopped inches from Angel's throat.

"Buffy," he said. "Easy. You know I hate being decapitated."

She lowered the ax. "Sorry. There were these rat creatures."

"Rat creatures?" he echoed.

She nodded toward the door. Scratching and squeaking could be heard from the other side. "They'll knock that door down, any second."

"Rats that can knock down a door?" Angel asked.

"Rats the size of poodles. The big ones, not those toys or miniatures."

"Poodles," Angel repeated.

"Look, just take my word for it," Buffy demanded. "You'll see soon enough if we don't get out of here." She looked at him. "How did you get in here, anyway? Where have you been? Where'd you come from?"

"Later," Angel said. "Long story. If the rats are going to get us, let's give them a surprise."

Buffy hefted the ax. "What I had in mind."

Angel reached up on one of the walls and removed a candle from its ghastly sconce. "I had a different idea."

"Ooh, fire good," Buffy said with a wry smile.

"But what to burn?" Angel asked.

Buffy strode to one of the weapons racks and shook it, throwing the weapons to the floor with a clatter. Then she raised her ax and chopped the wooden rack to bits. With the head of the ax, she shoved the bits against the door, which bowed inward from the pressure of the rats.

"Kindling," she said. "But hurry, because that door won't hold much longer."

Angel pulled a wall hanging off the wall and pushed it into Buffy's pile of kindling. He held the candle's flame to the dry fabric, and it caught immediately. He touched the candle to other parts of the wood pile, igniting little flames wherever he could.

By the time the rats broke though, a small fire burned before the door. Buffy and Angel passed through yet another door into yet another room—the castle seemed to be full of rooms, but Buffy knew that it was just as possible that there were only three and they just kept changing from moment to moment. This room didn't seem to contain anything flammable, so they kept running, through another door and into another room. Here they found pay dirt—big trunks full of elaborate clothing, fabrics like silks and satins, and simpler ones, more like cotton, Buffy thought.

They jammed the clothing up against the door and lit it with a couple of the omnipresent candles.

It caught like gasoline.

"Let's see them come through that," Angel said.

"It should slow them down," Buffy agreed. "But I think there's one other problem."

"What's that?"

Buffy waved a hand around the room. "There's no other door."

"Can't be done, man," Ren'chlad argued, running his fingers through his greasy, matted hair.

Disgusting, Spike thought. *Good thing he's already a vampire—I could be starving to death and I wouldn't take a bite out of* him.

"Anything can be done," Spike countered. "If you want it enough."

"You sound naïve," Malon pointed out. They sat in the shade of the big rocks, waiting for the sun to drop below the horizon. It was low in the sky, so soon they'd be making their nightly pilgrimage to the river to drink and fill the skins they carried back to their sleeping area.

"Listen, mate, I've lived plenty long enough to have the naïveté long since knocked out of me," Spike said. "What I am is a realist, and I know I'm not willing to be an exhibit for the rest of my life." Which, with a free-flowing river of blood and no natural predators, he knew, could be a very long time indeed.

Now he knew what Hell was. Not the place they told

stories about, the place he knew Angel had spent some serious down time in. No, it was an everlasting stretch of time with these apathetic fools in a vampire zoo, being observed by tourists on holiday like a bunch of chimps in a cage.

"Ain't so bad," Ren'chlad countered. "Plenty to eat. Nobody tryin' to stake you. Place to hide out when the sun's up."

"Not so bad," Spike repeated with a sneer. "Where you guys are from, do you have a Slayer? Someone whose job is just to hunt you down and kill you?"

"Something like that," Malon said. "We don't call him that."

"It's a man?" Spike asked.

"Yeah," Malon replied. "A kid, really. But tough."

"Ours is a girl," Spike said. "Young, beautiful . . ." He pictured Buffy in his mind's eye, wearing red leather pants and a sleeveless black top, a stake clenched in her fist and a determined gleam in her lovely green eyes. "Anyway, the challenge of it all—outwitting her, dodging her, outmaneuvering her—helps make life worthwhile, you know? The thrill of the hunt. The chase. Knowing that one wrong move could be your last. Without that, why bother?"

"Sounds stupid," Ren'chlad said.

"Yeah, well a bath sounds stupid to you," Spike shot back. "But some of us believe in soap and water—just not to drink. And we believe in living by our wits, using our heads for something more than rooting our hair."

"Hey," Ren'chlad said. Anger flashed in his eyes.

"What?" Spike asked, leaping to his feet. "Don't like it? Want to take a swing at me?"

Ren'chlad waved a hand at him, languidly. "Naw," he said.

"Leave him alone, Spike," Issak broke in. "He don't want to fight you."

"Looks to me like none of you want to fight anything," Spike said. "You just want to sit back and take what you're handed."

"Life's easy," Malon said. "Why stress?"

"Because easy's *boring!*"

"To you, maybe," Ren'chlad said. "Not to us."

Spike paced in the big rock's shadow. "I can barely believe you used to be vampires," he said. "Hunters. Merciless predators. Now look at you."

Ren'chlad smiled, exposing a mouthful of rotted teeth, and the gaps where some had fallen out. Stringy hair pasted itself to his cheek. "Pretty, ain't we?"

Spike had to turn away.

An hour later, the sun was gone and a sliver of moon poked above the horizon. *Good,* he thought, *a dark night. Perfect.*

The other vampires busied themselves gathering skins to carry down to the river. Spike watched them with contempt. They barely paid him any mind at all, used to his lack of respect or interest in their comings and goings. He had been here for three risings of the moon, though his internal clock didn't seem to match up with that, he knew. He figured the days here weren't much more than seven or eight hours long, if that—time seemed to pass at an accelerated rate. So a boring eternity would pass more quickly than it would back on his Earth, but it would still be eternity.

As the vampires trooped down to the river, Spike hung back. The rest of the group made a right turn, and Spike—feeling a pang of hunger that threatened to overwhelm him and send him to the river with the others—made himself go left instead. Toward the fence.

Malon had said "they," whoever they were, could electrify it at will. The implication was that they watched it at all times. But how could they? Spike didn't know how big the fenced enclosure was, but that very fact—the fact that he couldn't see one side of it from the other, and that none of the other vampires had claimed to have surveyed the whole thing—indicated to him the impossibility of monitoring every point on the fence at every moment. Spike was one man, alone—wouldn't they be watching the bulk of them as they went to the river for the night's feasting? He knew he was taking a chance, but it seemed like a calculated risk.

In a few moments, he was at the fence. It was no shorter than it had been the first time he'd seen it, and the four strands of barbed wire strung across the top looked just as sharp. But in the brief days between then and now, he'd realized that he was not a vampire who could stand to be cooped up in here for the rest of time. He needed to be out, to be free. He was a hunter, not a captive.

Spike shook out his hands and took a running start. A powerful leap landed him most of the way up the fence, fingers twining through the links. He used the momentum of his jump to keep his legs in motion, turning on the fulcrum of his hands, performing a gymnast's move to try to spin over the top of the fence.

He didn't quite make it. He gained loft, released the fence, and turned in midair, head whipping over his heels. But when he reached the peak of his arc and started down, he saw that he was coming down directly into the slightly-angled barbed wire strands. He put his hands down to tip himself away from the barbs and over the fence, and his hands caught on the barbs, his flesh tearing.

A moment later he landed flat on his back. He blinked

a couple of times, looked up at the sky. He was on the outside.

For a few minutes he just waited there. He'd touched the fence, if only briefly, and it had not been electrified. Did that mean his escape had gone unnoticed by the zookeepers? It was possible, he knew. He strained his ears to listen, but there was no sound other than the usual night noises of this place, the distant rush of the blood river, the chirps of unseen insects, the rustle of a breeze stirring the tall grasses. The night air smelled sweet, rich and fertile, but there were no unusual or unexpected scents that might indicate danger. Spike slowly, cautiously, rose to a standing position. He glanced back through the fence, at his former prison, and then turned his back to it.

No path marked this side of the line, no trail that might lead to freedom or capture. Spike was on his own, a pioneer striking out across unmapped territory. The same high grass grew on this side, so he pushed his way through it, heading in a straight line. He had no way to know which way danger was, so it didn't much matter where he went. He just wanted distance between himself and the enclosure. He could worry about an ultimate destination later.

As he walked, he found himself wondering again what had become of Buffy and Angel. They were supposed to be here somewhere, but there had been no sign of them. Had they met up with the people who ran the place? A zoo full of captive vampires would be great sport to them, he supposed. He liked to think that Buffy would have more class than that, but she was the Slayer, after all, whatever else he might credit her with. The person Buffy was one thing, the Slayer something else entirely.

Topping a hillside, he took another quick look back at where he'd been. He could still see the fence, far below him now, a sparkling line in the faint moonlight. Beyond that, he was able to make out the dark band of the river. The other vamps would be there drinking now, and probably wondering what had become of old Spike. He imagined stories would be told of him through the ages, now—the one that got away. *Cheryce would be proud of me,* he thought, then remembered that Cheryce was no longer in a position to be proud of anyone. He thought about her for a moment, sadly remembering the good times they'd had, realizing she'd never be able to introduce him to her friend who might be able to extract his chip.

He heard them first just as he started down the other side of the hill, into a sweeping valley that looked as if it might have inhabited structures in it. A drone like a mosquito, then like a whole troop of them, angry and determined. The sound quickly grew louder, and Spike knew it was no insect. He couldn't see anything in the dark sky yet, but he started to run just the same. Heading downhill, he moved quickly through the thick grass.

Louder and louder, the drone turned into a roar just before the first of them appeared over the top of the hill. Spike risked a look over his shoulder as he ran. They were some kind of flying sleds, with two helmeted occupants on each, standing up. One gripped what must have been the steering mechanism, and the other stood behind what could only be a weapon of some kind. A stun gun, Spike figured. If these were indeed zookeepers, they'd want to get their exhibits back safely and unharmed.

He threw himself flat on the ground, counting on the tall grass to hide him. Another glance revealed more of the sleds, at least six of them now, maybe more, passing over the hill he'd just climbed. As he watched through the blades of grass, one of them came to a hovering stop, just overhead. The one standing behind the weapon, a sinister-looking contraption mounted on a swiveling stand, swung its barrel around and pointed it directly at Spike.

Spike jumped up and began running again, cutting a crazy zigzag in hopes of avoiding whatever stun beam these blokes threw at him. Obviously that one had spotted him, and while he didn't like the idea of exposing himself, just laying there letting them blast him didn't seem like a good plan either.

As Spike leaped to his feet, the gunner fired his weapon. An explosion from the spot where Spike had just been nearly bowled the vampire over. *Those aren't stun guns,* he thought. *They're bloody well trying to kill me!*

Now the other sleds grouped around the first one, and more rays shot down toward the ground, all around Spike. Every time they hit, an explosion shook the earth, sending dirt and debris flying into Spike's face. He dodged and weaved, but the blasts came closer and closer.

Finally, one fired directly in Spike's path. The concussive wave slammed into him with the force of a physical blow. Spike went down in the grass again, and this time he didn't get up.

Inside the Gas-N-Go Mischa spotted a clerk and a single customer, a middle-aged man picking between competing brands of cream-filled cupcakes. The cop was right behind him, he knew, running from his car, no doubt drawing his weapon. Mischa didn't have time to think, only to act. He grabbed the customer from behind, one arm tight around the man's neck, and spun him so he faced the door, blocking Mischa's body with his own. The guy uttered a strangled cry.

The cop burst through the doors, gun in both hands pointed at Mischa.

"Freeze!" he demanded.

"You shoot, you'll kill this man first," Mischa replied. "I might just snap his neck anyway, if you don't drop that gun."

The highway patrolman held his bead on Mischa, as if gauging his chances of making the shot. Mischa was careful to keep the man in front of him, even bobbing his own head to make sure it was hidden behind his hostage's head at least some of the time. He didn't know if this cop was a good shot, but at basically point-blank range, he didn't want to give him a chance to play hero.

"Can't do that, son," the patrolman said. He was in his thirties, maybe, barely old enough to have a son Mischa's age. But he had that essence of maturity that sometimes came from having a uniform and a badge. "Why don't you just let go of him and let's work this out?"

The hostage nodded his support of that idea but Mischa just gripped him tighter, cutting off his air supply. The nodding stopped and Mischa relaxed his grip just a little.

"That's a good idea," the clerk said from behind the counter. He'd ducked down into hiding as soon as the cop had charged through the door.

"I do not want to hurt anybody," Mischa said. "But I have something very important to do, and I won't be stopped."

"Whatever it is, son, it can wait while we settle this," the cop offered.

"You have no idea what you're talking about," Mischa argued. "And I am not your son."

"No, you're not," the patrolman responded. He held his stance. The opening at the end of the gun barrel looked impossibly big and black. "But that doesn't matter. What matters is that no one does anything he'll regret later."

If I don't meet up with Alina, we might all regret it later, Mischa knew. She alone could work the Reality Tracer, so she held the world's future in her hands. He had to find her at the Grand Canyon, had to make sure she wasn't recaptured by her parents or anyone who'd force her to use it for their evil ends.

"I do not have time to explain to you," Mischa said. "So just listen. This man will die if you do not get out of my way. Do you want his death on your hands?"

"It won't be on mine, it'll be on yours," the cop countered. "I know you don't want that."

"One death is nothing compared to how many lives I am trying to save."

"Why don't you tell me about it, then? Maybe I can help."

"You would never believe me. Now, please move." Mischa increased the pressure again, and the man gave out a strangled *"Urk."* The highway patrolman took a step backward.

"Is that your car outside at the pumps?" Mischa asked his hostage. "The four wheel drive?"

The man nodded as far as Mischa's grip would allow him to.

"Keys in it?"

"Pocket," the man managed.

"Take them out and put them in my left hand," Mischa ordered.

"Don't do it, sir," the cop instructed.

"He's not the one holding your neck in his hands," Mischa growled.

The man reached into his pocket, fished out a key ring.

"The ignition key, please."

The man found that key, put it into Mischa's hand. The cop glanced at the hand as if he might try shooting it, but Mischa quickly moved it back behind his hostage's back.

"Now I ask you again," Mischa said. "Please get out of my way. We're going through the door, and I would like to do it in such a way that nobody gets hurt."

"I can't let you do it," the cop said.

"Then you're willing to kill this innocent man?"

The patrolman held his position for a moment longer, then lowered his gun and stepped to the side of the door.

"Think about what you're doing," he tried.

"I have to do this." Mischa kept the hostage between himself and the officer as he passed by him and backed out the door. He kept going, the man in step with him, also walking backward, all the way to the Nissan Xterra that waited by the gas pumps.

At the car's door, Mischa reached back with his left hand and worked the handle. The door swung open. *Now the hard part,* Mischa thought. He leveraged himself up into the driver's seat, still clutching the man around the neck. The patrolman had followed them outside and had raised his weapon again, drawing a bead on the driver's seat. Mischa hunched over in the seat; if he sat up straight he'd be too high up for the hostage and would be an easy target. Awkwardly, he fed the key into the ignition and cranked it. The SUV started.

Gunning the engine, Mischa put the car into gear, changed his grip on his hostage and shoved the guy straight toward the patrolman. At the same time he slammed his foot down on the accelerator. The vehicle lurched forward, and by the time the officer had a clear shot at it, his angle of fire had changed. He fired three times, his bullets striking the rear of the vehicle, shattering a rear window and punching holes in the back right fender.

Mischa pulled the door closed as he bumped up and over a curb marking the end of the Gas-N-Go lot. Beyond was nothing but open desert. Here at the fringes of the highway, the desert was trampled by cars and people. Plastic bags clung to the creosote bushes; soft drink cans scattered at their bases. An old electric range stood abandoned, its door missing, next to a bullet-riddled saguaro cactus.

Behind him, he heard the report of the patrolman's gun firing one more time, but the bullet vanished harmlessly into the desert. Mischa knew the guy would be on the radio soon enough, calling for helicopters or other help—but he also knew the cop couldn't follow him off-road in his squad car, so at least he had a head start. After he'd put some space between himself and the highway, he found an old, rutted dirt road, and followed it away from the setting sun.

Chapter 10

Los Angeles

"OF COURSE," WESLEY SAID, "THE DIFFICULT PART IS that she's in prison."

"Of course," Riley agreed. He sat, somewhat ill at ease, in Cordelia's living room. Alina sat on the floor working on her Reality Tracer, and Cordelia busied herself, as far as he could tell, by looking busy. "That would be a drawback."

"Quite."

"Unless we could get her out."

"Do you know a friendly judge? Or senator?" Wesley inquired.

"Maybe your Initiative goons can just storm the place," Cordelia offered.

"I don't think so," Riley replied. "I was thinking maybe something a little more discreet."

"You really *do* want to break her out," Wesley said, a wry smile crossing his face.

"It was your idea," Riley said. He found the man kind of amusing. Vaguely reminiscent of Giles, but somehow different at the same time. From what he'd heard, Wesley was capable of committing some violence when it needed to be done—a crack shot with a handgun, for one thing. Giles had talents of his own, but Riley had the sense that Wesley might be a little handier in a tough situation.

"Well, yes, but I didn't expect that we would actually do it."

"Isn't that kind of, well, illegal, for a straight arrow like you?" Cordelia asked.

"Maybe I'm not as straight as you think, Cordelia," Riley said, smiling at her. He wondered how Angel could put up with her. But then, he wondered how Angel could put up with Angel. He wouldn't be able to, for any length of time at all.

History has something to do with that, he thought. *A lot to do with it. The history of Buffy.*

And Buffy was what mattered here. If breaking Faith out of jail was what it took to make sure Buffy got home safely, then he'd do it if he had to kick down the walls single-handedly.

"What did you have in mind, then?" Wesley asked. "Chopper in during the dead of night? A commando raid? Tunnels?"

"I was thinking I'd round up some help."

"What kind of help?"

"Seems like something Gunn might be good at," Riley suggested.

"Gunn?" Wesley echoed.

"You know him, right?"

"Actually, I've never met him," Wesley replied. "He and Cordelia and I have seen each other, briefly. We haven't been introduced."

"We didn't know who he was," Cordelia explained.

"That too," Wesley confirmed.

"But you know how to find him."

"Sure we do," Cordelia said. "Or do we?"

"We know his neighborhood," Wesley pointed out.

"That might help." Riley got up from the couch and wandered to the shelves, eyeing the titles of some of the books. "Gunn came to Sunnydale and worked with us for a while. He's a good guy."

"Seems to be," Wesley agreed.

Alina looked up from her work. "Gunn?" she asked. "I like Gunn."

"You know him?" Riley asked.

"He saved me from some bad men," Alina said. "Is very brave."

"Yeah, he is," Riley said. "Brave as they come."

"I come with you? To find Gunn?"

Riley shook his head, smiling patiently at the young girl. "You not come with me. I'll go by myself. Those streets aren't safe at night."

"I could accompany you," Wesley volunteered. "An extra pair of fists, as it were."

"I think I'll be okay," Riley said. "But thanks for the offer."

"Anyway, don't you have a machine to fix?" Cordelia pointed out.

Alina threw a tiny screwdriver to the ground. "I give up," she said. "I cannot."

"You can't fix it?" Wesley asked her.

"No," she said, her lips fixed in a pout. "I will take it home to my father. He can fix."

"And then make you use it for evilly-type things?" Cordelia asked her.

"He will try," Alina said. "He will not succeed."

Riley watched her pick up her screwdriver and put away her tools. *Determined kid,* he thought. He'd only heard sketchy details about her past, but it sounded like she'd had it rough. He hoped she got through this mess and out the other side in one piece.

Faith headed back to her bunk after kitchen duty. She'd been assigned to dinner dishes, which meant two hours after the day's final meal, up to her shoulders in scalding hot water, scrubbing the filth off plates and flatware and trays. The women in this place seemed to have no sense of personal responsibility. She couldn't quite imagine how food and grime could get quite so caked on, unless they did it intentionally to make life hard for those with kitchen detail.

She had dish duty because it was a punishment, and she was punished because she'd made the wrong enemies. *Nothing new there,* she thought. *Spent my life doing that.*

This particular enemy was named Julia Swank. She was in Yorba Linda Ranch on racketeering charges, which was some district attorney's way of putting her inside when he hadn't been able to make anything else stick. Basically, she had run with a gang of dopers, and she had persuaded them to build a meth lab in the garage of one of them. They'd gone along with her scheme, cooking the drug and selling it on street corners. Finally, the garage had blown up, killing one of the men. Another one had turned state's evidence and fingered her as the brains behind the operation. Her connection was difficult to prove—she had never actually entered the lab, she never touched the drugs, she never sold any. But using racketeering laws, they'd been able to bring her down and put her away.

Now that she was inside, she wanted to continue running things her way. She'd made friends on the inside, guards and trustees and even, some said, the warden. Certainly, she got favors not granted the other inmates. Yorba Linda was a work farm, not as secure as a real prison, but Julia Swank had it easy even by these standards. She had a private cell, where most women had to share a bunk room with twenty-three other women. She was allowed visitors in her cell, when she wanted them, both from within the population and from outside. Only the cushiest jobs were assigned to her. She even had meals delivered to her cell, when she wanted them.

But Carrie Grimes, who had befriended Faith, had somehow found herself on Julia's bad side. Carrie was plain, petite, a bit on the mousy side, Faith thought. But sweet as could be. She was in for having kneecapped an abusive boyfriend. Instead of giving her the medal she'd deserved, the state of California had locked her away for ten years. Because she wasn't tough, didn't put on a front, and shied away from trouble, Julia Swank made a target of her.

Faith saw it happen once, and interceded.

The guards broke it up too quickly, and she had ended up with kitchen duty for two months. One more infraction, she knew, and it was solitary confinement.

That was a chance Faith was willing to take if it meant breaking Julia Swank's hold on the prison once and for all.

And tonight's the night it happens.

She'd had to use Carrie Grimes as bait, which she

didn't like. But Carrie was willing, so Faith didn't ask her twice, just explained the setup to her. Carrie would be straggling, moving slow about brushing her teeth and getting ready for bed. The other women would all be in bed while Carrie was still in the washroom. Since Julia was still looking for a chance to get Carrie without Faith around, her minions would report this to her, and some crooked guard would let Julia out of her cell. She and her thugs would catch Carrie in the washroom.

Which was when Faith would come in from kitchen duty. Having caught Julia and her gang in the act, she'd kick some major butt, and then get the guard who let Julia out busted as well.

It's a foolproof plan, she thought.

"What are you doing out?"

The voice stopped Faith short. It was one of the guards, Vicki Henderson. Short and blocky, with close-cropped auburn hair, she stepped from the shadows and stood in Faith's path. In her hands she held a baton.

"Just coming in from kitchen duty," Faith explained wearily.

"You should've been in before now," Henderson insisted. "You know what time lights out is."

"I know. I also know those women are a bunch of slobs, and if I don't get the dishes clean I have to do them again. So I stay as long as it takes."

"How do you expect to get to your bunk?"

"The doors aren't locked until eleven," Faith said. "You know that."

"Hell I do," Henderson argued. "Far as I'm concerned, when lights out is at ten, ten's when you should be in your bunk. You ain't, you get disciplined."

I really don't have time for this tonight, Faith thought.

She felt the seconds ticking by. Carrie would be in a lot of trouble if this guard delayed her.

"Listen, I'm sorry," she said. "I'll do them faster tomorrow night."

"Spending the night in solitary might help you remember that," Henderson threatened.

"I can't do that," Faith said. She had thought that Henderson was one of the guards who favored Julia Swank. Chances were, if she was out here right now, it was because she had just let Julia out of her cell to pay a visit to Carrie. She really didn't know any other way to explain Henderson's continual hostility toward her, other than the fact that she was an inmate and Henderson a guard, and some of the guards took that difference more personally than others.

"You will if I say you will." Henderson raised the baton, took a step toward her.

Faith reacted instinctively. She reached for Henderson as she was still in motion, her momentum, however faint, still pushing her toward Faith. She got the guard's right arm in her hand and yanked back on it, drawing it over her own right shoulder. Then she fell onto her back, kicking up with her legs. Henderson was pulled over her, launched from Faith's feet, and landed in a crumpled pile behind Faith.

By the time Henderson found her balance, Faith loomed over her, holding the baton.

"You're in a lot of trouble, Faith," Henderson told her.

"Me?" Faith asked. "Looks to me like you're the one in trouble."

Henderson pushed herself to her feet. "How do you figure that?"

"Because you want to live," Faith said. "And the only way I'm going to let you do that is if I have your word that this never happened."

"Are you threatening me?" The guard's face was twisted with rage. "Don't even think you can—"

"If you don't want to live, that can be arranged too," Faith reminded her. She tapped the baton against her own palm. "Your call."

Henderson glared at her for a moment, as if weighing her options. "Okay, this time," she finally agreed. "But cross me once more and you'll regret it."

"One of us will," Faith said. She exerted pressure on the baton, but not enough to visibly strain her, and snapped it in half. "Here," she said, handing the pieces to the guard.

Henderson looked in horror at the two halves of her baton. Her face white, she hurried away.

Faith picked up the pace, wanting to get to the washroom before Carrie was really hurt. She wended her way between the blockhouses containing bunks for the women until she got to hers, the building with a big 17 painted on the side. She tugged open the door, rushed through the bunk area, and back to the washroom. The washroom door was locked.

It wasn't supposed to be.

Faith gripped the knob, applied all her strength, and twisted it. It snapped open and the door swung free.

Inside, Carrie Grimes was backed up against a sink, struggling, panic in her eyes. Three women held her arms and her neck. Julia Swank stood before her with a long-bladed kitchen knife in her hands. At Faith's entrance, Julia swung around, pointing the knife at Faith.

"Just in time," Julia said. "Thought you might like to see your little friend get carved like a Thanksgiving turkey."

"No one gets carved," Faith said. "Except maybe you, if you don't put that down."

Julia lunged at Faith. Faith responded by kicking upward, a kick so fast as to be almost invisible, that caught Julia's wrist. The knife flew from her hand, straight up, and jammed into the ceiling. Julia grabbed at her wrist.

"That was a real mistake," she hissed, her teeth clenched against the pain. "Take her down," she ordered her minions.

Faith waited for the attack. The three women let go of Carrie, who remained where she was against the sink, tears streaming down her cheeks. Faith let the first one reach for her, and caught the woman's forearms in both hands. She yanked the woman forward, arms on either side of herself, and met the woman's face with a powerful headbutt. The sound of her jaw cracking and teeth breaking was a symphony to Faith. The woman fell to the floor, blood flowing from her mouth.

The other two reached Faith simultaneously, arms flailing, getting in a few punches. Faith took them easily. She drove her hands through the wildly punching arms, grabbing both women by the fronts of their shirts. With a mighty tug, she drew their heads together, about chest high. They struggled, grappling with her arms and striking her, but her strength more than outmatched theirs. With two quick knee jabs to their faces, both women were down.

Which left only Julia Swank. Her pretty face—the face that had inspired others to commit her crimes for her—was ugly now, red and twisted with rage. Her mouth curled down, lips parted, teeth bared like an animal. She had hooked her long, slender fingers into claws. She faced Faith at a crouch, coiled and ready to spring.

Faith thought she ought to let Julia live, because killing someone, even in self-defense, might extend her own sentence. *Even someone as useless as Julia Swank,* she thought.

On the other hand, judging from the fury with which Julia glared at her, she might not have a choice.

Julia had barely started her lunge when the building's front door burst open and the lights popped on. Six armed guards rushed into the building, moving between the bunks toward the washroom. All the women in the bunkhouse were awake now, whistling and hooting. Faith heard people exhorting her to kill Julia, and more than a few suggesting it should be the other way around. But with the guards closing in behind her, she backed away.

A moment later rough hands were pinning her to the ground. Cold handcuffs encircled her wrists and closed tight enough to pinch. Angry voices whispered in her ears, but she couldn't make out the words, only the tone. It took a couple of minutes to be brought to her feet again, by which time, she was delighted to see, Julia was also cuffed and under intense scrutiny.

"It's solitary for you," one of the guards told Faith. "Let's go."

"What about her?" Faith asked.

"She's no concern of yours," the guard declared. "But she's not supposed to be out of her cell. She's got some grief coming her way."

Armed with that knowledge, Faith knew she could handle solitary confinement.

Gladly.

Angel looked at the door they had just set afire. "Then I guess we use this one," he said. "Not much choice."

"It's just strange," Buffy replied. "All the other rooms had at least two doors. I guess there always has to be a last room somewhere."

"So if we go through this door, we'll have to fight our

way past some big rats?" Angel asked. He hefted a broadsword he'd taken from one of the wall racks. "At least we have weapons."

"Big angry rats," Buffy clarified. "And when I say big, I mean, big for dogs, not big for rats. Giant for rats. But that's not even the worst of it."

"What is?"

Buffy looks very serious, Angel thought. He liked her serious look. Brow furrowed ever so slightly, mouth a straight line, eyes intense. He didn't like it as much as he liked her happy look, but it was still a good look for her.

And I shouldn't be thinking that way, he thought. *That's history.*

"Well, I just came from that room," she explained. "And it was full of the big rat creatures. I didn't really notice much else about it, because I was in kind of a hurry. But, chances are, when we go back through that door, it'll be a different room entirely."

"Meaning what?"

"Meaning, rooms change here. You leave a room, you go right back through the door, and the room is completely different."

"So what you're saying is this is no ordinary house."

"Castle," she corrected.

"Castle."

"I guess you didn't get the outside view."

"I kind of came through a portal," Angel offered. "Didn't see much of anything."

"It's a castle. The big, dark, spooky kind. With interesting security features."

Angel studied the wooden door, which was now completely engulfed in flame. "I saw the suit of armor you fought."

Buffy looked confused. "I thought you said you didn't—"

"I was with this witch, in a different reality. She projected an image of you. Then she sent me here."

"Oh. So you didn't see the dragon?"

"No dragon."

"He said—well, after I killed him and he turned into a man, he said that I was supposed to save a princess in the tower. I'm thinking that she might be one of the kids, you know? From L.A."

Angel shook his head slowly.

"What?" Buffy asked. "Maybe I'm not explaining it very well."

"It's never boring," Angel said softly. Instead of elaborating, he gestured toward the door. "You know, if we don't go through it soon, it'll burn all the way through and then the rats will be able to come in."

"Better on our terms than theirs, you're thinking," Buffy said.

"Exactly."

Buffy raised the ax she'd found. "Follow me."

Angel almost protested, but decided not to. *Buffy knows our respective abilities,* he thought. *If she wants to be first through the door, then she wants to be first. She's not just saying it to be polite.* He stood back.

Buffy held the ax in front of her face, took two steps, and crashed through the flaming door. The ax took the brunt of the impact, smashing the door out of her way, sending shards of wood flying everywhere. Buffy flew through the space she'd made. Angel followed suit, punching a little more of the door out to make room for his larger bulk.

There were no rats to be seen.

The room was a large hall, with tapestry hangings on the walls and a red carpet running up the middle. A few randomly spaced chairs hugged the walls. Candles flickered in sconces and on iron stands.

"See what I mean?" Buffy asked. "This is not what it was before. It was much smaller, and full of rats."

Angel nodded.

"Do you think I'm crazy, Angel? If you think I've gone insane, just tell me, okay?"

"I don't think you're crazy, Buffy," Angel said. "I think this is a strange castle."

"Understatement of the year award," Buffy said.

"So the question is, if the rooms can't stay put, how do we ever find the tower we're looking for?"

Buffy shrugged, then pointed at the floor. "Follow the red carpet?"

They did so. It led to large wooden doors, ornately carved with scenes of medieval battle. Buffy and Angel each took one of the iron ring door pulls and tugged on them, holding their new weapons in their other hands. The doors opened smoothly.

On the other side was a narrow staircase, spiraling up and out of sight.

Los Angeles

The battle had started by accident.

A car full of Russian gang members sped through the streets of the Crenshaw district, after having thrown Molotov cocktails at a bar known to be frequented by Mexican gang members. The driver tried to race a yellow light, but it turned red before he quite made it to the intersection.

Heading in the other direction was a car loaded with Mexican gang members on their way to a Russian neighborhood to deliver some flaming destruction of their own. The car was loud with laughter, music, raucous jokes, semihysterical screaming, and fear. When the light turned green, the driver stomped on the gas.

The Russians' car slammed into the Mexicans' car, crunching the driver's side door panel and spinning the car three times in the intersection. It came to rest, finally, over the curb on top of two newspaper vending machines and against a bus stop bench. The driver's left leg was broken, and he was pinned inside the car. The others got out, guns drawn.

The Russians, also with guns drawn, exited their car, stalled in the middle of the intersection, and the firing began.

Word spread fast.

That had been almost forty minutes ago. Now Che crouched down in the mouth of a nearby alley. Several other Echo Park Band *camachos* stood around him. They were all armed. A dozen or so of their friends had shown up, and about that many Russians. They shot round after round at each other, but everyone had found cover and none of their bullets struck home.

"What do we do, Che?" Pepé Villaréal asked. "We ain't hittin' squat."

"I know, *ese*," Che said. "Lemme think."

"Ain't much time for thinking," Guillermo Montoya pointed out. "Listen."

They'd been hearing distant sirens for a few minutes now, but the sirens were closing in. The stutter of helicopters grew nearer, too.

"Dude, I know!" Che said, agitated. There was no way

this would turn into a big victory for them, and he was giving up on that goal. All he wanted now was to see at least one Russian fall under his attack before the cops shut them down.

Just one.

If I can hold my gun still enough to shoot.

He was nervous, scared really. He had to look tough and sound tough. Hell, he was tough. But a gunfight was serious business. People died. Che didn't want to be one of those people. Not for the first time, he thought about Nicky de la Natividad, refusing to share the secret of the Night of the Long Knives.

Invulnerability would be handy right about now, he thought.

"Those Russian *cabrons* can't just come into our neighborhoods and get away with it," Montoya continued. "They got to be put in their place."

"You want to just walk out there and tell them that?" Che asked him. "They got good cover over there. We got cover here. It's a standoff."

"But—"

"Listen," Che interrupted. "Those sirens are almost here. Cops will be all over this intersection in a few minutes. Maybe they'll flush some of the Russians out. You see any of them show up, you let them have it. Then *vamonos.* Vanish. You got to be invisible, dude. Let the Russians go down."

The other guys nodded their heads. From the cover of the alley, they waited.

The helicopters arrived first, blades chopping the night air and spotlights washing the streets. The guys pressed themselves flat against the wall when the light shone down the alley.

From above, a voice boomed.

"Everyone below, put down your weapons and lay flat on your stomachs. This is the Los Angeles Police Department. Put down your weapons and lay down with your hands behind your heads."

Villaréal aimed his gun into the air.

"Don't, man!" Che shouted, slapping at his hand. "You ain't gonna hit anything, but you'll show them where we are. Save it for the Russians."

Even as he spoke, a couple of Russians broke from the cover of parked cars, making a run up the street in hopes of getting away from the intersection before it was surrounded. Che aimed his nine. His hand was sweating, making it hard to hang onto the piece. He guessed that was why they patterned the grip, to make it easier to hold with damp palms.

Holding the gun too tight but unable to relax it, he led the Russian by a few steps, and jerked the trigger. The gun bucked up and his shot went wild. Next to him, a boom told him that someone else was shooting, too. Che aimed again, at the Russian who was now running in a crouched zigzag to present a harder target. He tried to anticipate which way the guy would zig next, and fired again, this time letting out a breath and remembering to squeeze the trigger instead of pulling on it.

His gun kicked after the bullet was fired.

The Russian buckled in the street. Two more bullets slammed into him, making his body jerk twice. Then it was still.

Che found himself trembling uncontrollably. He couldn't isolate the emotion that caused it. He thought it was a lot like terror, though.

Before he could put much thought into it, police cars

sped into the intersection, disgorging officers clad in riot gear and carrying shotguns. Che and his friends exchanged glances, and ran up the alley, away from the cops and the battle.

A block later, they were still running. A stitch had developed in Che's side, but he fought it, pushed on. His shirt was soaked with sweat, and he couldn't take in enough air.

Finally, he came to a halt, bent over and gasping for breath. Pepé Villaréal grabbed him on the shoulder.

"Look, *jefe*," he said.

He was pointing at something, a parked car next to the street.

"What," Che said. "It's a LeSabre."

"Under it, man," Pepé insisted.

Che looked again. Pepé was right. Underneath the car there was a strange shape. Someone hiding under it, he thought.

"One of the Russians?" Che asked.

"Probably," Villaréal replied. "One of ours wouldn't go under a car on this turf. This is our country—he'd go into one of the houses."

"Yeah," Che agreed. "He's probably strapped."

"Maybe," Montoya said. "But there's more of us." He aimed his gun toward the car. Che put up a hand to stop him.

"Wait," he said. "I want one alive."

After a moment's discussion, the three fanned out, surrounding the car. They each held their guns low, pointed at the shadowed form underneath it. Che spoke.

"We got you, man. Under the car there. There's three of us and we all got guns pointed at you. Now, we just want to talk, see if there's some way we can negotiate a truce. But if you move funny or fire a weapon at us, then we'll kill you. You got nowhere to go. You hear me?"

"I hear you," a voice from beneath the car said. It was thickly accented. *Definitely Russian,* Che thought. He smiled. *I killed one already. Next one's easy.*

"Throw out your strap," Che instructed the guy. "Nice and slow. Just toss it away from the car."

The guy didn't acknowledge him.

"Do it now," Che said. "Throw it away from you, into the street. If I count to five and you haven't done it, we start shooting."

The guy still didn't move. Che began to count.

Before he reached two, the guy under the car had skidded a weapon into the middle of the street. Montoya scooped it up and tucked it into his belt.

"Come on out," Che said. "Slow, with your hands where we can see them. We ain't talking with you under the car."

"Okay," the guy said. "I come out." He pressed his hands flat against the street and scooted out on his stomach. Che and the others rushed up to him, so by the time he got to his feet they were there. Che shoved him up against the car and pressed the barrel of his nine into the guy's nose, tearing the flesh there.

"Now we'll talk," Che said.

Chapter 11

Los Angeles

KATE LOCKLEY STOOD IN THE MIDDLE OF THE STREET, service weapon held at her side. Like a scene from *West Side Story,* the two gangs vanished into the night, Russians disappearing to the east and Mexicans to the west. The air still stank of gunpowder, and smoke hung thickly in the air like fog, filtering the white and red and yellow lights from the squad cars and ambulances that had converged on the scene. Sirens still wailed, and more were coming from various points.

Most of the cops in Los Angeles, she knew, were focused on the gang war—trying to disarm the gangs, trying to locate their leaders, trying to keep innocents out of the crossfire. Her case was something different—something she knew was as important, but which had fallen out of the public's eye when the bullets started flying.

The parents of those missing teens, though, were still concerned about their children, and Kate still had every intention of taking whatever steps were necessary to bring them home.

She didn't know if there was any connection between the gang activity and the disappearances. She knew Angel thought there was—and, as much as she was no Angel fan these days, she knew that he had a good sense for these things. He was despicable, a vampire, a creature of the night, and he had not been honest about it from the beginning . . . but he was a good detective and his instincts were sound. In fairness, she couldn't deny those things about him, even though she didn't like him.

"Everything okay, detective?"

She turned. It was a patrol officer named Perkins she'd met a couple of times before. He was thin, with red hair and a bushy red mustache, and his uniform always looked a little like a Halloween costume on him.

"Yeah, Perkins, fine," she replied.

"What a mess, huh?" He nodded at the bodies on the ground, the wounded being tended to by paramedics. "Kids are out of their skulls."

"Looks like it," she agreed.

"What makes 'em do that? Run with gangs, and all? Don't they know they're gonna end up dead?"

"You could answer that, Perkins, you could be mayor. Governor."

"Not me, Detective. I'm too ambitious. It's president or nothing." He gave her a wide, toothy smile. "Seriously, though, what do you think?"

She closed her eyes for a second, an image of her late father flashing before them. "I don't know, Perkins. I guess . . . I guess some kids just don't get what they need from their families, you know? From their parents. They feel powerless, they feel invisible. They need to get that, whatever, that sense of worth, someplace, and they find it in gangs. Doesn't seem to matter if they have money or not. It's about respect, I think, about finding a place that feels like home."

Perkins looked at her, maybe a little surprised at the thoughtfulness of her answer. "Could be, I guess. Me, I think it's just that they like to shoot guns and stuff, maybe."

Kate shrugged. "Hey, I'm no sociologist, but if you don't expect me to know anything, I guess I can talk a pretty good game."

He returned the shrug. "I don't know, I think you're pretty smart. Must be why you get the big bucks."

"Yeah," she laughed. "Real big."

She smiled and walked away from him, hoping she hadn't wasted too much time being sociable. The block was crawling with cops now, mostly clustered in little groups talking to each other about the battle they'd broken up. Kate walked through them, making eye contact with no one, hoping no one else saw her. She'd had an idea, had been just about to put it into effect when Perkins had interrupted her. Now she had thought it through as far as she was going to, which was, she knew, not far at all. If she thought about it, she might not follow up on it.

Assuming Angel is right about the connection of the gang war to the disappearing kids, she thought, *and assuming that his little trip to who-knows-where via Alina's machine doesn't pan out, then someone is going to have to get leaned on here in L.A. to get those kids back.* The Russians might know better who, or how. But they'd be less apt to cooperate than the Mexicans might if they thought she'd use what she got from them to go after the Russians.

So she struck out toward the west, after the Mexican gang.

Once she had moved out of sight of the police cars and the reassuring presence of blue uniforms, she felt very alone. The streets here were dark and quiet. Kate was a good cop, and she didn't doubt her own toughness. But even the best cop, alone in enemy territory, could become a victim. Being tough didn't mean being blind to the truth, and the truth here was that she had left the safety net of her fellow officers behind—breaking one of the first rules any rookie had drummed into her.

Instead, she was following one of the rules her father had instilled in her as a little girl.

"Sometimes you gotta make your own luck," Trevor Lockley had told his daughter. From the time she was very small, he had shared cop stories with her. She had listened breathlessly to his exploits, his tales of good guys and bad guys, hero-worshipping the old man even while other girls she knew doted on pop stars and screen idols. "We all have to live within the law, but the bad guys, they don't always follow the rules. That's what makes them bad. So to catch them, sometimes you have to bend the rules yourself a little. You can't always count on getting a lucky break when you need it, unless you do whatever you can to make that luck happen, and then keep your eyes open so you'll recognize it when you see it."

She smiled at the memory, even knowing where they were—walking on a hiking path in Griffith Park, on a sunny summer afternoon, eating ice cream bars they had purchased from a vendor with a cart—when he told it to her. He had illustrated the lesson with a story about a hold-up man he had caught by breaking into the suspect's apartment without a warrant, finding the evidence that would convict him, and then confronting the suspect with the certain knowledge that he was guilty. The guy had broken down and confessed, and the confession stuck. Those were different times, Kate knew. She couldn't get away with that today, and wouldn't even try. But the basic lesson—the idea that sometimes a cop had to think outside the box—had stayed with her.

In this case, thinking outside the box meant putting herself in harm's way, going into gang country with no backup in the middle of a vicious war, because a lone woman might be able to persuade someone to cooperate more effectively than a riot-suited squad would.

She scoped out the block before her. Every storefront was dark and protected by metal grillework. Graffiti coated bare walls of brick and stone. Cardboard covered broken-out windows, or duct tape held them together at the cracks. The gang members who had come this way had either faded into the buildings or kept going, as there was not a soul in sight.

And this, Kate knew, was only the first block of several that were controlled by the local gang. She swallowed, fighting down the fear.

This was territory rarely seen by outsiders. When the police needed to come here, they did so in cars, two officers at a time, and they were on the alert at every moment. Letting one's guard down could be suicidal.

Kate realized that the sense of security created by the fact that there was no one visible on the street was a false one. She could as easily be gunned down from inside a building, shot through an open window or from a parked car. Her hope was that she would not be—that a woman walking alone through these streets after dark would be an object of curiosity rather than a target. She wore plain clothes; there was no way they'd know she was a police officer until she identified herself as such.

She slowed at the corner, pressed herself against the brick wall and put only her head around to see what might be waiting where she couldn't see. She knew her footsteps had echoed down the quiet streets, so anyone around the corner would know she was coming. She wanted at least a fighting chance at seeing them the same time they saw her.

And there was someone there. Three young men, wearing the baggy pants and muscle shirts common to gang members on muggy summer nights. Their black hair was short. One sported a mustache and a bit of fuzz beneath his lower lip, while the other two were clean-shaven. Muscular arms, broad shoulders and deep chests indicated that they all worked out.

They leaned against an old Ford truck parked beside the curb, about halfway down the block. They saw her as soon as she poked her head around the corner, so she stepped forward confidently, walking straight toward them. Best not to let them think she was afraid of them, she knew. Fear was weakness.

Silently, they watched her approach. She stopped about six feet from them, put her hands on her hips. The one with the facial hair shifted position, spat into the gutter, and grinned at her. He had a gold tooth in front.

" 'Sup, babe?" he asked.

"I was looking for you," Kate replied.

"For me?"

"For any of you, really. Not you in particular."

"Because I could be of service to you, you know what I mean," he said.

"I'm sure you can." Now that they were talking, she wasn't as afraid. She still understood that the situation was dangerous, but she thought she could control it. "I'm reaching for a badge," she said. "Not a gun."

"Aw, man, you a cop?" one of them whined.

"You think anyone else would be stupid enough to brace three tough-looking *hombres* like you?" she asked. She drew her badge from the pocket of her silk jacket. "Of course I'm a cop. But I'm not looking to bust anybody."

"That's good," Mustache said. He seemed to be the natural leader of this pack. "Because I don't see no backup or nothin'."

"Don't need backup," Kate told them. "If I wanted to take you down, I'd take you down. That's not what I'm here for."

"Then what are you here for, tough lady?"

"You part of the little dust-up back there tonight?" She inclined her head in the direction of the gang battle, not taking her eyes off these three for a moment.

"We're just peaceful citizens havin' us a discussion about current affairs," Mustache said. The others howled with laughter. Kate smiled, too.

"I like to see that," she said. "I really do. Informed citizens. They're the best kind. But what I really am looking for, see, are some guys who were part of that battle, because I'm looking to come down hard on some Russian Mafiya types, and I need someone who can point me to their safe houses, their headquarters. I don't suppose any of you would know who might be expert on things the Russians have to hide?"

"Mama," Mustache said, "if you're looking to bust some of those freakin' Russians, you have come to the right place. Me and my *cholos* here, we're like, experts on

them. In fact, that's the current events we were talkin'
about—the Soviet menace."

"Well then," Kate said, relaxing her stance a bit and
putting her badge case back into the pocket. "Let's just
have us a little chat, shall we?"

Sunnydale

"We really ought to be getting home," Giles said.

"We really never should have left home," Xander
replied. "Or doesn't the fact that the city's overrun with
monsters mean anything to you people?"

"The monsters are why we're out here," Anya said.

"Can I just remind you what the word 'mortal' means,
Anya?" Xander shot back. "It means you can now be killed.
And me and Giles, well, we've always been mortal. So the
getting killed part? Not something we're unfamiliar with."

They were halfway across town, having headed out on
patrol, to see what they could do to combat the plague of
monsters overwhelming Sunnydale. Monsters they had
found, but though they'd vanquished a few of them, there
seemed to be a point of diminishing returns—they couldn't
destroy all of them, and when Anya had mentioned Joyce
and Tara, alone back at Giles's house, Giles had suddenly
become very concerned about them. Which was fine with
Xander, since it meant heading back to the relative safety
of a house with four walls and a door that locked.

"Believe me, I wake up every morning knowing what
'mortal' means, Xander," Anya said. "Some days, I even
think it's a good thing. It means you and I can grow old
together, instead of all alone like Giles is, and—"

"Excuse me," Giles interrupted. "But I am not 'all alone,'
nor do I think it would necessarily be a bad thing if I were."

"Right," Anya returned. "Occasional visits from your friend Olivia for the purpose of sexual gratification will certainly prevent you from becoming a lonely old man."

Xander was almost glad for the distraction of another creature, this one snakelike, except for the part where he had a humanoid head, neck, and shoulders grafted onto the body of a twenty-foot-long snake. It slithered into view around the corner and stopped, torso raised off the sidewalk, body and tail slithering and switching behind it, staring at them with an unmistakable fire in its eyes.

"It looks hungry," Xander pointed out.

"Yes," Giles agreed. "And I imagine we look more or less like lunch."

"It looks revolting," Anya said. "Not to mention dangerous."

"Definitely that," Giles replied. He hefted the ax that he carried. "But, fortunately, unarmed. I expect we can take him rather handily."

The snake-thing slithered a few feet closer to them, then opened its mouth. A long, reptilian tongue unfurled at them.

"Nasty," Xander commented. He noticed Anya didn't agree. Before any of them could act, the snake-guy retracted its tongue and spat at them. A gob of something struck the sidewalk directly in front of them. Where it landed, it fizzled for a moment, a thin wisp of smoke rising into the air. When the smoke cleared, Xander saw that the cement of the sidewalk had been eaten away, as if by a powerful acid.

"You said 'unarmed,' right?"

"Perhaps I was a bit hasty," Giles allowed.

"Perhaps," Anya echoed.

When that thing gets our range, Xander thought, *we'll be Swiss cheese.*

Giles apparently thought the same thing. "This might be a case when discretion is the better part of valor," he observed. He backed up a step. Xander and Anya mimicked him.

The snake matched them, slithering forward and then stopping and spitting again. They had stayed out of its range, though, and its acidic venom struck the sidewalk once more.

Glancing behind them to be sure they weren't walking into some other trouble, Xander took another couple of steps back. Giles and Anya followed suit, none of them willing to turn their backs on the snake-monster.

"It doesn't have much distance," Giles pointed out.

"And apparently it doesn't need much," Xander said. "Since it's got enough to keep anyone from getting close enough to attack it."

Anya nudged Xander's shoulder. "But we have a crossbow," she said.

Xander looked in his own right hand. "So we do."

"So use it already."

He tried to hand it to Anya, but she pushed it away. "You use it," he insisted.

"Xander," Anya replied. "Just do it."

They all kept walking backward as the snake-thing moved toward them, spitting its venom on the sidewalk.

"Oh, for heaven's sake," Giles finally said, a note of frustration in his voice. He waited until the snake was moving forward again, and charged it, swinging his ax in a wide arc. The snake-monster saw him coming, and jerked to a stop, lifting its head to spit. But Giles was faster, already in motion, and his ax sliced cleanly through the thing's neck. The disturbingly human-looking head spun around in flight before landing a good twelve feet away, long tongue hanging limply from its mouth. Where the tongue met the street, the asphalt sizzled and burned. The snake body twitched and writhed a few times, then fell silent.

Anya and Xander watched, open-mouthed.

"It quite clearly couldn't move and spit at the same time," Giles told them. "It only took a moment to observe that it could do one or the other, but not both. If you both hadn't been so busy quibbling you might have noticed as well."

"Sorry, G-man," Xander said.

"Something I have noticed," Anya said. "We've been talking and dealing with that creature for, what, five minutes or more? And that's the only monster we've seen. Nothing flying overhead, nothing skulking down the street."

"Yes, that's quite true," Giles agreed. "Perhaps they're thinning out a bit?"

"That's what I was thinking," Anya said.

"I'm all for that," Xander put in. "Thinning is good."

Sidestepping the creature's corpse, which seemed to be dissolving already, as if being eaten from the inside by its own venom, they continued their trip back to Giles's. Along the way they encountered only a small handful of monsters, nothing like the numbers they'd run into earlier. Giles's theory, much to Xander's relief, seemed to be true. He elaborated on it as they went.

"If the monsters were indeed coming into our world, our dimension, as it were, through those portals Buffy and Riley described, then perhaps the portals are closed. It's quite possible that we're seeing an end to the infestation—that as we defeat them, they're no longer being reinforced or replaced from whatever dimension spawned them."

"You just keep theorizing," Xander said. "Me, I'm just happy we don't have to wade through 'em to get home."

Spike woke up netted like a fish.

He must have been unconscious for a few minutes, he realized, because his captors had landed their freaky sleds and thrown a silvery net, made of some superstrong yet wire-thin filament, over him. The act of pulling it taut around him had roused him. And, quite frankly, ticked him off royally.

He tried to stand, but one of them yanked on the netting and he tumbled over into the grass. He kicked and writhed, trying to break free. The netting was too strong, though—even with his vampiric strength he couldn't tear it. As he twisted in the grass, they surrounded him, aiming weapons at him that looked like they came from the covers of science fiction magazines.

The bearers of those weapons were basically human-looking, but their skins held a strange orange cast, as if reflecting colored lights. Their outfits were of a shimmery material that looked similar to the netting itself. They seemed to have no facial hair at all, and their clothing covered every inch of their bodies, from fingers to the tops of their heads, so as far as Spike could tell they were completely hairless.

Now, with him surrounded, they allowed him to get to his feet, still confined within the net, which they held on to by long cables. Spike shook his head, straining against the netting. At his full height instead of on his back in the grass, he realized that his captors were barely four feet tall, the size of small boys. "I can take the lot of you," he said. "Just let me out of this netting for a minute." He took a step toward them, and was met by a blast from one of those futuristic ray gun–looking weapons.

A purple beam emanated from its tip, and Spike tried to dodge it, but the net kept him from moving far enough. He froze.

He remained conscious, though he could feel consciousness slipping away as if he'd been drugged, but he couldn't move a muscle. Rigid as a statue, he saw and heard the little men approach.

"This one's tainted," one of them said.

"Right," another replied. "We'll take it back to the Center and put it to sleep."

Then he was hoisted by three of them and carried to the sleds.

Los Angeles

Riley held his ground as the four men approached him from out of the shadows.

Either these are the guys I'm looking for, or I'm in for a fight, he thought, muscles tense, adrenaline raging. *Doesn't really make much difference to me one way or another, at this point.*

Since Buffy had left through the doorway, he'd been at loose ends—wanting to do what he could to help, but knowing that ultimately she was on her own, beyond the range of any aid he could offer. She had Angel, presumably, but that wasn't much comfort to Riley. He knew—*knew*—that Buffy was over Angel, but still he couldn't completely shake the old green-eyed monster that reared up whenever he thought about the two of them together.

I'd do anything for her, he thought. *I just have to hope she knows that.*

The four men stopped a few feet from him, looking

him up and down. "You look a little lost," one of them said. "Misplace the rest of your scout troop?"

"I'm looking for Gunn," Riley said.

"Might be your lucky day. Might not. Why you want him?"

"I'm a friend of . . . of Angel. And Buffy. Mostly Buffy."

"The Slayer?" the man asked. "Heard about her."

Another figure detached itself from the shadows and came toward them. "It's okay," this one said. "He's cool."

"Hi, Gunn," Riley said.

"What brings you into this neighborhood, Riley?" Gunn asked. "Thought you was back in Sunnydale."

"I decided I was needed more here."

"Know the feeling." Gunn took Riley's hand in his strong grip. "So what's up?"

Riley smiled. "I thought you might be able to help me. I need to break someone out of jail."

Gunn smiled, too.

Chapter 12

THE TOWER STAIRS WOUND UP AND UP AND UP.

"How high did you say this tower was?" Angel asked.

"I didn't say," Buffy replied. "But from the outside, it didn't look this high."

The steps were built from the same gray stone as the rest of the place. They were narrow and short, worn down from centuries of use, so the stone was slick and treacherous. The walls were rough rock except where generations of hands had smoothed out a line at about waist height.

"I don't like this kind of staircase," Buffy said. She kept moving one foot in front of the other. These short, uneven steps, some barely two or three inches high, were harder than taller, regular ones. "Have I ever mentioned that?"

"I don't think so," Angel replied. She couldn't see him, but she heard his ascent, right behind her. She'd rather be able to see him, given the bizarre nature of this castle, but the staircase was so cramped that if she could see him, he'd be right on top of her, leaving her no space to climb.

"Well, I don't. Just so you know."

"I'll keep it in mind."

"I heard the Statue of Liberty is like this. You know, in the torch? I don't know if it's true . . ."

"I don't either."

". . . but if it is, I don't ever want to go up there. Good view of New York, but I can get that from an airplane if I really want it, right? And anyway, New York? Isn't the appeal mostly indoors anyway?"

"Indoors?"

"You know," she explained. "Broadway shows, movies, nightclubs. Museums, I guess. All that cultural stuff. Nobody goes to New York for the scenery, do they?"

"I never have."

"See? And you've done everything."

"Not everything."

"Okay," she relented. *Am I babbling?* she wondered. *Babbling's not good. But then, neither is this staircase to heaven, which is so not good it's kind of freaking me out.*

"It's 'stairway,' isn't it?" she asked.

"What is?"

"Oh. Never mind. Thinking out loud. I do that."

"I've noticed."

What did he mean by that? Nothing sinister, she figured. *I was babbling. Have to knock that off.*

She kept climbing. *The stairs that never end.*

"Angel?"

"Yeah?" his voice drifted up from below.

"Was I babbling?"

"I don't think so. Maybe."

"Because I wasn't trying to. Babble, I mean."

"Okay."

She heard his footfalls behind her. Every now and then he, like she, slipped on the slick edges of one of the steps, and his foot made a scuffing noise.

Then his footfalls sounded like those of a lion, four legs padding quickly up the stairs. She heard the *chuff* of a lion's exhale.

"Angel?"

"Yes?"

"Just checking," she said.

Not a lion, then. That's good.

But it worried her that she had thought he might be a lion. He had been Angel when they started up the stairs. There were no side passages for Angel to go out and a lion to come in. There was only up, which they were going, and down, which they were not.

"Angel?"

"Buffy?"

"Do you think—never mind."

"No, what is it?"

"Do you think that a staircase can drive someone crazy?"

He was quiet for a moment, except for the continuing sound of his feet on the steps. "No," he said finally.

"How sure are you?" she asked.

"Not very," he admitted. "But if I had to guess, I'd say that maybe something in the staircase could make someone light-headed. Maybe even hallucinate. Lack of oxygen, or something. Why?"

"No reason," she said.

She kept climbing, ever winding to the right.

Behind her, following her up the stairs, was her father. He was getting tired of climbing, though, and wanted to just sit down and slide all the way to the bottom.

"Don't!" she cried.

"Don't what?" Angel asked.

"Angel. It's you." Buffy stopped. A moment later, Angel came into view.

"Of course it's me. Are you okay, Buffy?"

"Yes. I mean, I don't know," she said. "I thought you were a lion, then I thought you were my dad. Are these stairs making me crazy?"

Angel held her for a moment. She liked the feeling of his strong arms around her, but she broke away after a minute.

"Thanks," she said. "I'm okay."

"We've got to be pretty high up," Angel observed. "Maybe there is a lack of oxygen up here. Maybe the air's old and stale."

"But it's only affecting me?"

Angel tapped his chest, where his lungs were. "Vampire," he reminded her.

"Oh, right."

"You want me to go on alone?" he asked her. "Maybe you should wait here."

Buffy shook her head. "I'll be fine," she insisted. "Just don't turn into anything."

"I don't do that," he assured her.

"Even by accident, don't."

"Buffy," he said. Then nothing for a while. "Buffy!"

She blinked. He was staring at her, his head right in front of her face. His hands were on her shoulders. He looked worried.

"What?"

"Where were you?" he asked.

"I'm right here."

"I've been standing here calling your name," he said. "For at least a minute. You were frozen there, like a statue."

This news sent a chill through Buffy. *This place really is making me crazy,* she thought. "I . . . I don't know," she said. "I guess I just blanked out for a second. Shouldn't we be climbing?"

"I'm worried about you, Buffy. I think you should go back down."

"But there's someone up there who needs us," she argued. "The princess."

"I don't want you hurt," Angel said.

"I'm okay now, Angel. Really and truly. I'm back."

"If you start to feel strange again, you let me know," he demanded.

"Promise," she said. She turned away and resumed her climb.

Behind her, she heard Angel continue as well.

"Your name is Buffy Summers," he said.

Buffy. Summers.

"Your mom is Joyce Summers."

Joyce.

"Your dad is named Hank."

Hank.

"You live in Sunnydale, California."

Sunnydale.

"At 1630 Revello Drive."

1630. She climbed. The stairs wound on forever.

"You were born in 1981."

1981.

"You're the Chosen One. The Slayer."

Slayer.

She came around a bend, and suddenly the climb was over. At the top of the stairs there was a door. It looked incredibly old. It was built of three wide boards, banded together with rusted iron. A big lock, also rusted, hung from a hasp. It looked like it hadn't been opened in centuries.

A moment later, Angel joined her on the landing.

"Looks like we made it," he said.

"Angel?" Buffy said. She was smiling. He looked at her, his face a question mark. "You remember all that?"

"I remember," he said. "You wouldn't believe the things I remember."

She touched his arm, then turned back to the door. "End of the line," she said. "Everybody off." She pounded on the door. "Anybody in there?"

"Oh God, yes!" a voice cried from the other side. The voice was young, high-pitched, feminine. "Get me out, please!"

"We're coming," Angel said. "Stand away from the door."

"Kicking?" Buffy asked.

"I was thinking kicking," Angel replied.

"Works for me."

Together, they reared back and drove their right feet into the door. It splintered and flew from the hinges, crashing to the floor in the room behind.

A girl stood there, hands in front of her face. She was a tiny thing, wearing a blue man's shirt that was way too big for her. When she took her hands away, her face looked like she'd been crying for days.

"Are . . . are you . . . ?"

"We're here to help," Angel said.

"My name's Buffy Summers," Buffy told her. "That's Angel. We came to get you out of here. You're not from Los Angeles, by any chance?"

Tears sprang from the girl's eyes, but Buffy thought

they looked like happy tears, this time. Through the tears, she studied them. "Angel?" she asked.

"That's right," he confirmed.

"Cordelia's friend?"

"Yes. You know Cordelia?"

"My name's Kayley," the girl said. "Kayley Moser." She buried her face in her hands again, sobbing. Angel put a hand on her shoulder to comfort her, and Buffy stroked her arm, rail thin under the big shirt.

"She told me about you," Angel said. "We're here to help."

A few minutes later, they started down the stairs, Buffy in the lead, then Kayley, with Angel bringing up the rear. Buffy couldn't help smiling.

One down, she thought. *It's all downhill from here.*

The Xterra bumped and bounced over the desert landscape. Mischa worried every time he ran into one of the thicker bushes or taller cacti, and he felt bad for the path of destruction he left. But he needed to put some space between himself and the highway patrolman. He kept hoping he'd come across a dirt road—*this cross-country stuff is getting old,* he thought. *But at least the Highway Patrol cars can't follow me over this.*

Even with the headlights on, he couldn't see well enough to really chart a course, so he just kept it headed away from the gas station until he could no longer see the lights, then he turned in the direction he thought Arizona was.

Finally, his high beams picked out a tall electrical tower. Wires stretched from it in both directions. He reasoned that there had to be some kind of access roadway near it for maintenance vehicles. So he bounced and bucked toward it, and found that he was right. The road was rutted and washboard, but it was a road, and therefore better than cutting through the brush. Compared to what he had been doing, it was almost comfortable.

I'm going to make it, he thought. *I'm really going to do this. Don't worry, Alina, I'll be there soon.*

Then he remembered that he had to shield his thoughts, in case Alina's parents were scanning for him. It wouldn't do to let them know where he was headed.

He tried to think of the beach in Santa Monica, in the summertime. Hundreds, maybe thousands, of sweating bodies, jammed together on towels and beach chairs, baking in the sun. Music playing from hundreds of different radios. The scents of suntan lotion and soft drinks and picnic lunches and salt water all mingling together. The steady rumble of waves drowned out by the shouts of children, the happy laughter of young couples, the organized chatter of volleyball or Frisbee games. The *fwup-fwup-fwup* of helicopters . . .

That's not right, he knew. He forced the beach from his mind, listened. Definitely a 'copter, and not far away. He killed the lights, brought the SUV to a sudden stop, skidding a little on the soft sand. He opened the door, slammed it shut again, and turned off the dome light. Then he opened it again and climbed out onto the running board, looking toward the sky.

There they were. Two of them combed the desert, shining bright lights down toward its floor. Coming his direction.

I'm on a road, he thought. *The moon's bright. I can run without lights for a while, put some distance between them and me. I can do this.*

He plopped back down behind the wheel, turned the

key. The engine sputtered and died. He turned it again. A click. He tried once more. Another click.

He got out, walked around the SUV. There were several bullet holes in it, and his stomach sank. He climbed in again, turning the key far enough to turn on the electrical system. The gas gauge line was on the E and the little gas pump icon was lit up. In his haste, he hadn't even noticed. The tank had been full, back when he'd stolen the car. *One of the bullets must have punctured the tank,* he thought. *I've been leaking gas all over the desert.*

On the bright side, it didn't blow me up.

The helicopters closed in.

Mischa knew the vehicle would be no more help. And anyway, he'd be harder to spot on foot. As the hopelessness of the situation, the certainty that he'd failed Alina, weighed in on him, he struck out across the desert, with only the light of the moon to guide him.

Los Angeles

Wesley braked the Plymouth Belvedere outside the Vishnikoff home. "There you are," he said.

"We'll wait here until you're inside," Cordelia added. "Just in case."

"Thank you," Alina said. "For everything." She climbed from the car, the Reality Tracer clutched against her side.

"We'll be fine," Willow said. "But thanks for the lift and, you know, the conversation."

"Oh, no trouble at all," Wesley said. "I'm just sorry we can't stay, but you know. Duty calls."

He had told them that he and Cordelia were on their way to locate a transdimensional demon they'd once known, in the hopes that this demon could help with the whole idea of portals and doorways. Alina had tried to convince them that it was useless—that the Alternities were not simply separate dimensions, but separate realities. "Is like, what is American metaphor?" she asked. "Apples and bananas?"

"Oranges," Cordelia said. "But I get the idea."

"Still," Wesley chimed in. "We've got to try everything we can."

"Very well," Alina relented. "You try that."

Now she crossed the yard to her parents' house, accompanied by Willow, Nicky and the Flores family. Wesley and Cordelia had decided they'd be safer staying with the Vishnikoffs than waiting alone in her apartment. *Plus,* she had thought, *I want to* have *an apartment when I get back.* Alina had smiled at Cordelia's thought processes.

Inside, some of the staff took Willow, Nicky and the Floreses to a room where they could wait—and Willow could perform the ritual that would prepare Nicky to go through a portal, though they weren't telling the staff that—and her parents came into her workroom to see her. She pointed at the machine, resting on its usual table, and spoke in English just to upset them.

"Tracer is broken," she said. "Fix, please."

Her father responded in Russian. His fists were jammed into his pockets. "So you can steal it again?"

She switched to Russian now too. "So I can repair some of the damage I've done."

"Repair?" her mother asked. "What does that mean?"

"I've torn apart families," Alina explained. "I've made parents lose their children. I've made people disappear."

"For the State," her father declared.

"What State?" she asked. She felt tears welling up inside her, and she wanted to make her case before she cried. "There is no State! You're living in the past, both of you. Dreaming of Soviet glory! Wake up! The Soviet Union is gone! Nothing you do will bring it back!"

"Our plan will work," her father insisted. "Americans will cooperate with us to get their children back."

"Americans might give you money," Alina countered. "Dollars, that's all. Is that what you want?"

"Dollars are powerful. It's what they respect," her mother offered.

"But they won't buy a country that doesn't exist."

"With the money and American support we can—"

"You need more than just American support," Alina said. "You don't even have Russian support!"

"Of course we do," her mother said, her voice stern. Her mother had always been the driving force in the partnership, Alina knew. Her father had been smart, technically. He'd understood the theory, and he had been able to apply it to the machine. But her mother had manipulated his purposes, his reason for continuing the research. She was the political one. He was simply her tool. "You don't know. You aren't in the meetings we have, the long conversations—"

Alina cut her off again. "I don't have to be," she said. "I can hear their thoughts just fine after the meetings. When they come to see how things are going. Out in the street, at the bakery where Mischa works. Anywhere there are people who know about your plan, I know what they think of it."

"And what do they think, smart girl?" her father exploded. "They think it's pretty damn smart!"

"They think the Americans will pay money," Alina replied. She was shaking with anger and couldn't rein it in. "They like that part. That's all they want, just the money. I used to tell myself that they'd go along with it, that they'd be happy when the Soviet Union was restored. That you were both geniuses, and everybody would see it when things came together. But I was kidding myself."

"Your father is a genius," her mother said simply.

"Yes, and so are you. But you're both blind. All these people around you want is the money. They're criminals," Alina insisted. "They protect you, protect your precious machine and your not so precious daughter, because they know it will pay off in the end. Not in a new Soviet State, just in dollars! Once they have the money they'll forget you ever existed."

"I don't believe you," her father said. He started for the door.

"Don't go out that door," Alina warned.

"Why not?"

Alina couldn't answer him. There was nothing she could do to him now, no threat she could make. He had spent his life wanting one thing, and she had already told him she would never give it to him. She tried never to hear her parents' minds, and they were skilled enough to block, anyway. But a sense of defeat rolled off him like waves rolling from the sea.

"Just fix it," she said. "It isn't too late to make things right again."

Valerya and Alexis Vishnikoff looked at each other. They were silent. Finally, Valerya shrugged and walked from the room. Alexis looked at his daughter again. She knew what he would say before he said it.

"Get out of the way. How do you expect me to fix it with you standing there?"

Alina retreated to a corner, pressed her back into it and sat down on the floor. It had been a while since she'd tried to reach Mischa. As much to retreat from her father's presence as anything else, she summoned up a mental image of her friend and listened for him.

". . . failed Alina . . ." she heard.

Mischa!

In her mind, she cried out to him.

And when she knew he heard her, she began to weep.

Chapter 13

THE WAR WAGON ROLLED TO A STOP IN THE DARKNESS OF A back road, a quarter mile from the Yorba Linda Ranch, just over the San Bernardino County line from Los Angeles. Riley felt like he was on another Initiative mission, except that the men and women of Gunn's crew, while seemingly as brave and disciplined as any soldiers he'd ever known, were anything but military in dress and appearance.

He climbed from the truck and met Gunn in back, where he was already unrolling a chart on the truck's bed. Someone else—Chain, Riley thought the guy's name was—held a mini Maglite on the chart for illumination.

Gunn pointed to a building. "This is where Faith is bunked, according to what we hear from inside," he said. Riley had been amazed that Gunn had been able to find out so much so quickly, just by making a few phone calls. But Gunn was tapped into the city's streets, and many of those on the streets had put in time inside, he figured.

"There's forty women in this unit," Gunn continued. "Lights have been out for a couple hours now, so hopefully they're all asleep." He turned to Riley. "Riley, you know Faith, so you gotta be the first face she sees, to make sure she don't freak and start yelling or something. Anyone raises a shout while we're in there, it's all over."

"Okay," Riley agreed. "But first we've got to get in there." He indicated lines on the map. "This is the outer fence, right?"

"Twelve feet tall, razor wire at the top, electric," Gunn said.

"How many guards?"

"Two guards walk the perimeter constantly. Takes thirty minutes to make the circuit. Otherwise, there are guards in the towers at these corners of the inside wall," he poked a finger at four points on the map, "with searchlights. They may or may not be looking at any point on the fence at any time."

"Nobody said this would be easy, did they?" Riley asked.

"Not that I heard."

"Good. Because it won't be."

Riley could see Gunn's smile in the dark. "Easy's for suckers."

"Glad you feel that way."

They moved out toward the first fence in a line, spaced a dozen feet apart except for Riley and Gunn together at its head. Both held sections of wooden broomstick, notched at one end. Gunn carried a bolt cutter with rubber grips as well.

Twenty feet from the fence they met Pike, who had been standing lookout since they'd arrived.

"Thought you'd never get here," Pike whispered.

"Status?" Gunn asked.

"Guards came by . . ." Pike looked at his watch. "Seven minutes ago."

"Twenty-three minutes to get in, get the girl, and get out," Gunn said.

"What are we standing around for?" Riley asked. He and Gunn continued toward the fence. The others hung back, still spaced out to make accidental detection less likely.

The fence was a standard link fence, strung between tall steel poles, with the razor wire Gunn had mentioned strung across the top. Riley put a hand close to the links and swore he could feel the electrical field.

"Looks pretty tight."

"Why we brought these." Gunn held up the bolt cutter. He knelt next to the fence's base, placed the cutting blades around a section of the heavy fence wire. "Keep an eye out."

"I'm watching," Riley said. "No movement in the towers. They're sleeping or playing cards or something."

"No work ethic anymore," Gunn whispered. "Be the downfall of modern society." He clipped the wire and moved on to the next section. There was a spark when his bolt cutter touched the fence, but the rubber grips kept him safe.

After a moment, the fence had been cut in enough spots to make it not as taut at the bottom as it had been. Riley and Gunn inserted their broomstick sections, catching the wire in the notches, and raised the bottom of the fence a couple of feet higher. Jamming the other ends of the sticks into the dirt, they created a space three feet across and two high that people could slide under.

"Cake," Gunn said.

"Freeze," Riley hissed. He had spotted some motion in the tower off to their right. A guard appeared at the opening, looking off into the distance. Gunn and Riley both stood stock still, waiting and hoping. Apparently the guard didn't see anything amiss, and he didn't beam the searchlight down on them. After another moment he turned away.

"Okay," Riley whispered. "Let's go."

He dropped to his stomach and crawled under the fence. Gunn came right behind him. At Gunn's signal, two more of his crew, one male and one female, came running out of the darkness, dropped, and came through the fence. Gunn held up a hand, signaling the others to wait where they were.

There was no more discussion for now. They were inside the first obstacle, but there were more to go, and with every moment their chances of being discovered grew. Riley knew that Gunn understood this, and he didn't seem to care. When he found out the purpose was to help Angel and Buffy, he'd been more than willing to do whatever it took, regardless of the risk.

What is it about Angel that inspires that kind of loyalty? he wondered. *Buffy has it too—her friends would lay down their lives for her in a second. And how do I get some of that?*

No time to think about that now, he realized. They crossed a wide no-man's land between the outer fence and the inner wall. The wall, he knew, would be a challenge. It was ten feet tall and well-lit, the guard towers were right on it, and one couldn't cut through it with a bolt cutter. Gunn had claimed to have a solution to the problem, but he hadn't told Riley what it was. *Better put it into play, if it exists,* Riley thought. *We're here.*

They stopped at the base of the wall. It was built of whitewashed cinder blocks, and was taller than Riley could reach. Light splashed over the top of it. The prison officials were concerned about people breaking out, not in, so security efforts were mostly dedicated to watching the insides of the walls and fences rather than the outsides.

Still, Riley felt uncomfortable. From this angle he couldn't even see inside the tower lookouts. There could be automatic weapons being pointed at them all right now, and he wouldn't know it until lead began to fly. *Where is Gunn's solution?*

Gunn tapped Riley on the shoulder. "Best cover your ears," he said simply.

Riley did so. A moment later, a deafening siren began to wail from inside the prison.

"We've been spotted!" he said, alarmed.

"Chill," Gunn assured him. "It's called a diversionary tactic."

"This is a diversion? Alerting the whole place?"

"To an incident—a fight—on the other end of it. Everyone'll be paying attention to that, and not to us."

Riley shook his head. "I hope you're right."

"Trust me, dog," Gunn said casually. He made a cradle with his hands, and Riley stepped into it. Gunn boosted him up, and he got a grip on the wall's top, hoisting himself up.

Inside, he could see guards running away from the wall, between low-slung buildings. He glanced down at Gunn. "Looks good," he said. "They're leaving this area as fast as they can."

"Won't take long to stop the fight," Gunn said. "Then they'll be coming back to their posts. We got to hurry."

Riley pulled himself to the top of the wall and dropped down the other side, fully aware that he landed in the wash of floodlights. He hit the ground as he landed, knowing that a prone figure was harder to spot than an erect one.

A moment later, Gunn followed, and then the woman who had accompanied them. The fourth one, with no one to boost him, remained on the other side of the wall.

"Riley, this is Sheila," Gunn said. "Sheila's been here before."

"Got it," Riley said. *Nothing like an ex-con to guide us through a prison,* he figured.

"This way," Sheila said, barely acknowledging his existence.

Big on manners, too, Riley thought. But he followed her, moving at a half-crouch away from the wall. The diversion had worked, though; no one paid the least attention to anything happening at this end of the prison farm.

The buildings were single storied, with doors at both ends and barred windows lining the walls. Even with the shrill sirens shrieking through the night, lights remained off inside the buildings. Riley figured they were probably on timers, and could only be turned on during lights-out hours from some central control panel.

Mercifully, the sirens stopped as they moved between the dark buildings. "So much for anyone inside being asleep," Riley said quietly in the sudden stillness.

"They may not be asleep but they'll be in their beds," Sheila whispered. "During an alert, anyone gets out their bed finds herself in a lot of grief. And you'd be surprised what these girls can sleep through."

"I'll take your word for it," Riley said.

She led the way to the building Gunn had pointed out on the map. There was a big number 17 painted on the building's side. "That's it," Sheila announced. "Doors are locked at night."

"No problem," Gunn said. He fished in his pockets and came out with a device that looked almost like a flashlight. Carrying it to the lock on the near door of unit 17, he held it against the lock and pushed a button. There was a quiet whirring noise. After a moment, he removed it.

"After you," he whispered with a bow. The door swung open. He tucked the thing back into his pocket. "I like to think of it as a master key," he said.

Sheila and Riley went into the unit while Gunn stood guard at the door. Two rows of bunks, two high, flanked a central walkway. The only illumination came through the screened, barred windows. Riley's guess had been right—in the faint light, he could see that most of the women here were awake, staring at him and Sheila with undisguised interest.

"Sheila," one of them said. "You brought us a present?"

"Hush," Sheila said. "We looking for someone named Faith."

"Faith? Bunk thirty-six," the woman said. She rose up onto one elbow, examined Riley closely. "You sure he can't stay and play?"

"Sorry," Riley said. "We're kind of on a tight schedule."

"What they all say," the woman said. She dropped back onto her bunk. "You won't find Faith in her bunk, though," she announced. "She's in solitary."

Sheila and Riley turned around and walked out of the unit without another word. Gunn looked at them quizzically as they came out alone.

"Solitary," Sheila explained. "Girl's been breaking the rules."

"Faith?" Riley added. "Imagine that."

"Lead the way," Gunn said.

Sheila took them through the maze of bunkhouses to the solitary block. It was a lone building, standing next to the inner wall. One narrow window, placed high up in its adobe wall, provided the only illumination. Next to the window was a door. In front of the door stood an armed guard.

"You or me?" Gunn asked.

"I'll do it," Riley offered. He had been hoping they'd be able to do this without hurting anyone. These people were just men and women doing a job, after all, and they were on the side of the good guys.

But he needed Faith, and Faith was behind that door.

He stepped out of the shadows, walking purposefully toward the guard as if he had some business there. The guard noticed him, lowered his rifle so that the barrel pointed at Riley. "Who are you?" he demanded.

"Whatever happened to 'who goes there?' " Riley asked. "Not good enough for you?"

"Don't make me ask it again," the guard snarled.

"California Prisons Commission," Riley bluffed. "We're conducting some tests here tonight. You might have heard the results."

"I heard something."

"You'll get a good write-up," Riley promised him. "You're on the alert. What's your name?"

The guard relaxed his stance a bit, and Riley moved in fast. With his left hand he batted the gun to one side so it wouldn't shoot him if it was discharged accidentally, and with his right hand he swung at the guy's windpipe, dislodging it. The guard choked and dropped to the ground. Riley knew he had a few moments before he'd have to right it again, or the guard would die. He had to use those moments well.

He snatched keys off the guard's belt, unlocked the door. "Faith?" he called into the darkness.

"That sounds like a soldier boy I once knew," Faith's voice called back. "And I do mean 'knew.' In the biblical sense."

"Don't remind me," Riley said. "Come on. We're getting you out of here."

Faith appeared in the doorway. She was dressed simply, in a prison jumpsuit. Her long hair gleamed in the light from the yard, and her big brown eyes flashed. *She's a beautiful young woman,* Riley thought, angry at himself for even thinking it, *even in jail clothes.* "I'm paying my debt to society," she said. "Last thing I need on my record is a jailbreak."

"Thought you'd jump at the chance," he replied. "The way I remember it, your record was never a big concern."

"Maybe I'm a changed girl," Faith said.

Riley snorted.

"It can happen," she insisted.

"I'll believe it when I see it. Anyway, we've worked that out. We've got some people on the inside, and we're going to make it look like a hostage situation. You're not an escapee, you're a prisoner."

"Listen, Riley," Gunn hissed from the shadows. "We need to get going, here."

"Maybe I won't go," Faith suggested. "I could yell right now, call for the guards."

"Faith . . ." Riley responded, half-tempted to let her. He knelt down, restored the guard's windpipe. The guy would be sore, but fine. "Buffy and Angel are in trouble. Maybe bad trouble. They need help. Help I can't give them. It's got to be you."

"Angel?" Faith asked. "I don't owe Buffy a thing. But if Angel's in trouble . . ."

"Seems to me you owe Buffy plenty."

"Then we see it differently," Faith declared. "I'll help Angel, though. Let's go."

Strangely, as Buffy and Angel descended the stairs from the castle's tower with Kayley Moser in tow, the staircase didn't turn into anything it hadn't been on the way up. "I thought this was the castle of changeability," Buffy said.

"Maybe that's only on the way in," Angel said. "Maybe once you're all the way inside, it stops transforming."

"Makes as much sense as anything else about it," Buffy replied. "I'm just hoping we don't run into any rodents of unusual size on the way down."

"You saw those, too?" Kayley asked. "I used to watch them from the tower, sometimes. They'd run in circles on the streets, like they were racing or something."

"Probably chasing someone for dinner," Buffy guessed.

"I never saw them eat anyone," Kayley said. "But they looked big enough to do it."

"I can vouch for that," Buffy assured her.

At the base of the tower, the castle was quiet. Candles still flickered in many of the rooms they passed through, but everything else seemed quiet. No rat-creatures, no other hazards presented themselves. The path to the main doors seemed obvious.

"I swear it was a lot harder coming in," Buffy said.

"I believe you," Angel agreed. "I saw the rats, remember?"

"Yeah, but you cheated by beaming in or whatever that was."

"Maybe the castle wants to keep strangers out," Angel offered, "but doesn't care who leaves."

"And again I say, it makes as much sense as anything," Buffy said. "I can accept pretty much anything at this point."

A few minutes later they stood on the plain outside the castle walls. "I really want to thank you guys for getting me out of there," Kayley said. "But—and don't think I'm not appreciative of what you've already done—what the hell do we do now?"

Buffy met Angel's glance. *He doesn't know either,* she thought. She shrugged.

"Well, we have more missing kids to round up," Buffy told her. "But how do we find them? Or get them home? Basically a big question mark there."

"How'd you get here?" Kayley asked.

"The proverbial long story," Buffy replied. "But the short version, though a door from Sunnydale."

"Sunnydale?"

"Told you it was long," Buffy said. "And to make it longer, Angel came from, where again?"

"I don't really know," Angel said. "From L. A. to some other place, and from that other place to here, following Buffy."

"And what about the witch who sent you here?" Buffy asked. "Think she can be any help now?"

"I doubt that she's alive now," Angel replied. "She was dying."

"It's never simple with you, is it?" Buffy asked him. He didn't answer, but then, she hadn't really expected him to. "It'd be nice if we'd hear from Will and Tara and Salma's grandmother," she continued. "Or get an Instant Message from Alina's machine."

"That'd come in handy, right about now," Angel agreed.

But somehow, Buffy didn't see it happening anytime soon.

Spike regained consciousness as the sleds jerked to a stop outside a long, low building. He realized that the building, set into the side of a hill, would have been almost impossible to see from any angle other than this one. From here, though, a wall with no ornamentation was plainly visible. There was a single open doorway in the center of the wall, and the sleds had parked in front of it.

He tested himself. The ray seemed to be wearing off—he was able to move his feet and his hands. He didn't dare try anything more complicated, because he didn't want them to know he had come around. He kept his eyes nearly closed, just open enough to let him see his surroundings.

A moment later, a couple of the little orange men lifted him off the sled to carry him inside. This, then, was where they'd be "putting it to sleep," as they'd so delicately phrased it. The thought angered him all over again. He had to make a move before they got him inside—who knew how many would be waiting in there, or what technology they'd have.

He twisted suddenly, breaking their grips and dropping to the ground with a thud. *Well, that was a bloody awful start,* he thought. But at least he was out of their hands. He got his feet underneath him and slammed his still-netted body into the nearest little guy. The man went over beneath his assault.

Around him, the others scrambled to his side. "It's awake!" he heard one cry out.

Getting his fingers through the netting, Spike grabbed the fallen one's weapon and writhed, bringing the gun up to point at one of the other little men. "Don't call me 'it!' " he shouted, squeezing the trigger. The purple beam shot out again, and the little man froze. Spike held the trigger down and played the gun across some of the others.

As he did, he realized that he was fighting them—and feeling great about it. Either the chip was gone, or these orange buggers really were evil. Either way, the thrill of combat charged through him. This—surrounded by enemies, draped with a net, using an alien gun against its owners who wanted to kill him—this was the best he'd felt since he'd heard that Cheryce had died.

It ain't heaven, he thought. *But at least it ain't Hell.*

Chapter 14

THE MOON CAST A SILVER GLOW ON THE DESERT FLOOR, illuminating Mischa's way. Crossing it on foot was a struggle. *Every plant out here,* he thought, *seems to have thorns or barbs or stickers of some kind.* He already had tripped once and caught himself on his hands, only to find that his hand had landed on a cholla cactus. When he yanked his hand away, a round ball of thorns was stuck to it. He batted it away with his other arm, but many of the almost invisible, hairlike thorns were apparently still embedded in his flesh. His hand throbbed and every time he ran it across another surface, it made a rasping noise.

There's nothing like this in Russia, he thought. *That I've ever heard about, anyway. Maybe Siberia . . .* He knew that Siberia was vast, spreading across nine time zones, and while his general impression of it was a vast frozen icefield, he knew intellectually that there must be more to the place than that. Nothing he'd encountered, though, in his homeland or here, had prepared him for the bizarre landscape of the Sonoran desert.

The way before him was fairly clear, though. The plants, most of whose names he didn't know, were widely spaced. The hardest part of negotiating his way was that the ground was uneven. Though a given stretch of it might look flat from a distance, up close it was anything but— unseen rocks, animal burrows, broken areas where occasional streams flowed and churned the earth all made the footing treacherous. Then there were times when he found an easy path, down the center of a wash, for instance, but before he knew it he was headed into a canyon with steep walls and no way out. On those occasions, he backtracked, trying to keep a course charted by the moon and stars, headed for where he thought the road would cross his path. He had tried to drive parallel to the road, knowing he'd need to return to it eventually to get to the canyon. But he'd gone farther afield from it than he'd thought, or it had turned away from the course he thought it followed.

Mischa? he heard, inside his head.

Alina, he thought. *I'm here. I'm trying to get to you.*

Hurry, Mischa, she replied. *I need you.*

I know. I'm trying. I'm coming.

Are you safe?

He glanced at his palm, burning with the pain of the buried thorns, his ankle, scraped on a boulder. *I'm fine. The helicopters are gone, landed by the car, I suppose. So far no one has followed me here.*

I'm glad, Mischa.

Me too. Nothing will get in my way now. I'll be there soon. A few hours on the road.

Be careful, Mischa. I have to go now.

Be safe, Alina. Soon . . .

Soon . . .

Finally he saw a smudge of light against the horizon. Setting his sights on that, he pressed on, dodging the cacti and barbed succulents. The light grew, turned into a gas station/truck stop sign standing atop a tall pole. Salvation.

As he started down a gentle slope toward the truck stop, looking at the dozen or so big rigs parked in its lot while their drivers ate dinner, showered, or slept, he heard the dull roar of helicopters in the background. So they hadn't given up once he'd abandoned the stolen vehicle, as he'd hoped they might. He was a criminal now, an animal to be pursued no matter what.

Well, I'll lead them on a merry chase, then.

He rushed down the hill into the floodlit parking lot. Now instead of canyon walls, the steel walls of huge trucks rose up around him, legends and logos and pictures painted on their sides. Some of the big machines rumbled, smoke rolling up into the sky, disappearing at the top edge of the dome of light cast by the tall floodlamps. Stealing one, Mischa knew, would just land him in the same situation he'd been in before, with the police chasing him in the other direction, only this time at the wheel of an unfamiliar vehicle. The SUV had handled largely like a car, but an eighteen-wheeler was another beast altogether, he knew.

Mischa's psychic skills had never been even close to Alina's. Not even in the same league. But he had some abilities, which was the only reason the Vishnikoffs let him stay around. And Alina had taught him a few things, helped him hone what skills he did have.

Time to put it to use, he thought.

He saw a trucker returning to his rig from the coffee shop. The guy wore a ball cap with a New Jersey Devils logo on it. He was skinny, his face gaunt and pockmarked, and a scraggly black beard clung to his chin like Spanish moss to a tree limb. In one hand was a steel thermos, and in the other a ring of keys. Mischa couldn't tell what the man's truck contained; its sides were plain white, with what seemed to be random letters and numbers painted in one corner. Mischa presumed that meant the guy hauled whatever he could, rather than working for any particular company. The cab was painted a bright yellow, and a badly drawn cheetah adorned the doors, with the words "RJ FREIGHT" under it.

Mischa presumed the driver was RJ. He stepped from the shadows as RJ inserted a key in the driver's side lock.

"Excuse me," Mischa said.

RJ spun, startled, his eyes wide. "Yeah?"

Mischa caught the driver's gaze, held it. He stared into the man's dark eyes, boring into his mind. Keeping the man's eyes locked, he sent his thoughts like a dark tendril across the space separating them, into RJ's mind. He felt no obstacle there, no attempt to keep him out. RJ, then, didn't know about psychic assault, had never developed the ability to protect his own thoughts. Mischa gave up on verbal communication, and went straight to mental.

I need a ride.

"You need a ride," RJ said, his voice suddenly taking on a rasp.

I need a ride to Los Angeles. You will take me there. Quickly, and without argument.

"To Los Angeles," RJ echoed. "Fast."

No one must know.

"No one." RJ unlocked his door and climbed into the cab. He leaned across the bench seat and unlocked the passenger door. Mischa crossed in front of the cab and climbed up into the seat. RJ started the engine.

Los Angeles

Willow watched Alexis Vishnikoff work on his knees, the Reality Tracer open before him. Over the years, he explained, he had developed a tool kit specifically for working on the thing. He knew every bit of its schematics, inside and out. The device was more complicated than a supercomputer, but to Alexis it seemed as second nature as checking oil is to anyone who drives a car.

After a few minutes, he closed the access hatch, screwing it down tight. "There," he said. He glared at Alina, then allowed Willow to share in his angry glare. *Like I'm the one who broke it,* Willow thought. Remembering what Alina had said about how he had treated her since her power had surpassed his own and his wife's, she gave him back some of the same. *Grrr. Nasty old man. Cool name, Alexis, but still . . . grrrr.*

"It is fixed," Alexis continued. He rose and went to stand beside Valerya, who watched with her arms folded stubbornly across her chest, her mouth set in a thin line. *She doesn't look,* Willow thought, *like she has ever smiled in her life. How does anyone become so joyless?* "And I hope that you will have realized by now that you need your mother and me, and have had enough of disrespecting us."

Alina barely spared them a glance. Since their earlier argument, she had been quiet, aloof. Now she looked at Willow instead of at her parents.

"Are you ready?" she asked.

"Alina," Alexis said.

"Father, we've agreed. I will only use it to try to return those I have already sent away. I need Willow and her friends to help me locate them in the Alternities."

"Come, Alexis," Valerya said, uncrossing her arms long enough to tug on her husband's hand. "We are not needed here. We're only in the way."

"Yes," Alexis said. Something in the tone of his voice reminded Willow of her own father's voice, on the day she'd started at UC Sunnydale. Willow hadn't gone away to school, but she did move into the dorms, and her father, helping her pack and go, had been oddly glum, as if the realization that his little girl was growing up had set in all at once. Willow had wondered what he'd have thought if he'd known how she spent many of her nights, helping Buffy fight evil and all. That part of her life had been invisible to her parents, but if they'd known about it, they might have been less affected by her moving out of their house. The dorm, they'd have figured, couldn't possibly be any more dangerous than the Hellmouth.

Alexis followed his wife from the room, leaving Alina, Willow, and a glowering Nicky, who sat in a corner worrying at his fingernails. The Flores family was already ensconced in some other part of the house—Cordelia and Wesley had dropped them all off and then left. Alina turned to Willow. "That is better," she said. "I could not have concentrated, knowing that they were watching."

"Well," Willow said, "there's plenty of concentrating to be done, right? I mean, are you ready? To, you know, send Nicky through and find Buffy and Angel and those other kids? Because, if you are, I need to get in touch with Tara and Doña Pilar." She had worked with Nicky while Alina's father repaired the Reality Tracer. He wasn't the most cooperative subject she'd ever worked with—there was so much anger in him, it scared her. But he was determined, and that helped. And he'd undergone the Night of the Long Knives ritual, which satisfied the still-theoretical aspect that people who went through had to have been through a reality shift of some kind.

"I am ready," Alina assured her.

"I've been ready," Nicky said. "Can we get this going or what?"

Willow tried to blank out her mind, to contact Tara, but before she could there was noise in the hallway and a knock at the door.

"What is it?" Alina called out.

"You have visitors," someone announced.

"Expecting anyone?" Willow asked her.

Alina shrugged. "I do not know what to expect anymore."

The door to the workroom opened and Buffy's hunky boyfriend came in. "Riley!" Willow declared, excitedly. Then she saw who accompanied him. "Oh, and Faith."

"Hi, Will," Riley said.

Faith stopped in the doorway, regarding her with those big dark eyes. "I see the second string is in the game," she said.

"We're not second string," Willow protested, feeling a flush of anger. "Anyway, Buffy's kind of missing."

"I heard the whole sad saga from GI Joe," Faith said.

"Faith is here to help," Riley reminded Willow. "She's agreed to go through after Buffy and Angel. If the Tracer's fixed, that is."

"It is fixed," Alina promised them. "With Willow's help, I will be able to send her to the correct Alternity, and then she can help guide the others back."

"You sound confident," Riley said.

"I am."

"Her dad's like the king of all Reality Tracer repairmen," Willow put in.

"He built it," Alina added. "He knows how it works."

"That's a plus," Faith said. "I'd hate to, you know, get stuck someplace I didn't want to be."

Like jail? Willow thought. But she kept her mouth shut.

"What is this?" Nicky demanded, rising from his spot in the corner. His fists were clenched and anger clouded his face. "I'm supposed to go through. I need to get to Salma."

"We know," Willow assured him. "We can send him to Salma and Faith to Buffy, right, Alina?"

"There should be no problem," Alina said. "With the Reality Tracer functioning correctly and you to help guide them on the other side, we can send anyone through. As long as—"

"As long as what?" Faith asked.

"I think I know what she means," Willow cut in. "We have this theory—actually, I don't know if it's really a theory or more of a hunch, but anyway, we think that for people to be able to go through the portals and into the Alternities, and then come out again, safely, that they need to have some kind of experience of their own that helps them survive the trip. Some kind of experience with alternate realities, maybe some kind of flip-flop. Like you and Buffy exchanging bodies. Angel having a soul, then not having one."

"My Night of the Long Knives?" Nicky asked.

"That would probably cover it," Willow agreed.

"But what about Salma? Does this mean I won't be able to bring her back through safely?"

"I don't know," Willow said. There was no time for anything but brutal honesty, but she hated the way his face fell when she said it. "Maybe if you're there to guide her. But we know that some things, and most people, can't just go through and then come back in one piece, or without being horribly transformed in some way."

"I am sure she'll be fine if you're there," Alina said. "In theory, at least, the portals respond to the people who are sent through. One of my parents' goals was to continue to refine the device so that anyone could travel in both directions safely, but they haven't quite achieved that yet."

"This really sounds encouraging," Faith said. "So I might get over there, find Buffy and Angel, and then when I try to bring them back through, we'll all be turned into ground beef or something?"

"No," Alina replied. "The three of you will be able to return. I believe the other kids will too, if you're there to show them the way."

"She believes," Faith echoed. "Well, I'm feeling so much better about this now."

"Look, let's just do it," Willow said. "The longer we talk about it the worse things might be getting."

"Okay, whatever," Faith said. She put her hands on her hips. "I'm ready."

Willow went back to blanking her mind, though it was a little harder with Riley and Faith crowded into the room. She mentally drew a plain white blind across the window of her mind's eye. When everything was white, she conjured a picture of Tara's pretty face, eyes closed as if in slumber.

After a moment, Tara's eyes opened.

Willow?

Hi. It's me.

I can see you.

Are you ready? We're going to send Nicky de la Natividad through to where his sister ended up, and then send Faith through to help show Buffy and Angel the way home.

I guess I'm ready. What about Doña Pilar?

I'll get her next. Hang on.

Holding onto the image of Tara, Willow called up Doña Pilar's lined, friendly face. The same routine repeated itself, as Doña Pilar became aware of her presence. In a moment, the three women were all in communication, triangulated around a mental image of Alina, hooked up to the Reality Tracer. At the edges of her consciousness, Willow heard a faint hum as the Tracer powered up.

She heard Alina's voice, as if through ears plugged by airplane travel or too much swimming.

"Are you ready, Nicky?" Alina asked.

Nicky's muffled voice replied in the affirmative.

Find Salma. The thought belonged to all four of them at once, Willow, Doña Pilar, Tara, Alina. *See Salma.*

Then they *could* see her. She was alone and frightened, a line of trees looming behind her. But whatever it was that scared her was in front of her, not in the trees but coming across the grassy plain that spread before her. It was out of their field of view.

"Go, Nicky," Alina said.

Willow could sense motion in the room, though most of her mind was otherwise occupied. Before Salma, she saw a portal appear.

Nicky stepped through and the image faded from sight.

Buffy now, their thoughts said as one. *See Buffy.*

There was a moment's vertiginous motion and then Buffy crystallized. Angel stood close beside her, a spectacular stone castle at their backs.

Touch Faith. Hold on to Faith.

Faith materialized into view, though not her surroundings.

"Go, Faith," Alina instructed.

Before Buffy and Angel, a portal opened. Faith stepped toward it.

Buffy was about to comment on Angel's Instant Message line—*been spending much time online lately?* or something like that—when the shimmering field that she had come to know as a portal's apparition grew before them.

"Portal," she said, somewhat redundantly.

"Do we go through?" Angel asked. "Or is something coming this way?"

Buffy braced herself for either answer.

"You mean you don't know?" Kayley asked. "What good does it do for you to rescue me from the castle if you don't know where you're taking me?"

"We're kind of playing this by ear, okay?" Buffy said. "At this point we don't know a lot more than you do."

"Cordelia made Angel sound like some kind of superhero," Kayley complained. "So far, I can't say I'm all that impressed."

"Cordelia has a tendency to exaggerate," Buffy said, knowing Angel would not come to his own defense. "But in this case she's not far off."

"I say we go for it," Angel said. "Wherever it takes us, at least it'll be motion."

He started for the portal, but before he could take two steps, someone came through from the other side.

Not just someone, Buffy realized. *Faith.*

"Great," she said. "Now the portal's breaking people out of jail."

"It just so happens, Buff, that your boyfriend broke me out of jail."

"Riley? Why would he—"

"To save your butt, though I'm not sure why he'd want to."

"You? Save us?"

"Buffy," Angel said. "Faith—"

"I know, I know. Faith's changed. Heard the drill. I'll believe it when I see it."

"Then start believing," Faith insisted. "Here I am. You think I'd have been able to get here if I wasn't sent through after you?"

She has a point there, Buffy realized. As much as she hated to admit it, sending Faith after them probably made sense. More sense than sending Riley, who, while tough and experienced, was no Slayer.

"Are you in contact with them?" Angel asked.

"Alina, Willow, Tara, Doña Pilar," Faith said. "The whole sisterhood."

"Then what are we supposed to do?" Angel asked.

"What now?" Faith said. Buffy realized she was not speaking to any of them, though. Her gaze was toward the sky, and she seemed to be paying attention to something none of them could see or hear. After a moment, she pointed behind them, where yet another portal materialized as the one she had come through vanished. "Through there."

"Just like that?" Buffy asked. Following Faith blindly seemed like a supremely bad idea, in spite of Angel's protestations that she had changed. Buffy had seen scant evidence of any change, and she couldn't shake the image of Riley and Faith locked in heated embrace—even though she knew the image was wrong, that when Riley had been with Faith she was in Buffy's body, not her own.

"Buffy, we don't really have a choice," Angel insisted. "If she's in touch with home, we need to do what she says."

"But how can she prove that she is?" Buffy queried.

"We have to take her word for it," Angel said.

"It's not like you two know anything," Kayley commented.

"True," Buffy replied. "But . . ."

"I'm going through there, Buff," Faith said. "Because that's where Alina's telling me where to go. You can come with me or not. But if you don't, I'm not coming back for you again."

"We'll come," Angel said. He looked at Buffy. "We'll come."

Buffy shrugged. She didn't, she knew, have any better ideas. "We'll come."

The soldiers had her in sight, Salma knew. They raced across the meadow on the backs of their strange beasts, bearing directly toward her. She could take refuge in the trees behind her, but that would only be temporary. The forest was dark and thick, underbrush and brambles choking the space between great tree trunks. Movement would be slow and difficult, and she didn't know her way. If she managed to evade the soldiers, she'd surely be lost, and how would that be an improvement?

So she resolved to meet them here. She had no weapons. She couldn't hope to beat them.

But she could make them kill her.

That would be preferable to allowing them to return her to the Worm's tunnels, or to wandering, lost and hungry, in a dark forest until she died of exposure.

She braced herself for their onslaught.

But before it happened, a portal opened before her and a familiar form stepped out. It vanished as soon as he came through, blinked away, and then returned in a heartbeat.

"Nicky!"

"Salma!" he shouted, joy brightening his face. He rushed to her, swept her into his arms. She clutched him tightly, knowing all the while that the soldiers were almost on them.

"Nicky, you're alive!"

"I'm just glad that *you* are!" he replied.

"I-I am fine, now," she said. "But we can't stay here. The soldiers—" She indicated the advancing troops. The ground shook under their charge.

"Into the portal," Nicky commanded. "I'll watch your back until you're safe."

"We'll go together," Salma declared. It was hard now to be heard over the thunder of the soldiers, the roar of hooves, the creak of leather, the clash of steel.

"It's one at a time," Nicky shouted. "You first. I haven't found you just to lose you again." He pushed her toward the portal. "Hurry!"

"You're coming too!"

"I'm right behind you!"

She stepped toward the portal. As she did, the dust churned up by the soldiers enveloped her. Now she could smell their mounts, hear their raised voices. Another moment and they'd have her. She pushed through the portal, turning as she went to see how close behind her Nicky was.

But Nicky remained on the grass, as if rooted there by the spears that suddenly sprouted from him, making him strangely resemble a human pincushion. The soldiers surrounded him, some of them looking her way with wonder and puzzlement on their faces, others intent on her brother. On finishing him off.

"Nickyyy!" she shouted, and then she was gone.

Chapter 15

Los Angeles

Wesley and Cordelia looked up at the seedy hotel. A pink neon sign flickered BRI HTON AR S—the G and the M had gone out, and Wesley was certain there were no buildings even remotely resembling this one in Brighton—above the doorway. The windows were mostly covered by venetian blinds or faded, tattered curtains, but some were open. The bluish glow of TVs shone through them, and tinny voices and laugh tracks wafted on the air.

"You're sure this is the place?" Cordelia asked in a hushed voice. Again.

"Quite sure," Wesley told her. He'd been telling her this ever since they'd parked Angel's car and three young men who looked like they'd be as at home in a prison yard as on a street corner had given it the once over, as if adding up what they could get for parts. "Second floor. Room two-thirteen. You heard the man."

"I didn't hear a man," Cordelia corrected him. They had approached the hotel, but now stood just beyond its doors, so no one inside could hear or see them. "I heard a demon. With blue skin and scales—*scales!* I don't trust him a bit."

"He knows that if he lied to us, he'll answer to Wesley Wyndam-Pryce," Wesley said.

"Oooh, he's probably shaking in his hooves."

"Look, Cordelia," Wesley said. "The fellow—all right, the demon—said that there was an Oden Tal female holed up in here. It's not Jhiera, but they all owe us a favor, don't they?"

"Maybe they owe Angel a favor. I think all they owe you is a slap for that leering and groping bit you did."

He turned on her. "I did not grope!"

"So you admit to the leering?"

"There may have been a little leering. But no groping."

"Okay, Wesley. If we trust your demon informer and we think there's an Oden Tal female up there, let's go up. Maybe you're right and she can help with the dimension-hopping stuff."

"I don't know," Wesley confessed. "I've been thinking it over and I believe that Alina's probably correct. Interdimensional travel is probably nothing like traveling between the Alternities."

Cordelia took his arm, dragging him toward the hotel door. "Too bad," she said. "No chickening out now. Let's go." She shoved the door open. Wesley expected someone to raise an alarm, to try to stop them.

No one did. A desk clerk looked up from behind his cage of bulletproof plastic. A couple of residents watching an old black-and-white console television in the lobby glanced up, then looked back at the screen.

Cordelia marched up the stairs, Wesley right behind. They stopped in front of the door with a lopsided metal 213 nailed to it.

"They can be quite dangerous, you know," Wesley said.

"Only if they're turned on," Cordelia replied. "You go in first, we'll be fine."

Wesley took offense at that but didn't see how it could be argued. He knocked on the door. A gruff voice responded.

"Yeah?"

"Wrong room?" Wesley whispered.

"If you're an Oden Tal female, we need to talk to you!" Cordelia called. "Don't worry, we're friendly! And not at all attractive."

"Cordelia!" Wesley chastised.

"A little white lie," she said. "Hello?"

The sounds of someone unlocking the door came from the other side, and a moment later it swung open. A large, unshaven man stood there dressed in a stained white undershirt and striped boxers, with black socks on his feet. He looked at them both.

"You're not Chinese food," he said.

"Indeed we're not," Wesley agreed.

The man shut the door and locked it again.

Wesley and Cordelia looked at each other.

"Demon informants," Cordelia said. "I keep telling you, never trust a demon informant!"

Salma stumbled as she fell through the portal, falling to her hands and knees in damp grass. Her last view was of her beloved brother Nicky's death at the hands of the soldiers who chased her, and then she was passing through, that lurching, stomach-turning experience, but even this was minor to her compared to losing Nicky again. *He saved me,* she thought, tears streaming down her cheeks. *This all started because he disappeared—because he joined a gang and wanted to perform a spell that would make him accepted, make him one of them. And now he's gone, and I'm alone again.*

But she wasn't. When she lifted her head, wiped the tears away from her eyes with the back of one filthy hand, she saw people standing in a semicircle around her, looking at her. Behind them, a dark castle loomed, but it didn't look at all like the one from which she had escaped.

"Salma?"

"Buffy! Oh my God, is it really you?" she screamed.

"Last I checked," Buffy said. "Around here, I don't take anything for granted, though."

Salma rose unsteadily to her feet. She didn't know these other people—a tall, handsome man; a dark-eyed beauty about Buffy's size, but with a toughness in the set of her jaw and the cock of her hips; and a tiny girl who swam in an oversize blue shirt, a lost look in her eyes.

"That's right, you could be me," the dark-eyed girl said, a touch of sarcasm edging her tone.

"I think I'd know if that happened again," Buffy replied. She didn't sound happy about the prospect. Salma figured she would never know or understand everything about who Buffy was or what she did. But she was glad to see a familiar face.

"Nicky's d-dead," she said, her voice hitching. "He pushed me through the portal, and the soldiers . . . the soldiers got him." She felt the tears again, felt the sobs rise up in her. Buffy came to her, put a comforting arm around her shoulders, drew her into a hug. She could feel the strength in Buffy's arms, and she felt safe there.

"Just like Buffy," the dark-eyed girl said. "All cuddle-cuddle and no action. No wonder the boys like me better."

Buffy released Salma then. "I guess if you're going to have to put up with these people, you might as well be introduced," she said. She pointed to the dark-eyed one first. "That's Faith, over there with the mouth. Tall, dark, and brooding is Angel. And the one whose clothes don't fit is named Kayley. She was one of the disappeared, too, like you."

"Hi," Kayley said shyly, waggling her fingers in Salma's direction.

Salma worked to bring her tears under control. "So . . . so you don't think I was specially targeted? I was just another one of the kids who vanished?"

"I don't know for sure," Buffy said. "There's a lot about this we don't understand yet. But chances are, you just got zapped because you were a teenager—Alina said the machine was basically picking teenagers at random and sending them through."

"Alina? Machine?" Salma asked, completely lost. "What are you talking about?"

"I keep forgetting when you disappeared," Buffy said. "You didn't know a lot of what we found out." Buffy filled her in briefly on the Reality Tracer, Alina and her parents, and the way they had been sent through in search of the missing teens.

"So it wasn't all Nicky?" Salma asked when she was done. "His spell . . . ?"

"We think his spell was partly responsible," Buffy said. "We think the fact that he was messing around with magick in Sunnydale at the same time Alina was trying to work the machine in L.A. made portals open in Sunnydale, which let the bad stuff in."

"The shadow monster?"

"Among others, yes. The shadow monster seemed to have been somehow attuned to Nicky, and therefore to you. I thought it was trying to protect you, but maybe it was just trying to keep you from finding Nicky."

"Is it still there?"

"I don't know," Buffy said. "Being . . . here, and all."

"Speaking of which," Kayley interrupted, "can we go home now?" The girl looked nervous, Salma thought, maybe even more frightened than she herself was. She wondered what horrors Kayley had been through since being snatched from her home.

"We kind of have to round up the rest of the disappeareds," Buffy explained. "That's what we came here for."

"Oh," Kayley said, disappointment evident in her voice. "Right. Sorry."

"We'll get you home as soon as we can," Angel assured her. It was the first time he'd spoken. Salma found his voice reassuring.

"So what are we standing here for?" Faith asked. "Just like the view?"

"I don't exactly know where to go," Buffy replied.

"You don't need to," Faith said. "That's what I'm here for."

"You're still in contact?"

Faith waved at no one in particular. "Hi, Alina," she said. "What's shakin'?" She paused for a moment, as if listening to something no one else could hear. "Looks that way," she said finally. "Through there."

Faith pointed to a spot a few feet away from the group. There was more grass there, but that was all—there was nothing to go "through." Salma thought maybe she was crazy as well as brassy and just the slightest bit rude. But as she watched the spot, a golden glow began to form, and in a minute, a portal hung there in the air.

"Through there?" Buffy asked, sounding uncertain.

"That's what Alina says," Faith reported.

"And it'll take us where?"

"Where we need to be, I guess."

Buffy looked at Faith, as if examining her face would disclose any hidden motive or agenda. After a moment, she shrugged and turned to the others. "Stick together," she said. "We don't want to lose anyone now."

Spike kept tugging on the trigger of the alien gun. The little orange sods dropped like flies—or froze like flies, he realized, was a more appropriate analogy, since the gun had the same effect on them that it had had on him. Others aimed their weapons at him, but he dodged their blasts, his legs—basketball-player long, compared to theirs—carrying him out of harm's way. He ran up a slight mound and jumped behind it, hitting the ground and rolling. At the same time, he was able to snake out from beneath the netting that had held him. When a couple of the orange aliens appeared at the top of the rise to look for him, he blasted them from his prone position. They stayed where they were, miniature statuary on the crest of the hill.

"Come on!" Spike shouted when no more of them appeared for a few moments. He rolled to a sitting position, so he could swivel more quickly in case they were trying to flank him. "Don't tell me you've already given up! I haven't had this much bloody fun in days!" The chip didn't hurt him a bit, and he'd almost forgotten that combat could be so joyful.

Motion from the corner of his eye caught his attention,

and he turned, bringing the raygun up to shoot. But what he saw froze his finger on the trigger.

"Slayer?"

"Spike? What are you doing here?" Buffy demanded, stepping from a glowing portal. She was a bit the worse for wear—clothes torn oh so fetchingly, a few bruises on her face and arms—but still as lovely as ever. "I thought you were back in Sunnydale, helping to fight monsters!"

"You know my wandering ways, Buffy," he replied, waving the gun casually as he did.

"You want to put the gun down, Spike?" Angel asked.

A whole crew of people stepped from the portal. Buffy, Angel, Faith—*Faith?* And two kids he didn't know, who looked lost and terrified.

"Thought you were locked up," Spike said to Faith.

"Thought you'd have been dusted long ago," she retorted. "I don't know why Buff lets you slide."

"It's because of my charm and good looks."

"Get real."

"Listen, kiddies, there's a whole bunch of little creepy-looking orange aliens going to come over that hill any second with rayguns like this one," he said, ignoring Faith's comment. "If they shoot you, you'll be frozen for, I don't know, twenty minutes or so, I reckon."

"And now your delusions are getting more serious?" Faith asked.

"He's got one of the guns," Buffy pointed out. "So maybe not delusional?"

Angel nodded toward the hill Spike raved about. "I don't know about little orange guys," he said, "but there's a big blue one."

Spike whirled, following Angel's gaze. The surly vampire was right—where he'd been expecting more of the little orange buggers, instead a vaguely human-looking thing with deep indigo skin looked down at them. The creature was powerfully muscled, his neck as big around as a stout tree back on Earth, his arms like poles, his legs so solid they almost seemed to grow right out of the ground. His clothes were ragged, simple things—a strip of fabric for a loincloth, another that ran diagonally across his chest, both tan, as if these creatures hadn't invented dye yet. He stared at them through small eyes shadowed by a heavy brow that slanted, caveman-style, to a row of raised ridges, almost fins, Spike thought, that ran down his back. He seemed to be at least a dozen feet tall, or maybe a little more than that.

"He's a new one on me," Spike admitted.

"Try the gun, Einstein," Faith suggested.

Spike looked at it as if he'd forgotten he still carried it. With a shrug, he aimed it at the blue man-thing, even now taking a giant step toward them. He squeezed the trigger, and the now-familiar ray shot out, enveloping the blue guy in its glow.

The blue guy took another step.

"No good," he said, shaking his head. "Maybe he's too big."

Buffy, Faith, and Angel all took up positions beside Spike, ready to take the thing on. "You never did tell me what you're doing here, Spike," Buffy said.

"I followed you through the bloody door," Spike told her. "Thought you might need a hand, and it wasn't like I had Cheryce at home to keep me there. But instead of ending up where you went, I came here—vampire paradise, if you don't mind being a dumb animal on exhibit."

"Meaning what?"

"Meaning, whatever else there is on this planet, these

lot here are running a vampire zoo! And since I wasn't willing to sit and preen for 'em, they decided it'd be a good idea to do me in."

"So this is all self-defense. The gun, and everything."

"Yeah," Spike said with a smile, remembering the thrill of battle. "The kind I haven't been able to enjoy back home lately. I can kick their little skulls in and feel absolutely first-rate doing it."

"You guys want to keep jabbering, maybe you should get a room," Faith said. "There's gonna be some serious blue butt-kicking going on here in a second."

Spike tore his attention away from the Slayer. The blue meanie still lumbered down the hill, slow but determined. The sight of four of Earth's toughest vampire Slayers and vampires arrayed against him didn't give him a moment's pause.

Then Spike noticed something at the top of the hill— another massive blue head swinging into view. "Oh, wonderful," he said. "He's got a twin."

The second giant topped the hill and started down after the first. Just for giggles, Spike gave him a shot with the raygun. Nothing. He tossed it aside. "Looks like it's the old-fashioned way," he said. He paused for a moment. "Anyone got any ideas?"

"Yeah," Faith put in. "My idea is let's have a party!" She started up the hill at a run. Buffy followed her, then Angel. Spike brought up the rear.

Faith reached the blue giant first. He hesitated, slowing his descent to move into a defensive stance, crouching a bit and shifting his weight backward since he was on a downhill slope. Faith hurled herself into the air, lashing out with a strong right foot that slammed into the monster's chest. He responded by swatting her out of the air like a bug. She hit the ground with a sickening thud and rolled.

Buffy glanced at her, but devoted the bulk of her attention to the blue monster. Following through on his swing, he was off-balance just the slightest bit. Buffy feinted as if she were going to make a Faith-style leap, but at the last moment she changed course and passed him, going farther up the hill. He turned at the waist as she passed by, trying to keep her in sight. But Angel and Spike were closing from the front, so he couldn't take his eyes completely off them. Spike saw the look of confusion cross his prehistoric-looking face just as Buffy buckled his left knee with a sharp kick from behind. Almost as if they'd choreographed it, Angel charged him from the front at the same time, causing him to swing one of his gigantic hands. The combination threw him completely off-balance, and he fell, a great crashing tumble that sounded to Spike like a redwood falling in a forest. Spike had to dodge one of the huge hands as it flailed toward him.

Once the giant was down, it wasn't over. He was already clawing at the earth, trying to regain his footing. Buffy and Angel both began pounding on him with fists and feet. The blue man grunted and moaned under their assault. Spike joined in, enjoying the feeling of flesh pulping under his fists once again.

But the second one came down the hill more quickly, and more carefully, than the first one had. By the time the downed giant sank into unconsciousness, the other, leaning backward and keeping one hand in contact with the ground, for stability on the slope, had almost reached them.

Faith rose, wiping herself off and cursing under her breath. *That isn't like her,* Spike thought. *The old Faith would be swearing at the top of her lungs. Maybe jail's rehabilitating her, after all.*

Hate to see that happen.

"Look out, Buffy!" Faith called, pointing up the hill at the advancing blue man-thing. *As if Buffy hasn't already seen it,* Spike thought. Faith was a slayer, but Buffy was *the* Slayer, as far as he was concerned. Without peer.

"Thanks!" Buffy shouted. She spun just as the giant reached for her. She dodged the hand, punching at the big, grasping fingers. The blue man yanked his hand back and took another lumbering step forward. His expression was grim, but a half-smile played across his features, as if he knew something no one else did. Spike doubted that was true—the big galoot looked giant in every way except mentally. His idea of a plan seemed to be to swing again at Buffy—barely missing her—while ignoring the advance of Angel, Faith, and Spike. Buffy danced just out of his way, jabbing at his grabbing hand again.

Angered, he tried one more time. This time, Buffy sidestepped the hand but caught the wrist in both of her hands and pulled. Angel and Faith ran past the giant as he struggled to tug his arm from her grip. Working soundlessly—again, Spike had the sense that they'd prepared these moves, but he understood that it just came from working together—they each chose a leg and pushed as Buffy pulled.

The giant went over onto his head and shoulders and tumbled down the hill past them.

"Bigger they are—" Spike began.

"Don't say it," Buffy ordered.

"In fact, don't say anything," Angel said. His tone was sharp. He was not a happy-go-lucky sort at the best of times, but even his limited patience seemed at an end.

"What's bugging you?" Spike asked.

"You are. You shouldn't even be here, and we have better things to do, and here we are risking our necks to save you."

"You don't need to save me," Spike insisted. "I'm perfectly capable of saving myself."

"Didn't look like it to me. It looked like we saved your scrawny hide."

"I think I've had just about enough of you, Angel," Spike threatened. He reared back and aimed a right jab at Angel's manly jaw—and the pain in his head felt like his brain was exploding in its skull cavity. He lowered his arm.

"Thought I was all healed up for a minute there," he said glumly. "Thought maybe I didn't have a chip here."

"Looks like you do," Angel observed. "So you'd better try cooperating with us. Do what you're told and we'll let you tag along."

"Boys," Faith called. Spike turned to see her standing in front of a portal that had materialized on the side of the hill. "If you're through with your testosterone rally, we have places to go."

Spike noticed that both blue men were getting to their feet, looking up the slope at them like it was dinnertime and they were the main course. "All right," he said, somewhat halfheartedly. "I guess you'll probably need my help, so I'll come with you."

"Thanks, Spike," Buffy said, sounding just a bit too cheerful. "Are you still in touch with Alina, Faith?"

"That's why I'm standing here saying 'let's go this way,' Buff. You think I'd just make it up?"

"Wouldn't put anything past you."

"Ladies," Angel said, stepping between them. "No more rallies."

They stepped through.

* * *

It felt strange, having someone else inside her head, but that's what it felt like to Faith—as if she carried Alina along like a passenger. The Russian girl seemed to be able to see and hear everything that Faith saw and heard, and they could converse without actually using their voices. She even saw Alina's face, faintly superimposed over everything she looked at, as if she were seeing Alina's reflection in a mirror.

She could feel Willow's presence, too, along with Willow's friend Tara and the old lady, Doña Pilar, but she couldn't *see* them like she could Alina—they were more like shadows without substance in her mind.

She was happy to put up with the strangeness, though, because it meant that the contact hadn't been broken, that Alina, through the science of her Reality Tracer and the magick, or whatever it was, of her highly developed psychic powers, was genuinely leading her from point to point among the nearly infinite number of Alternities. Alina could open portals at will now, and better than that, she knew where they'd lead.

Alina guided Faith, and Faith guided Angel, Buffy, and the others. That felt strange, too—*but good strange,* she thought. *They're following wherever I take them. They're respecting me.* That was new. And she liked it, a lot.

She took them through the portal from Spike's hillside, and it opened inside a vast city—buildings as far as the eye could see, in every direction. Masses of people moved briskly along crowded sidewalks, bumping and jostling each other with every step, but uttering barely a word when they did. Everyone seemed inwardly focused, as if, with this many people in one place, privacy could only be achieved by ignoring everyone except oneself.

Julianne Mercer was here, in this city. The pretty brunette had vanished from a Cowtown Burger Ranch, and she still wore the uniform when they found her on the hundred and ninety-third floor of a building—about halfway up its total height. She had started down the stairs when she arrived at its uppermost level, but she'd had to stop to rest and scrounge food occasionally, so she still hadn't made it to street level.

Another portal took them to a strange landscape where steam erupted from wide fissures in the earth, and flames danced along jagged lines like earthbound lightning, and the dominant beings were hunched over, wizened creatures with sharp fangs and a serious yen for human flesh. Cheerleader Julie Mazullo had wound up here, and had spent what seemed, to her reckoning, about nine hours hiding in caves that were nearly as hot as ovens, and full of human bones.

Through the portals again, after battling several of the human-hunting things, Faith led the growing group to what looked like a paradise, with big, healthy trees bearing ripe, inviting fruits, beautiful flowers, sweetly singing birds, curious but shy little mammals that looked like they belonged in a Disney cartoon. The downside was that it was all the domain of a feudal lord who kept it pristine by instructing his soldiers to impale anyone who dared disturb his paradise—the hundred or so staked bodies scattered among the trees and plants looked like *Titanic* survivors dog-paddling to keep their heads above water. Two teens, a boy and a girl from El Segundo, had vanished together and had ended up here. The girl had, so far, escaped being impaled. The boy had not been so lucky.

Buffy looked brokenhearted. "No one said you'd be able to save them all, Buffy," Faith told her.

"But I wanted to," Buffy replied. "Can you imagine telling his parents what happened to him?"

Faith touched Buffy's arm—an alien gesture, to her, showing Buffy affection or concern. Buffy forced a smile, and then looked away quickly.

Really gets to her, Faith thought. *After all this time, saving people's lives day in and day out, to miss just one still tears her apart.* But she knew standing around here dwelling on the failure wouldn't do anybody any good—there were still more places to go. Alina opened another doorway, and they went through.

Tony Tataglia, Halka Czornik, Joe Frost, Eric Vicente—kids none of them had ever heard of, spirited from every part of Los Angeles while Alina's Reality Tracer was set to randomly pluck teenagers—they found them all, rescued them from danger if need be, convinced them to leave seemingly pleasant existences in a couple of cases.

Tony Tataglia refused. They located him, in the reality where Angel had found himself sidetracked by Tan-kia's peril. Tony had found himself the only man in a court of young women—he was the center of attention, and he loved it. Buffy and Angel had argued with him, until Faith finally pointed out that there were more waiting to be rescued, and they couldn't force him to accompany them. When they passed through the next portal, Tony waved good-bye with a broad smile on his face.

As the group grew larger and larger, Faith felt more and more Pied Piperish, though not in that creepy way the real story went. She knew she was not taking the kids away from their families; she was bringing them home.

That made all the difference.

Chapter 16

Los Angeles

"Is REALLY WORKING!" ALINA SAID EXCITEDLY. HER FACE looked like that of a schoolgirl who just got a note from a boy she likes—*or a girl,* Willow amended—her smile showing lots of teeth, eyes gleaming, nose crinkled in delight. Of course, Willow couldn't really see her, but she, Tara, and Doña Pilar all remained psychically linked to her, and a visual manifestation of Alina came with that. They could all "see" one another, as if they stood together in a room of pure white with the faintest hint of rose petals scenting the air.

Of course it is, Willow said. *You said the Tracer would work, and we told you we could handle the rest.*

But it . . . it is so wonderful! Alina thought, apparently remembering that she didn't have to speak out loud.

Yes, child, Doña Pilar agreed. *It is. But do not lose your focus now. There is work yet to be done.*

I know, Doña Pilar. I'm sorry.

The hardest part, Willow knew, was yet to be done. They had managed to lead Faith through the Alternities, one after another, following the faint energy trail the Reality Tracer maintained on each one of them. The gang had been able to round up almost all the missing kids.

But now they had to be brought home—safely—through the portals. That, no one was quite sure, could be done. They *thought* it could, as long as one of the people who could, theoretically, travel safely through the Alternities, guided them through the right portal at the right time. But that was all guesswork, really. No one had actually done it.

So far, since getting the Reality Tracer fixed, it had worked like a charm. And the work that she had done with Tara and Doña Pilar, practicing the lines of communication, had paid off. There hadn't been a single hiccup on this end.

Which, she thought, *is usually when things get jinxed.*

"That's the place," Che said. "According to those Russian dudes we worked over, they're real careful to guard this house."

"Which means," Pepé Villaréal said, "there's something in there they don't want us to have."

"You got that right," Che agreed. "So we need to get in."

He glanced down the line. This was a major operation—the biggest he'd ever been part of. There were ten cars here already, parked on every side of the intersection of Mount Vernon and Fairway, with at least three or four guys per car. Another half-dozen were on the way. Every man was strapped with at least a handgun, several with autos, some with shotguns. A couple of grenades were in the mix, too, and cans of gasoline, bottles, and rags, for Molotov cocktails.

The freaking war had gone on long enough. Che met with some of the other *jefes* after they'd learned of this place, and decided that hitting here would help bring it to a quick and victorious finish. Anyplace the Russians were so protective of would have to be a good strategic target. The Russian guy they'd snagged after a battle down in Crenshaw had warned that this house was well fortified, defended with many troops. He'd died before he could spill much more detail than that. *But that was okay,* Che thought. *We got the address and we got the warning. We know how to take care of ourselves.*

So far, he hadn't seen any activity at all from the house. It was pretty obvious, if someone bothered to look out a window, what was going on. The house was surrounded by Echo Park and East Side Kings, Latin Cobras over from Sunnydale, even some Valley Flash, down from Bakersfield.

If only Nicky gave me that secret, Che thought. *I had that Night of the Long Knives going for me, I could just walk in there, invincible, and throw everybody out of the house.*

But Nicky had refused, had insulted Che by breaking into his house and threatening him, and then had vanished into the night. *The next time I see Nicky, I kill him,* Che vowed. *Just whack him right there, on the spot. No hello, no good-bye.*

After tonight, he just might lead a raid on the de la Natividad house, just for laughs. *Show those rich folks how the other half dies.*

Che heard engines, caught a glimpse of cars heading up the road without headlights. The rest of his people, then. He had noticed movement in some of the surrounding houses, fluttering curtains, porch lights shutting off. He half-expected the cops any time. But they'd show up with lights and sirens, he knew, not quiet and dark. He willed his reinforcements to get into place quickly, so they could take the house before the cops did come.

There was something in that house Russian gangs were willing to die to protect.

Che wanted it.

Whatever it was.

When the other cars had pulled into place, their occupants spilled onto the streets, he gave the signal.

As one, fifty guns boomed.

Glass shattered. Outside ornamentation—white-painted shutters, porch lights, security lights, window boxes—were blown to bits. Chunks of wall blew out.

A haze of smoke hung over the street. Che gave another hand signal, and the firing stopped. His ears ringing, Che studied the house.

It looked like a hundred bullets had hit it . . . but little real damage had been done, he realized. There weren't rooms behind the windows, just more walls—walls that looked like galvanized steel, walls that withstood the punch of the bullets, denting but not allowing penetration. Same thing behind the walls—none of their bullets had actually gone through. They'd done cosmetic damage, but no genuine progress was made.

"Dude," Villaréal said. "That's just freaky. It's like a fort or something."

"Something, yeah," Che said. "So it'll be tougher than we thought. Makes it more fun."

He raised his arms to give the signal to resume firing, but stopped when he heard a whirring noise from the house, a sound like a dozen tiny electric motors humming to life.

And then he saw where the noise originated.

From vantage points around the house, sections of the steel walls slid open revealing narrow slots, not much more than an inch wide, a couple of inches high.

From the slots poked the barrels of big guns. Not rifles, not pistols.

Machine guns.

"Down!" Che cried. He threw himself to the dirt behind an El Dorado.

The guns started to bark.

There were only maybe twelve of them, but the noise was more deafening than Che's guys' fifty guns. Big, loud cracks, one following the next with hardly any space between. And the bullets that flew from these guns were huge, smashing into the cars, hitting Che's men, trashing houses across the street, punching out lightposts, raining death all over the intersection.

"Take 'em out!" Che ordered, screaming to be heard over the din. "Take 'em!"

He raised his gun over the El's hood and fired back, aiming for the slots, figuring he could hit the gunmen or at least plug or damage the barrels.

He might as well have been blowing bubbles at it.

"Keep it up!" he commanded. "Don't let up!"

He kept firing, leading by example. He saw his men do the same. Arms stuck up over the doubtful cover of cars, guns more or less pointed at the house. The fusillade continued. Chunks of plaster flew everywhere. Metaljacketed slugs slammed into the steel inner walls, ricocheted off with a *zing,* kicking up sparks.

Al somebody, a guy Che knew from Bakersfield, came running over at a crouch. He dropped down behind the El, a sawed-off shotgun cradled in his arms. Blood dripped from a cut over his eyes.

"Dude, you're hit!" Che said.

"It's a scratch, a ricochet off a car, I think."

"Cool," Che said. "What's up?"

Al avoided his gaze. There was a quaver in his voice. "I think we're pulling out, man."

"Pulling out?" Che spat in the street. "You can't, *ese*. We're under serious fire. We need every gun we can get!"

"Guns don't matter, Che. Look at that house. We've been shooting at it for five minutes. Any other house, this many bullets going into it, everyone inside would be dead by now. There'd be big freakin' holes in the walls you could drive a truck through. But this place? It's like all we've done is tick them off."

"Then we need to finish the job, that's all," Che insisted. The sight of Al was beginning to make him sick. One scratch, a little blood spilled, and the guy was ready to walk away. *Sometimes you need to make sacrifices,* Che thought, *for friends. Put their needs over your own.*

"The thing is, this isn't really Bakersfield's war," Al went on. "It's an L.A. thing. It don't concern us."

"This is everyone's war," Che hissed. He leaned in close to Al, put one hand on the guy's shotgun so he couldn't raise it. The hand he used happened to be the one clutching his nine, so the barrel wagged in front of Al's chest. "These guys, these Russians, they ain't gonna stop in Los Angeles. They're everywhere. East Coast, Midwest, all over. Them and the Eastern Europeans, they're the new Sicilians, you know. They want to run everything. That includes you and me, Bakersfield and L.A. Everything. We don't stop them now, then we're just rolling over for them."

Al nodded, more frightened now. "I know, Che. But my guys, they don't want to die here."

"Everyone goes sometime, Al," Che replied.

"Sometime. Not today."

Che leaned down on the shotgun, pressing the barrel of his nine into Al's chest. "Today for you, *amigo,* you try to leave us here like this."

"You-you'd do that?" Al asked. Terror widened his eyes. His lips quivered now, a thin line of drool escaping them. "You'd just off me right here?"

"Right here, right now."

"Th-them other guys were r-right," Al stammered. "They said you was nuts, Che. Just crazy, they told me. I always stuck up for you, y'know? I always said, not Che. He's got ideas, he's got *cojones,* that's all. He ain't afraid to think big."

"You're right about that, Alberto," Che agreed. He felt very calm now, pressuring Al even as the thunder of the big guns continued to roar, all but drowning out the *pop-pop-pop* of his own people's weapons. "You are definitely right. I do think big. I guess your problem is you just think small. You think nothing can ever touch Bakersfield. You're over there in that valley, across the grapevine. You think it's still 1949 or something, you can wear a zoot suit, swing your chain, impress the ladies. Well, news bulletin, Al. It's not. Now you got to have big ideas and the stones to back them up or you're as extinct as the dinosaurs."

Al seemed to know what was coming. He shook his head violently, back and forth. Spittle and mucus flew, and he made a kind of hitching noise, like a sob stuck in his throat trying to get out. Che maintained his composure, still feeling an amazing calm as he squeezed the trigger of his gun. There was a loud report, a spray of blood up his arm, and Al fell into the street. His arm flopped out from behind the car, and was instantly blown off by a burst from the house.

"Grenades!" Che screamed. "Cocktails! What are you people waiting for?!"

At that direction, some of the guys began pouring gasoline into the soda and beer bottles, stuffing rags into the mouths, and dripping some more gas onto the rags. Others held grenades in their hands, nervous. Very few of them had ever actually used one.

"Here," Che demanded, holding out his hand to one. "Give it over here."

The guy handed him the grenade. Che put his back to the El Dorado, took the grenade's pin between his teeth. "Like this," he said, mouth clamped around the pin. He pulled the grenade away, pin remaining in his mouth. He spat it out, counted to five, then hurled the grenade backward, over his head and the El. Then he spun around to watch it land.

It bounced twice in the yard and came to rest up against the wall of the house. Half a second later, it went off, a tremendous burst of light and noise and force. Flame shot up the wall, sheeting one of the gun slots. Che felt a concussion wave all the way back at the El.

When the cloud of smoke cleared, the gun at that slot was quiet, its barrel blackened.

A cheer went up from the guys.

"It works!" Che shouted. "Take out those other guns, now! Let 'em have it!"

Others threw grenades at the house, and Molotov cocktails followed, exploding against the house's walls and spreading flame everywhere.

"We'll bake 'em out," Villaréal said gleefully. "Just like an oven!"

Che nodded, smiling. *All it takes are some stones,* he thought. *It ain't no magick spell, but it's all right.*

When the thunder started, Alina's first thought was that a storm had blown in off the ocean. But it didn't stop, didn't roll away like thunderstorms did. It just built.

"What is that?" she asked, concern in her voice.

Do not break your concentration, Doña Pilar instructed.

"But . . ."

It sounds like shooting, Willow agreed. *Lots of it.*

Willow—are you okay?

I think so, Tara. A little scared.

My daughters . . .

Sorry, Doña Pilar. I'm worried about Alina. And me, I guess.

I'm worried about Willow, too.

The thunder transformed into a rapping noise, and gradually it broke through Willow's consciousness. Someone at the door of their room. She heard a voice.

"Willow! It's Riley! Willow, open up!"

Riley . . .

Willow, no! Doña Pilar's "voice" warned.

But—

Then she broke it off, rushing to the door. She spun the lock and yanked it open.

"Riley, what's going on?"

"Firefight," he said. "It's some kind of all-out invasion."

"Of this house?"

"This house has some defenses you wouldn't believe," Riley said. "And more troops than I thought. You'd almost think it was an Initiative post."

"You'd almost think that," Willow said. "I'd think it sounded scary."

Riley nodded. "Yeah, okay. It is, kind of. Scary. But so far, so good. The house is holding up. You're safe in this room, and I've got the Floreses squirreled away in another fortified room."

"What about you?" Willow asked. "You know Buffy would have my head if I let anything happen to you."

"I'm being careful," Riley assured her. "Believe me. I have no interest in getting in the middle of this fight. But that won't stop me if I have to." He looked around the room. "How are things going in here?"

"They *were* great," Willow confessed. "Until the gunfire interrupted us." She didn't mention his persistent pounding on the door. "But now I'm afraid we've lost contact."

Riley looked freaked. His fear for Buffy was palpable, matched only by Willow's own.

"But you can get it back, right?" he asked, hopefully.

"I think—sure." She bit her lip and smiled painfully. "Absolutely, Riley."

He ventured a halfhearted smile. "Go for it. I'll watch your back."

"'kay," Willow agreed. "Be careful. Stay safe."

"Got it," Riley said. He left, and Willow locked the door behind him.

Her gaze met Alina's, and the Russian girl's eyes filled with tears.

"We've lost them!" she wailed.

"She's gone," Faith announced, as she looked around, her eyes widening. Her voice felt strangely weak.

"What do you mean, gone?" Buffy asked.

"Like, gone! How many things does that mean? Not there! Vanished! Kaput! Gone!"

"Gone," Angel echoed.

"I'm not hearin' this," Spike said, shoving his fists into the pockets of his leather duster. "I am not hearing this. Am I?"

"I think you are," Buffy said. "Isn't he, Faith?"

"Look, I don't know what to tell you," Faith said. "She was there in my head, and then she was gone."

Spike waved a hand around them. Portals opened and closed like hungry mouths in a bird's nest, winking in and out of existence. All the teenagers looked on at them, worry etching lines in their young faces. Beyond them was a landscape of urban decay, burned-out buildings never made by human hands, fallen towers, piles of smoldering rubble dotting the horizon. "So what do we do?" he asked. "Which one of these doorways goes home? Because I have to tell you, I don't like this neighborhood one bit."

"Look, I can figure this out," Faith said. They had landed here through the last portal, picking up the final missing kid, a friend of Gunn's named Marcus. "Just chill, okay? Give me a minute."

But she didn't feel as confident as she hoped she sounded. She'd liked taking the lead, having Alina guide her through one portal after another. She'd been in control, and the others had to look to her to show them the way. She had led them without a single wrong step. She'd felt—she almost hated to admit it to herself—she'd felt like a Slayer.

Now it was all gone, all the certainty and confidence. She was as strong as ever. She could fight anyone, and win. But the whole leadership ability thing was as fragile as a robin's egg, and it was tied to being able to direct them all through the right portals, and now that was gone.

Defeat wasn't in Faith's vocabulary, though. She knew that at another time, she'd have taken advantage of a situation like this to step through one of the quickly vanishing portals, leaving the others behind, along with the rest of her jail sentence. A Slayer could get along anywhere, she figured. Especially someplace where they didn't know her, where she didn't have a record or a rep to live up to. She could pop through one of those doors and make herself queen of some new world.

Six months ago—hell, six weeks ago—I might have done it, she thought. *I would have done it.*

Put a different way—if Angel hadn't seen something in that hole where my soul's supposed to be . . .

. . . I wouldn't be who I am right now.

She looked at the others, who were looking at her— looking up to her, willing her to help them—and felt stronger than ever. She felt . . . good.

I gotta take my temperature, she thought. *I must be feverish or something.*

"Look, Slayer junior," Spike interrupted her thoughts. "I don't want to put any pressure or anything on you, but the locals are starting to come out of their houses. And they don't look like they bloody well like visitors."

Spike was right. A variety of creatures—*monsters,* she supposed, *would be the word*—shuffled toward them. Monsters of every color and description, from tiny, many-fanged anklebiters to towering beasts with thick necks and clawed feet. They flew, they writhed, they shambled. There must have been a hundred of them.

"Spike," Buffy said carefully. "Do they look familiar?"

"They look like sodding monsters, Buffy," Spike snapped. "What more do you need?"

"I mean, the types of monsters," she pressed. "The sheer numbers of them."

Beside her, Angel nodded. Faith wasn't with the program, and felt stupid. *B's always gotta be the smart one . . .*

"Thinkin's what I do best," Spike shot back. "Or second best. Wait a second . . ."

Buffy pressed. "You see what I'm getting at?"

The bleach-blond vamp took inventory at the gathering groups of the gross and the restless. "Kind of converging," he said, "massin' for a rumble.'"

"Or for something else," Angel put in. "Awful lot of them."

"Not really. Those are as many as live around here," Marcus said. "Property values are all gone to seed." He looked grateful at the fantastic four, Slayer, Slayer, vampire, vampire. "Now you see why I was glad you folks showed up."

"Gettin' warmer," Spike said. "Lotta monsters, some we seen in the ol' dale . . ."

"So this was the reality that opened onto Sunnydale!" Buffy went on, her excitement building. Angel nodded.

"But which door is it?" Faith asked, as the portals blinked around them.

"That door's closed, remember, Slayer?" Spike pointed out. "No guarantee any other one will take us to Sunnydale. It's just as likely to drop us in Pomona or some other hellish place." He shivered. "Aging boomers and ladies with blue hair."

"Right now, I'd settle for Pomona," Faith told him. "I'd kiss the ground in Pomona."

"You never did have any standards," Spike flung. "And those monsters? They're coming closer. Pick something!"

Things shambled toward them. Tall and purple, amorphous, jellylike beasts that rolled along, leaving trails of animal bones and slime; green tentacled lumps; a couple of Lindworms, and horned, furred beasts that looked like a cross between a yak and Sasquatch picked up their scent, becoming aware of the group of humans. The smell was unbelievable as things slithered and rolled and slid along the ground. The kids started to panic, and Angel and Buffy moved into attack mode as Faith looked at the portals.

Wink, wink, wink. They came and went, sometimes staying for a minute or more, sometimes scant seconds. *Alina?* she thought. *Willow? Where are you?*

"What are we supposed to do?" one of the rescuees piped up.

"We're going to die!" someone shrieked.

"Chill," Faith barked, then took a breath. "It's gonna be okay." She glanced at Angel, who nodded grimly.

"We'll make it okay," Angel gritted back.

Chapter 17

F<small>EAR WAS AN UNCOMFORTABLE SENSATION FOR</small> F<small>AITH</small>, panic even more so. Right now, she felt a little of both, and together they threatened to overwhelm her. She knew she could kick monster tail when necessary; so could Buffy, Angel, and Spike. But even the four of them—four of the toughest fighters their Earth had to offer—couldn't hope to take on an entire dimension of angry creatures, especially with close to fifty teenagers in tow who they had to keep safe.

"Where do we go, Faith?" Spike questioned. "Pick one already!"

"Do you think I should?" Faith asked, to no one in particular.

"Wherever we end up, it couldn't be much worse than here, could it?" Buffy asked. "I mean, unless we drop straight into the land of killer clowns, or something, which, you know, clowns. Brrr!" She shivered.

"Okay," Faith replied, with a faint grin. *Summers, you're such a geek.* She pointed to a portal, at random. "That one."

Some of the teens started to file toward the portal she indicated—which, suddenly, winked out of existence.

She said, "Or not."

"Hang loose," Angel advised her. "Try to find Alina again."

Behind her, she heard the sounds of the monsters coming closer—roars, groans, the clank of armor and chain, the creak of leatherlike skin, the huff of breath and the gnashing of teeth. *No time left even for eenie meenie minie moe,* she thought. They needed to be out of here, and it needed to be—

"Right there!" Willow's voice sounded inside her head, almost as clearly as if Willow stood next to her.

"Willow?" Faith cried, glancing around.

"You see her?" Angel asked her.

"No. Not like I saw Alina." Faith brushed her hair out of her eyes. "She's in my head."

Buffy glanced at her sharply. "You're lying. You don't want to go back."

Then the monsters charged, just as if someone had shouted, well, "Charge!" Rushes of green and blurs of seeping wounds and tentacles and whiplike tails and fangs came at them.

"Stay focused!" Angel barked at Faith, as she got ready for slayage, coming up beside him and Buffy as they raced toward the creatures. "Work on the portal!"

"But—" she protested.

"Faith, do it!" Angel insisted. "You're the one who can do it!"

Then he and Buffy took on the first phalanx of attackers, moving in the same kind of coordinated-but-unplanned ballet of violence she and Buffy had gotten so good at—synching up, going for it, with roundkicks and hard chops and rabbit punches to the soft or squishy places. Hunks of monster went flying as the two did their thing; the kids started to freak and scatter, and Faith realized that if she didn't hurry up and pick, they were going to lose the teenagers and probably just plain die.

And then . . .

Faith saw the Mayor.

He stood smiling in a nimbus of shimmering light, his arms outstretched, in his human form. He wore a chambray shirt and a pair of khaki trousers, and he looked the same as he had in life. With the same brownish hair, the same twinkle in his eyes, he was there again, for her. Evil, yes, but he loved her. He believed in her. He cherished her.

And there was the picnic, spread out on the checkered cloth behind him. Chicken and potato salad, sodas in cans. An old-fashioned straw basket; there was probably chocolate cake inside, maybe even homemade, not simply purchased at the bakery section of a grocery store . . .

"The road not traveled," the Mayor whispered. "We can do it, Faith. We can have it."

The world around her seemed to shift, to become a kaleidoscope of flickering bits and pieces, so very insubstantial and unreal. Everything that had happened to her wafted around her like paper-thin pieces of film negatives, losing definition, blurring into options that she had tried to pretend she didn't have.

"You can roll that reel back up," the Mayor assured her. "Take it out of the projector and come with me, Faith. I'll protect you. I'll take care of you."

* * *

"Faith! Figure it out!" Buffy shouted.

A towering hunk of fangs and talons sliced at her. Suddenly blood spurted across her cheek at the same time that a piercing, sharp jab ripped through the small of her back. As she tried to land a good, hard double sidekick somewhere where sharpness was not, she thought, *Damn, we're gonna lose this one.*

"Angel?" she shouted, but the roars and growls and screams were so thick that it was like she was seeing sounds. Chaos whirled and dervished all around her, and there was so much of it, so thick and relentless, that she couldn't pick out one object from another. She was surrounded by stuff of the bad—skins and hides and teeth and stingers and nothing good, nothing that was a friend, nothing that could save her or help her save anyone else—

Angel walked up to her in the gentle sunshine of the glade. Droplets of water glittered in his hair and his eyelashes. He chuckled and held out a hand to her. He was holding a fresh, juicy peach, and he had taken a bite.

She took his hand, and his flesh was warm. His fingers curved around hers and brought her gently to him. Her knuckles rested on his chest, and the steady, good rhythm of his heartbeat thrilled her.

He lifted the peach to her lips and she bit into the succulent, sweet fruit. It was the most delicious thing she had ever eaten in her life. He caught a little trickle of juice coming from the side of her mouth and his smile grew.

"Come live with me, and be my love," he said. He seemed to glow with love and warmth, all his attention

focused on her. His world was her. "We can be here, to-gether."

"Yes," she said. "We can."

They could live here, and marry, and have children. She could have children with Angel. She could be a mother.

She could lay down her weapons and bring life into the world. What greater destiny was there? To be Angel's Chosen One, and spend her days basking in his joy, bringing him pleasure, receiving so much in return.

"Come with me," he urged. "Buffy, it's not too late. Walk through the portal and—"

"Oh, crikey, we're doomed," Spike wailed. "We're gonna bleedin' die!"

"Not if I can help it," Buffy shouted, pummeling a solid wall of red, oozing monster slab in concert with Angel. *"Faith!"*

I've been tempted before, Angel thought.

But this time, you are offered a true alternate reality, said a figure standing in a brilliant silvery-white light. *The Powers That Be give you this change. It's no test.*

Step through, Angel. It's the peace you seek. The lifting of the burden.

There will be no retribution. No consequences.

Only peace.

And Angel, the only vampire in the world who had a soul, saw nothing but the light. He had no visions of other lives, or of loved ones—not even Buffy. All he saw was that precious, beautiful glow, and it began to spread over him. Warmth and ease seeped into every fiber of his being, the very fabric of his soul.

Rest, weary one.

He closed his eyes and began to let go.

And then he opened them and joined Buffy as she rabbit-punched the slab, driving it backward. She flashed him a nod. "Thanks."

"Stop panicking!" Faith shouted, rounding up the frightened teenagers like so many cows.

"What do we do?" one of them bellowed at her, his face a total mask of fear. He had a goatee and a shaved head, an earring, and he was so scared his nose was running. "Tell us what to do!"

Faith realized they had placed their destiny in her hands. Handed it over, trusting her. She had brought them here. She had to get them out.

Then she felt Willow, strong and real. She could see the redhead, hands joined with the other girl, eyes closed, Tara somehow there and not there. And Riley, and guns, and *holy cow, grenades?*—and she knew, suddenly, that for her, there was only one door: the one marked with her name, and her destiny.

Come, Willow urged. *Don't be afraid.*

The portal shimmered directly in front of her.

I go through it, I might die, she thought.

Come. Willow was there, solid, real.

She grabbed Shaved Head by the shoulder and hustled him to the portal. "That one! Hurry! Go!"

The teens reacted to the urgency in her voice—and to the slew of monsters closing on them, Angel and Buffy totally outnumbered, backing up toward her.

"You're sure of that one, Faith?" Angel asked her, as kid after kid began leaping into the light, and disappearing.

Faith hustled them, thinking of *Titanic,* which she had seen in prison five, maybe six times. "Willow says that's the one."

"Willow? I thought you were communing with Alina," Spike yelled, his voice suspicious.

All Faith said was, "Change of plans."

She and Angel shared a look. She raised her chin.

"Hell," Spike said.

But as he stepped toward the portal, it vanished just as suddenly as the last one had.

"Nice move, Slayer Junior," Spike said, coming up short. "You've just lost all those sodding kids we've been chasing around after."

"No!" Faith screamed, fear and rage and frustration pouring out of her in equal measures.

Then an enormous, furred thing roared up on two legs, hovering over Buffy and Angel, and Faith flung herself toward it, knocking Buffy out of the way.

"Portal," Angel shouted at her. "Faith, concentrate!"

"Gotta . . ." Faith said, as the one of the creature's arms arced downward and slammed into the ground, inches from her toes. The ground split, smoke and fire skyrocketing upward like a geyser of oil.

"Come," Willow said.

Willow's presence was stronger than this. Faith could almost see Willow, as if she stood on the other side of some semitransparent windowpane, with those other two, Tara and Doña Pilar, standing behind her.

"It's okay," Willow's voice said. "Look."

And as Faith glanced around, she realized all the kids were gone. It was just her, Spike, Angel, and Buffy. And a jillion monsters.

"They've gone home," Willow said. "It's your turn."

A new portal opened. It flickered, then stabilized, hovering about two feet off the ground.

Without a word, Faith grabbed Spike and shoved him through. He disappeared.

"Angel!" Faith yelled.

"You go, Faith," he yelled back.

"I have to be last," she said. "In case there's some other change of plans."

"Buffy. You," Angel shouted to the other Slayer, as she twirled in the air, executing a great 360-degree turn and slamming both heels into the thigh of the furred beast. The monster tottered slightly backward as Buffy landed in a squat.

Before Buffy had time to rise, Faith grabbed her wrists and heaved her through the portal.

"You next," Faith said to Angel, as he flicked his attention from the tall white thing to the portal.

Then to her. They shared a look.

He thinks I'm gonna bail, she thought, hurt. *Thinks I'm looking for the way out.*

"I'll see ya," she promised.

The raging creature regained its footing and lurched toward them both.

Angel stepped through the doorway. Faith watched him go, and took a breath. Then, as Willow's form gazed at her, Faith said, "Coming, Willow," and stepped through, too.

For an instant, there was the gut-churning sensation of everything and nothing, all at the same time, and then she came out on the other side.

Angel's look of pride was the first thing she saw.

Buffy didn't recognize the place—the Vishnikoff house in Hawthorne—but Alina and Willow were there, with a little machine she guessed was the Reality Tracer. Alina looked stressed but happy to see them. Willow, though physically present, was in a trance state, not really there at all. Then, when Faith stumbled into existence, Willow's eyes snapped open and a beaming smile crossed her face.

"You're back! All of you!" Willow cried.

"What about the kids?" Buffy asked her, looking around.

Willow nodded. "Good. Alina had the hardest time figuring it out, especially with all the noise and, like, shooting and stuff going on, but—"

"Shooting?"

"—but she rigged it so the kids would all go back to exactly wherever they were when they vanished in the first place. Kind of iffy for some of them, but safer than here. They'll have only hazy memories. Everyone will think they were drugged."

Alina nodded, looking very tired but pleased.

"That's great, but shooting?" Buffy repeated. She could hear it, though this room seemed to be pretty well insulated. Angel and Faith were moving through the room, all three of them looking at Willow for clarification.

"Well, we're kind of under siege or something like that," Willow explained. She made a face. "Kinda medieval, huh?"

"I'm up to here with medieval," Buffy said. "What siege?"

"War," Willow explained. "Gangs, who want the Reality Tracer, and other bad guys, and . . . where's Spike?"

Buffy glanced around. "Didn't he show?" Then she said, "Where's Riley?"

At that moment, she locked gazes with Angel and she

thought, *This is reality. This. Riley. Not . . . not anything else.*

As if he had read her mind, he moved away from her. *Keeping his distance. Like I should keep mine.*

"Is everyone okay?" Angel asked. "Alina?"

"This house—it looks like a regular house, from the outside," Alina told them. "But the walls, the windows, all reinforced steel, bulletproof. We can survive for a long time in here. And surely the police will come."

"Which, seems like, your folks might not like," Buffy pointed out. "Since they'll want to come inside and all."

"Never again will I use that machine," Alina announced, and there was something in her voice—a sense of letting go, of surrender—that touched Buffy deeply.

Reality check for her, too, Buffy thought. *She's gonna be okay, somehow, after all this is over for her.*

Before anyone else could speak, the door burst open and Riley strode in. He crossed to her and swept her into his arms, his lips finding hers. She gave him this moment, and let herself rest in his arms, then pulled away.

"Firefight," Riley shorthanded. "The Vishnikoffs' friends have some good gear, but they're kind of outnumbered. The Flores family is here, Angel, in one of the internal safe rooms. They're fine."

"Good," Angel said.

"What's the plan?" Faith asked brightly.

"Kick ass," Buffy said, grinning at her.

"On board." Faith threw back her head and laughed.

Outside the house at the corner of Mount Vernon and Fairway, the scene resembled an urban battleground. Members of the Echo Park Band, along with Latin Cobras from Sunnydale and members of a dozen other His-

panic gangs, had bullied people from their homes, surrounded the house with cars, and used those homes and
cars as cover from which to fire on the Vishnikoff house.
Russians inside the house returned fire through special
gunports built into the walls. The neighboring houses, by
this time, were bullet-riddled, windows smashed, walls
missing chunks. Every car on the block had lost its glass
and tires.

Sirens wailed as police and paramedics closed in on
the area. Even in full riot gear, the police were hesitant to
get too close, because the gangs felt no compunction
about firing upon them as well as each other, and there
was a lot of lead flying through the air. The police surrounded the neighborhood, hustled residents out of their
homes to safety, and hoped to at least contain the worst of
it. At some point, the combatants would run out of ammo,
and then they could go in and sweep up.

Kate Lockley paced furiously behind the police lines.
She had learned about this place from the Mexican gang
members she had met, but by the time she got here, the
firefight had begun and she'd had to hold back. Then the
locals had shown up. She was way out of her territory
here; her badge granted her permission to stay, and no
one was likely to take the time to shoo her off, anyway.
But she didn't know any of these cops, and no one from
her own division would show up here, this far from home.
The force here consisted of Hawthorne cops—most of
them, she guessed—some L. A. County Sheriff's officers,
even some Staties. There was talk about bringing in the
National Guard, with tanks, if things didn't quiet down
soon. Kate thought that might not be a bad idea. She just
didn't want the house razed, or breached by the gangs,
before she could get in there. She had a feeling, which the

rumors the Mexicans had heard seemed to confirm, that inside that house was the key to everything that had been going on. The disappearances, the gang conflict, even the oil field fire in Sunnydale she'd heard about—all of it centered somehow around the Vishnikoffs.

She had confirmed, driving one-handed and using the mobile computer terminal being installed in all LAPD vehicles, that the house she'd been told about did indeed belong to the Vishnikoffs. Further, she had found that there was something unusual about its construction—it had been built during the postwar housing boom, along with the rest of the neighborhood, but after being sold to the Vishnikoffs a few years before, it had been torn down and rebuilt from scratch, to look identical to the house that had stood there before. From the outside. Every indication was that it was quite different on the inside, but the records, the inspection reports—all the paperwork pertaining to the construction job—had been stolen from city offices.

She *had* to get into that house.

As she stared at it, willing herself inside, she heard the growl of a big truck, grinding through the gears as it approached. It was moving fast.

Mischa had thought his own psychic abilities were pretty impressive until he'd come to know Alina, and learned just how powerful a mind could really be. Now he realized his abilities were little more than parlor tricks, the things anyone with a little training and practice could learn to do if only they accepted that they could.

Fortunately for him, most people had not figured out what their brains were capable of, which meant that even someone with his limited skills could overcome their resistance. At the moment, that meant the driver of the eighteen-wheeler he'd commandeered back at the truck stop in the desert. They'd driven nonstop, Mischa gripping the driver's mind and directing him every mile of the way, pushing the limits of his own endurance and the truck's huge engine. All the way, Mischa had worried about Alina. He hadn't dared try to contact her mentally—all his earlier attempts had been fruitless, and he didn't want to relinquish control of the trucker long enough to do it again—and though he used the driver's cell phone to call the house in Hawthorne, no one had answered all night.

Now, Alina's neighborhood came into view—and it was surrounded by police cars, ambulances, armed officers in helmets and body armor. Mischa's eyes widened at the sight, but RJ, the driver, remained hunched over the wheel, staring straight ahead, his eyes reacting to the changing road conditions and nothing else. Mischa felt sorry for the man—when he was finally freed from Mischa's mental grip, he'd wonder how he got so far off course and how his newly filled gas tank could have become so empty.

Some of the police officers saw the truck bearing down on them, and they shouted, waved their arms, raised their weapons. Mischa ducked behind the dash in case they opened fire, and willed RJ to keep going. RJ had no choice in the matter. He sped on, shifting up as the ground leveled off at the top of the rise.

Mischa heard screams from the police, heard the reports of guns and the frightening sound of bullets punching through the truck's metal skin. But the big machine kept rolling, even as its front bumper plowed through the tail end of a police car parked sideways across the street. Metal screamed, glass broke. The truck kept going.

Taking another look out the windshield, miraculously untouched, Mischa saw that they had come through the police line. Ahead of them was the house. It was surrounded by cars, and behind the cars, gang members with guns fired at it. But as the truck thundered its approach, they stopped looking at the house and turned to look at the Mack instead, expressions of fear painting their faces as it came. Mischa aimed the driver at the corner the house sat on. Two cars had been parked on the lawn.

The huge truck lurched onto the sidewalk. Gangsters scattered before its relentless approach. Finally, at the last possible moment, Mischa willed the driver to brake, and the man stomped down on the pedal, locking it. The truck barreled into the parked cars, crashing into them, demolishing them, and skidded as it did so, its trailer fishtailing behind it, threatening to tip the whole vehicle with unchecked momentum.

Mischa was out the door even as it came to a shuddering, smoking stop, and running for the house.

Kate Lockley, in the wake of the truck's passing, broke into a run behind it, drawing her service automatic. *This is it,* she thought, not really knowing what "it" was. She just had a feeling that the truck was the thing that was going to break the situation wide open, and she wanted to be there. She knew it was stupid, reckless—she wasn't even wearing a Kevlar vest—but she didn't care.

When the truck stopped and the young man jumped out, she froze, fixing him in her sights. A dozen gang members pointed weapons at her. The young man ignored all of them, making for the front door. Oddly, the people inside the house didn't fire at him.

"Hold it!" Kate shouted. "I'm going in with you."

The young man looked at her for a moment, then turned away, heading up the walkway to the house without answering.

"Anyone goes in that house, Mama," one of the gang members called, "we all do!"

The young man was almost at the door when it burst open, and some familiar figures charged out. Angel, Buffy and her boyfriend, the military-looking guy whose name Kate couldn't remember, if she'd ever known it, Faith and Willow emerged from the house at a run. Buffy took a running leap, twirling over twice in midair, and landed in the midst of some of those who held their guns on Kate. Fists and feet flew, and in an instant, they were disarmed. Angel aimed himself at another clutch of gang members, whipping an automatic rifle from the hands of one and using it to knock the others aside. Faith—who Kate had heard had been abducted from the jail in some kind of hostage grab—dove toward a man who held two automatic pistols, slamming him in the gut and driving him to the ground before he could fire either one. Riley hurled himself at a couple of gangsters trying to beat a retreat, wrestling their guns away.

Watching all this, Kate didn't even see the guy lying on the ground with a shotgun until he already had her in his sights and his finger was closing on the trigger.

"Kate, look out!" Angel shouted.

She turned, feeling like suddenly things were happening in slow motion.

Angel launched himself into the air, but it was too much ground, even for him, to cover before the gun discharged.

She heard the boom as if it were far away somewhere, saw the puff of smoke and the burst of fire from its muzzle, saw the shot as it rushed from the barrel, scattering as it came toward her. She knew that when it hit her it would still be concentrated enough to rip her to shreds.

But it didn't hit her.

It stopped, in midair.

Kate could see each individual pellet of shot, so many tiny beads of steel, hanging there, frozen in time.

Then, after stopping there for a moment, it all dropped harmlessly to the ground, bouncing on the walk like a sudden, tiny rain shower.

Still in slo-mo, Kate turned back to the house. *That isn't something,* she thought, *that Angel or Buffy can do. Unless they've got talents I haven't heard about.*

But when she looked at the house, she saw a Mexican man standing in the doorway, middle-aged, a little paunchy. She recognized Rojelio Flores, whose police report she had read after Angel took up his cause. His face was flushed with effort, sweat poured from his forehead and soaked his shirt. He stared at the shooter, and, following his gaze, Kate saw that the man's shotgun had removed itself from his hands and was floating into the air, a dozen feet up and rising.

The young man from the truck started to push past Flores, but then Alina appeared in the doorway, stepped through, and ran into his arms. They held each other tight for a long moment.

For Kate, the apparent slow motion timing of things stopped then, the normal accelerated rate of the world resumed. Voices shouted, feet slapped pavement—the cops advancing on the corner. No more guns were fired, though. The battle, it seemed, was over for now.

"Buffy, is my friend Mischa," Alina said excitedly. "He has just come from Arizona."

Buffy chuckled. "I saw. In a big truck."

"Not all the way from Arizona. And I hope the driver isn't hurt," Mischa said.

"He's not," Angel informed him. "Just really confused."

"That's good."

Alina led the way inside the house—she and Mischa first, followed by Buffy, Angel, and the rest.

"I'm going to want some explanations," Kate said. "And fast."

"You want the truth?" Angel asked her.

She scowled at him. "I'd like that. But I also want something I can tell the two hundred cops who will be here in about thirty seconds."

"Swamp gas is always a good one," Willow suggested. "Or mass hallucination."

"Thanks loads," Kate said. "I take it your little machine is working again, Alina?"

"For now, yes. But I intend to destroy it."

"That'd be an excellent idea," Kate agreed.

Alina pushed open the door to her room, and froze just inside it. Buffy released Riley's hand and came up behind her, shoving past Mischa. "What?" she asked.

But as she entered the room, she saw what. There was another portal there, hanging in the room. Two people were stepping through it even as she watched.

"Mama!" Alina called out, emotion making her voice quake. "Father!"

The man in the portal started to turn around at the sound of his daughter's voice. Buffy thought maybe he would come back, but he just looked at Alina, love and regret mingling in his eyes, and then the portal was gone as if it had never existed. Alina's parents had disappeared.

"No!" Alina cried. "Come back!" She rushed to the

machine, but before she even reached it, smoke began to billow from inside it.

"Look out!" Willow shouted. Buffy grabbed Alina and yanked her away from the Reality Tracer, spinning around so the girl's body was shielded by her own. As she did, it exploded with a bang, bits of metal and plastic flying all over the room. Buffy felt some of the debris bite into her back and legs.

When she released Alina and turned back, Riley was already on his knees, looking at the ruined shell. "Looks like they planted a small charge in it before they went," he said. "Not enough to hurt anyone, just a little shaped charge to wreck the machine." He paused, looking at Alina, concern etching his attractive face. "Like they didn't want to be followed," he continued. "Or brought back."

Alina sobbed in Mischa's arms. Buffy put a hand on her shoulder, but knew there was really nothing she could do to make it better. The girl's parents had walked out on her, abandoned her here when their political dreams fell apart.

Riley seemed to understand immediately. He held Buffy in his strong arms. "Maybe there's another reality out there," he said, "where their Soviet Union still exists, or even a more benevolent one, someplace the principles of Communism aren't marred by the totalitarians who ran this one. Maybe where they've gone, they still have a daughter. There's no telling, is there?"

Buffy shook her head. "Not with so many possibilities," she said.

"An infinite number of them."

"An infinite number. And we can only see one at a time."

"Buffy," Riley said softly. "The only one I want to see is the one with you in it."

Unexpectedly touched, she pressed her head against

his chest, listening to his heart. Surrounded by her friends, Willow, Angel, even Faith, she realized that one reality at a time was good enough for her, too.

A moment later, the police stormed into the house and they all went outside. Buffy looked around at the wreckage, the shattered glass and broken houses, the truck piled amid the cars, but also at the grass and the trees and the sky. A bird fluttered past overhead. She took it all in, eyes wide with the wonder of it all, determined not to take any of it, this whole wonderful world, for granted, but to see everything there was to see as if for the first time. Too much of her life was spent in the dark, in the shadows, moving unseen beneath the range of human existence. She knew that wouldn't change; that was her calling, her reason for being. But, she understood now, it didn't matter if the world saw her.

It only mattered that she saw it.

Epilogue

FAITH AND KATE LOCKLEY FACED EACH OTHER ON THE lawn outside the Vishnikoff house.

"You're, umm, not a hostage anymore, are you?" Kate asked her.

Faith hesitated. Then she stepped forward, holding out her wrists for the handcuffs. "Guess not," she said.

"I don't want to cuff you," Kate informed her. "I have a feeling you helped these guys . . . do what, or how, or where, I don't know and I don't want to know. But if you were on their side, you were probably doing something good."

"Probably," Faith agreed. She hugged Angel and even Buffy, ever so briefly, and then let Kate take her to a waiting car. *I can make it to the end of my sentence,* she knew. *I've toughed out worse things.*

The others stood and watched as they piled into Riley's car. It was way overcrowded until they dropped Alina and Mischa at the de la Natividad house.

Willow had talked to Doña Pilar, who in turn spoke with Salma. Of all the teenagers who had been snatched away into the various Alternities, Salma, with some magickal assistance from her grandmother, was the only one who remembered all of it. She knew what Buffy and Angel had gone through to get her back, and she understood Alina's role in the whole thing. She had also been told about Alina's desertion by her parents.

When they arrived at her front door, Salma's pretty brown eyes filled with tears. She had lost her brother, and the memory of that was still fresh, an open wound. She reached out and scooped Alina into her arms, and the two heads bowed as the girls burst into tears.

Buffy had a feeling Salma wasn't coming back to Sunnydale.

Salma released Alina and said, "We have extra rooms. Lots of them." She glanced at Mischa, and both the Russians brightened and looked at each other.

"We have much to offer," Mischa said.

"I know," Salma replied. She turned to Willow. "You will come and visit? My grandmother wants to teach me so many things."

"Yeah." Willow touched Salma's cheek. "Blessed be."

"Blessed be, Willow," Salma murmured, taking Willow's hand. "Give Tara *besitos de* Salma." She wrinkled her nose. "Little kisses."

"I will." Willow's eyes shone. "I can't wait to see her."

They swung by Cordelia's apartment next, to drop Angel off. Cordelia met them at the door.

"Yay!" Cordy cried. Then she grew serious. "It's over?"

"It's over," Angel assured her.

Cordelia looked puzzled for a moment. "What is it that's over? I'm drawing a blank."

People all over the city had already forgotten the disappearances—as far as the city was concerned, they'd never happened. Only those who'd gone through the portals or been connected to the witches remembered. And their spotty memories allowed people to fill in their own explanations: drugs, runaways, adolescent rebellion.

"I'll tell you later," Angel said.

"Well, I suppose you all want to come in and finish off the few scraps in my refrigerator," she said warmly.

"There is actual food in it," Wesley said from behind her. "I made a run to the store, and I mean that quite literally."

"We'll, ahh, just get out of your hair now," Buffy said. "Now you see us, now you don't."

Riley put his arm around her shoulders. He held out his hand to Angel and said, "It was a good fight."

"What was?" Cordelia asked. She turned to Wesley. "Are we missing something?"

Wesley shrugged. "That wouldn't be unusual."

Then Buffy said, "Thanks, Angel." She held out her hand, and he took it, gave it a squeeze and a light shake. "For everything. See ya."

He held onto her hand for a moment longer than he should have, his eyes burning into hers. "Yeah," he finally said, his voice hoarse. "See you."

Giles stood outside his front door watching the sunrise. He rubbed his hands together, relishing the warmth that distant orb cast down on our little world. In the first light of a new day, Sunnydale looked like people wanted to think it really was—a peaceful, somewhat sleepy southern California bedroom community, a place where young people could start families, watch them grow up, and retire, all in harmony with nature and their neighbors.

One would hardly know the place sat on top of a Hellmouth, he thought.

"You aren't that crazy guy who scares the milkman, are you?" Xander said from behind him. Giles turned. Xander came outside, rubbing his eyes. Anya followed him, looking as bright-eyed and cheerful as she always did. She was human now, Giles knew, but she didn't seem to require much sleep.

"Umm, no, no I'm sure that I'm not," Giles said.

"There is no crazy guy," Anya told him. "He's just teasing you."

"You know the Xan man, loves to tease," Xander said.

"I know, Anya. But thanks, just the same." Giles turned to Xander. "I was just, umm, noticing how few monsters there are about this morning."

"Like, none, that I can see," Xander noted.

"Exactly. We made it through the worst. I believe they're gone now."

"Do you know that for a fact?" Anya asked.

"It's true," Tara said, joining them from inside. "I can . . . sense it. The portals are closed, and the monsters who came through are gone. Or dead."

"We did lots of monster killing," Xander observed. "We should get an award or something."

Joyce Summers followed Tara out. "I think our reward is getting to live in a Sunnydale that's not full of monsters."

"Except, of course, the usual ones," Anya added.

And my reward is getting to live in a home that's not full of this lot, Giles thought. *Though, really, if I were going to share living space . . . there would be worse people to share it with.*

He looked at his friends, blinking and stretching in the morning sun, and realized that, as bad as things sometimes seemed, they really couldn't be better.

Cordelia felt a pang after the old gang left. *Poor things, going back to Sunnydale.*

She turned back to Angel and Wesley, settling down in chairs. Phantom Dennis rustled some papers in the kitchen. She thought about what it was like to go into the Sunnydale Mall and be greeted by name at all her favorite stores. Or to walk up to the concession stand at the Sun Cinema, and have Mark, the tall, hunky film major who worked there part-time, say, "The usual?" and hand her one of the room-temperature bottles of water he kept on hand, just for her.

But here's good, too, Cordy decided, as Angel picked up the TV remote, thought about it, put it down and closed his eyes. Wesley turned the page of a book he was reading.

"Coffee?" she said.

"How nice," Wesley murmured, not looking up at her.

She smiled to herself and went into the kitchen.

Riley and Buffy took the front seats; Willow sat alone in the back. Of Spike, there was no sign.

Buffy held Riley's hand as he drove. She'd been feeling invisible, she knew, like she was out there every night fighting for people who didn't know she existed or care if she lived or died. And then she'd found out that there was a whole range—an infinite range—of other realities out there, places where she didn't exist, places where she did, or some aspect of her did. Places where her parents had never divorced, where she had never broken up with Angel, even places where Buffy Summers had never become a Slayer.

"It's tough, knowing there are options," Riley said quietly.

"Doesn't matter." She smiled at him, but something in her teared up. There was a hollow feeling in the center of her chest, as if little pieces of her heart were breaking.

"It matters." Riley watched the road, then glanced at her. "You're a fighter. You want something, you go for it. It's not right, you try to change it." He looked back through the windshield. "I'm a warrior, too, Buffy. We're the kind of people who take action."

"But this is our battlefield," she told him, placing her hand on his leg. His serious expression softened, and she felt a little better. As if the broken pieces were knitting back together . . . in a different way than before, and not without scars. But they were still parts of her heart. They were not lost, or missing.

"This is where we are who we really are," she said, her voice catching, but only slightly. "Playing the hands we were dealt."

"Nothing wrong with a discard to get a better hand," he ventured, covering her hand with his before he downshifted.

"From the same deck, Riley," she murmured. She looked at him. "I like knowing that the sun will come up again and again, and that people I know and love walk around under it."

"Or hide from it," Riley said, very quietly.

"Or hide from it," Buffy agreed. A fresh, bittersweet tang underscored her reply.

In the backseat, Willow was asleep, a gentle smile wreathing her face.

"But I'm going through this with my eyes wide open. In the sun, Riley. I just . . . I just want people to . . . to really *see* me when I'm there. While I'm here."

His gaze was intense, unblinking. "I see you, Buffy Summers."

"I see you, Riley Finn." She let him see deeply into herself, hoped he knew how much she loved him.

Riley tugged on her hand to point out a mother horse running through a grassy field in the morning light, her long-legged brown foal by her side. The two watched them trotting along, their hides gleaming in the light of the new day.

"It'll be good to be home," Buffy said quietly.

"We *are* home." His voice was gentle but strong. There was a sureness in it that soothed her, comforted her.

Faith. Angel. Cordelia, she thought. *Take care, in that big city.*

She let go of the whispers in her heart, forced the merest sheen of tears back down, and let the light shine through the tender, new healing places in her soul.

"Yes," she said. "We're home."

London, 1880

Where the bloody hell? Spike thought. And then he knew:

He was not Spike, not quite yet. He was still William, fleeing the scene of his humiliation with tears in his eyes and a pulse in his veins. His one true love had laughed at his poetry and at his tender confession that he loved her. Said she was above him in station, and who the hell did he think he was?

I went through a different portal than the others, he realized.

Then there they were: Angelus, the vicious vampire Angel had been before his soul had been restored. Darla, Angel's beautiful sire, she of the blond hair and black, unbeating heart.

And Drusilla! His dark-eyed, mad darling, and his own sire.

The three were walking toward him, wicked smiles on their faces, savage bloodlust in their eyes.

She will change me now, William thought. *My life as Spike will begin.*

In that precise instant, he was overcome with mortal terror. With a cry, he dropped his papers. He was frightened completely out of his wits.

No, I want it, he thought, baffled. *I want to be a vampire.*

But as the deadly trio drew near, gliding like vipers, every instinct for survival snapped into focus. Fighting for his very life, William ran down the wet, dark street of London town, fleeing as if Heaven itself demanded it.

What the devil? he thought, but blind panic robbed him of further thought, and the young, bookish man raced down the lane, lost beyond reason, gibbering with fear.

At the end of the street, a sharp, brilliant light popped into existence before a wooden gate. It gleamed like a beacon, like a bonfire, and he raced for it, running so fast he thought his heart might burst.

Oh, dear, God, help me, he thought. *Save me!*

The light burned brightly as if it waited for him—either to carry him to heaven or burn him into a hellish pile of cinders.

"Help!" he screamed, and dived toward the light.

The End

Nancy Holder is the bestselling author of forty-eight books and many short stories, articles, and essays. Alone and in collaboration with other authors, she has written sixteen *Buffy* and/or *Angel* projects for Pocket Books. Her work has been translated into two dozen languages, and has appeared on the *Los Angeles Times, USA Today, Locus,* and other bestseller lists. She is currently working on the second book of this trilogy with her coauthor, Jeff Mariotte.

She lives in San Diego with her daughter, Belle, their dog, Dot, and two kittens named Sasha and David, and all five consider themselves honorary members of the Hart/Mariotte continuum. In her spare time, Holder belly dances . . . and sleeps.

Jeff Mariotte has written, alone and in collaboration with other various authors, two novels about the superhero team Gen[13], one novel about Xander Harris, two novels about Angel, and the nonfiction *Watcher's Guide, Vol. 2.* He has also written more comic books than he cares to count. He is a co-owner of Mysterious Galaxy, a specialty bookstore in San Diego, and Senior Editor for WildStorm Productions/DC Comics.

He lives in San Diego with a variety of people and animals, and would like to find time to visit the desert.

SPIKE AND DRU:
PRETTY MAIDS ALL IN A ROW

The year is 1940.

In exchange for a powerful jewel, Spike and Drusilla agree to kill the current Slayer—and all those targeted to succeed her. If they succeed with their plans of bloodlust and power, it could mean the end of the Chosen One—*all* of the Chosen Ones—forever....

A *Buffy* hardcover
by Christopher Golden

Available from Pocket Books

Everyone's got his demons....

ANGEL™

If it takes an eternity, he will make amends.

Original stories based
on the TV show
Created by Joss Whedon
& David Greenwalt

Available from Pocket Pulse
Published by Pocket Books